Sarah retrieved the lamp and twisted the peg. The outhouse door swung open on its own, and she gasped.

"Momma?" Sarah asked as she held out her lantern.

No. A ruined version of Molly stood in the doorway. Before her disappearance, people often commented on the sixteen-year-old's beauty, but in the last twenty-eight days birds pecked out her pretty blue eyes, and maggots now swam in the sockets. Molly's head hung to the left at an odd angle. Her skin looked mottled with patches of gray, blue, and black. A beetle crawled out of Molly's half-opened mouth and darted back in.

Sarah's heart leaped to her throat, and she jumped back. She lost her footing, fell onto the outhouse seat, and dropped the lantern to the floor. She bent to retrieve it; thankful the glass globe did not break. Sarah looked up and saw an empty doorway.

Impossible, she told herself. *Must've dozed off, had a nightmare, and woke up when I dropped the lamp.*

Her heart still pounded in her chest, and Sarah took a deep breath to calm herself.

Holding the lamp before her once more, she crept out…

Praise for Robert Herold and
THE EIDOLA PROJECT

"A ripping yarn! The narrative is lurid, lean, and delightful."

~Lisa Jones (Professional Editor)

~*~

FINALIST in the Launch Pad Manuscript Contest
(as *Haunted Heart*)

~

As a pilot script:

WINNER of the Wildsound Festival
FINALIST in the People's Pilot Awards
SEMI-FINALIST in the Nashville Film Festival

The Eidola Project

by

Robert Herold

An Eidola Project Novel

This is a work of fiction. Names, characters, places, and incidents are either the product of the author's imagination or are used fictitiously, and any resemblance to actual persons living or dead, business establishments, events, or locales, is entirely coincidental.

The Eidola Project

Contact Information: info@thewildrosepress.com

Cover Art by *Debbie Taylor*

The Wild Rose Press, Inc.
PO Box 708
Adams Basin, NY 14410-0708
Visit us at www.thewildrosepress.com

Publishing History
First Black Rose Edition, 2019
Print ISBN 978-1-5092-2406-7
Digital ISBN 978-1-5092-2407-4

An Eidola Project Novel
Published in the United States of America

Dedication

To Scott Wyatt, Sandy Nygaard,
Cheryl Hauser, Laura Peterson,
and Barbara Extract (wherever you may be)
for your tremendous help in crafting this novel.

~

To Al Runte for your support & for your expertise on trains. And to Gerry Hall and Amy Johnson, the alphas of beta readers!

~

To Lisa Jones, whose review and advice
buoyed my spirits! (Pun intended.)

~

To Sherri Good for your wisdom, guidance,
and humor in the editing process.

~

And to Ruth,
for your love and support all along the way.

Chapter One

Almost a month after Molly's disappearance, a full bladder forced Sarah Bradbury awake in the middle of the night. Try as she might, sleep would not return. She could not deny the inevitable—she needed to pee.

Sarah groaned, pushed away the ratty quilt, and sat up. For the thousandth time she wished her father would allow her a chamber pot, but she'd spilled one once, four years ago, when five-years-old, and that was the end of that. Pitch-black darkness filled her room, so she fumbled around on the small table next to her for a lucifer.

Sarah located one and struck it on the rough surface of the unpainted tabletop. Sulfur filled her nostrils and she sneezed, nearly dropping the burning matchstick. After lighting the wick in the old metal lamp on the bedside table, she shook the lucifer to extinguish its flame. She then raised the little metal arm on the kerosene lamp, which caused a small glass globe to lower over the burning wick. The lamp provided faint light, but enough to find her way. She pushed her red hair back from her narrow face and stood.

Easing open the bedroom door, Sarah crept down the hall past her parents' room, hoping beyond all measure she hadn't woken them. She tiptoed into the wider area of the house that served as kitchen, eating area, living room, and entryway. She lifted the metal latch on the door with the greatest of care and eased outside. Dew covered the rough boards of their front porch and the well-worn path through the yard to the outhouse. The moisture caused dirt and grass to adhere to the bottom of her feet as she trudged along.

The previous day's overcast sky looked rent apart, as though some celestial demon raked its claws first one way across the night sky, then the other. Patches of stars shown between the many small clouds. For a moment the full moon appeared, then scuttled behind a cloud, causing its outer edge to glow.

Sarah pulled open the outhouse's wooden door and held the lamp before her, peering within. Empty. One night a raccoon found its way in there, and they both had a fright until the critter scampered out. Sarah did not wish to renew the acquaintance.

She stepped inside, pulled the door shut, and twisted the peg that held the door closed. Sarah put the lamp on the floor, hiked up her nightgown, and sat on the seat—a plank with a hole in it. A pile of newspapers sat next to her, and after relieving herself, she tore off a piece of one sheet to wipe herself dry.

Sarah retrieved the lamp and twisted the peg. The outhouse door swung open on its own, and she gasped.

"Momma?" Sarah asked as she held out her lantern.

No. A ruined version of Molly stood in the doorway. Before her disappearance, people often commented on the sixteen-year-old's beauty, but in the last twenty-eight days birds pecked out her pretty blue eyes, and maggots now swam in the sockets. Molly's head hung to the left at an odd angle. Her skin looked mottled with patches of gray, blue, and black. A beetle crawled out of Molly's half-opened mouth and darted back in.

Sarah's heart leaped to her throat. Recoiling, she lost her footing, fell onto the outhouse seat, and dropped the lantern to the floor. She bent to retrieve it; thankful the glass globe did not break. Sarah looked up and saw an empty doorway.

Impossible, she told herself. *Must've dozed off, had a nightmare, and woke up when I dropped the lamp.*

Her heart still pounded in her chest, and Sarah took a deep breath to calm herself.

Holding the lamp before her once more, she edged out. Nothing unusual. She made her way around the side of the house, but as she turned the corner to the front, there stood Molly.

Sarah turned and ran. Over by the outhouse, she looked over her shoulder and saw she wasn't being followed. She stopped.

If Molly were a spirit, nothing prevented her from appearing somewhere else.

Sarah shivered despite it being a warm night. She rubbed her arms, feeling the goosebumps beneath her fingers, and looked back toward the house.

What does she want? Soon, curiosity overpowered her. Sarah crept back toward the front of the house and peered around the corner. Molly still waited there, facing Sarah, but neither said anything. The supernatural figure turned and shuffled across the matted grass of Sarah's front yard and went out onto the road leading from the farmhouse.

Sarah dashed up onto the porch to where her father left his boots under the awning. She put them on over her bare feet but did not bother to lace them. She clomped after Molly. The moon emerged from behind a cloud, and now Sarah could clearly see Molly walking ahead. After about a mile, Sarah stumbled into a pothole and fell. This time Molly waited for her.

They headed down Old Mill Road. Molly stopped and pointed, so Sarah came up and looked where indicated. She held the lantern before her, but no more kerosene remained in the lamp and the flame became a thin blue line which guttered out. A canopy of trees blocked the moonlight, and she could make out nothing ahead in the darkness. When Sarah looked back, Molly had disappeared.

Sarah wondered for a while what to do, then she used the heel of her right boot to carve a line across the dirt road and found enough rocks to make an arrow of them on the shoulder. She hoped the markers would be visible in the daytime.

When she got home, her father waited for her with a switch in his hand. He slapped it against his palm a few times for effect. “You fixin’ to run off like Molly?” he asked, despite Sarah’s young age. “You got a boy you’re seein’, same as her?”

He commenced to beat her backside raw. Between tears and shouts of pain, Sarah tried to tell him what happened and he beat her all the harder for lying.

From her parents’ bedroom, her mother emerged. Heavy-set, like her husband, with a perpetual sheen to her face. Her hair, a wild rat’s nest, often stayed uncombed throughout the day. She regarded the beating with mild interest, then complained about how Sarah had tracked dirt into the house.

Whatever Sarah said didn’t matter, so she quit saying anything.

When her red-faced and sweaty father spent his fury, her mother put a hand on his damp back. "Come, Honey, sit down at the table. Looks like you worked up an appetite this morning."

Later, when Sarah left the house to go to school, she did nothing of the sort. Her backside ached and she wasn't sure she could sit at her desk. It even hurt to walk, but she did it anyway, compelled to retrace the steps she traveled last night.

The farms and homes along the way looked as always and were mundane in their familiarity. Fields appeared bright green with early summer growth. Corn, rye, barley, and pumpkins, all popular local crops, flourished in the morning sunshine.

Eventually, Sarah turned down Old Mill Road and left the farms behind. The road led into a wooded area—thick with second growth that grew back once the mill, which rotted away long ago, closed.

Will I be able to find the spot? What will I find?

A half-mile along, Sarah spotted the line she scraped across the dirt road and the rough arrow made of stones. She surveyed the gooseberry bush blocking her way. Sarah weighed her options. Brave the thorny bush or find some way around it. She chose the latter and managed to find stinging nettles instead. Her right calf stung and began to break out in a blistery rash. She tried rubbing soil and spit on the affected area, achieving some relief, and pressed on until she stood where she figured her markers lay on the other side of the brush.

Sarah started walking away from the road and noticed a terrible smell that hung heavy and rancid in the air. Sarah placed a hand over her mouth and nose, trying to use it as a filter. A few feet beyond, she found Molly's corpse lying face-up on some green leafy foliage. The remains of the girl looked exactly as last night, including the beetle in Molly's open mouth.

Seeing this in the light of day with the added smell of putrefaction became too much for her. Sarah vomited.

After a while, nothing more would come up, yet she still gagged. She needed to move away from the site and the terrible scent. Now what? Go to the police or tell Molly's father?

Sarah decided Mr. Scott, Molly's father, deserved to know first. She retraced her steps back to the road, careful to avoid the patch of nettles.

The Scott's farm, like many New England farms, was lined with stone fences—people needed to do something with all the rocks they dug up. Molly's father used much of the farm for pasture instead of growing crops, but the animals she saw as she approached the house looked poorly. A thin shabby horse and a similar-looking mule stared at her with impassive eyes. Four Holstein cows lowed in pain, imploring her to milk them as they crowded around the gate to the fence.

Sarah knocked on the door and looked through the nearby window. Bertrand Scott slept at the kitchen table, next to a bottle of gin. After many knocks, she managed to rouse him. Bleary-eyed, the man struggled to his feet and staggered to the door, unlocked it, and swung it wide.

Seeing her, he growled, "What do you want?" His breath stunk of gin, and a filmy line of dried saliva ran along the inner edge of his chapped lips. He grimaced in the morning sunshine and held his right hand to his head in evident pain. "Go away," he snarled.

The man teetered back to the chair at the kitchen table, plopped down, and massaged the sides of his skull.

"I saw Molly last night," Sarah told him.

Mr. Scott sat up, suddenly alert.

"She's dead," Sarah added.

Mr. Scott came at her, and Sarah flinched, afraid he would hit her. Instead, he grabbed her shoulders and gave her a little shake. "My girl—dead?" he asked.

Sarah gulped. "Yes, sir."

"How do you know?"

"Her ghost visited me last night."

Molly's father let go and turned away in disgust. "Go away."

"I know where to look. I marked it last night where she showed me, out on Old Mill Road. I went there this mornin' to check—makin' sure it weren't a nightmare. She's there all right."

Mr. Scott turned back and looked at her. "What was she doing way out there?"

"I don't know. Perhaps she'll tell me next time."

"You're crazy."

"No, sir, I thought maybe so, but I just come from where she's layin'. I could have gone to the sheriff, but I thought you should know first."

The man's eyes bore into her, but she held up under the scrutiny. At last, he stood and went to the sink. He stuck his head beneath the pump's spout and worked the handle until water ran over his head. Eventually, he stood up and pushed his sopping hair back from his face. "Let's go."

Outside, Mr. Scott retrieved his horse and hitched him to the buckboard wagon. He climbed onto the plank seat and motioned for her to do the same. When she climbed up next to him, he stared straight ahead and said in a threatening voice, "If this is some sort of sport, our next stop *will* be the sheriff's."

Molly's father shook the reins and they rode off.

Every bump and pitch to the wagon awakened fresh pains in Sarah's raw backside. By the time they reached Old Mill Road, tears clouded her eyes and ran down her cheeks.

Sarah swiped the tears from her face and studied the roadbed ahead. The shadows cast by leafy trees above made it difficult to see details in the road as they went along.

"Slow down, will you?" she said.

At last, she found the spot, more by gut instinct than anything else. She yelled for him to stop. The two climbed off the wagon and went around the gooseberry bushes as she had done before.

When they found Molly's body, Mr. Scott let out a wail and dropped to his knees. He picked up one of her rotting hands and held it to his chest.

Later that morning they drove the wagon into town to present Molly's remains to the sheriff. The sheriff came out of the jail, followed by Mr. Scott and Sarah, and drew back the canvas draped over Molly's body. He turned a little green.

The sheriff threw the tarp back over Molly and retreated a few steps. He looked up at the sky for several long moments then leveled his gaze at Molly's father. He put a hand to his holstered gun. "Bertrand, I have to ask you to step into a cell on suspicion of murder."

Bertrand Scott, already ashen, turned whiter still. "What?"

"You heard me. I've had doubts about you from the start, out there in the boonies with your daughter. You and Molly fought, no doubt, and you did something you probably now regret. You couldn't live with yourself after what you'd done, cooked up this crazy story, and got this girl here to buy into it."

Bertrand struggled to speak. His mouth worked up and down like a fish out of water. Tears ran down his cheeks. At last, he found his voice, as he clenched both his eyes and his fists, but only one sound came out, a wracking heartfelt moan.

The sheriff glanced at Sarah and back at Bertrand Scott. The lawman became suddenly conciliatory. "Step inside, Bertrand, and we'll sort this thing out. Don't make me have to pull my sidearm or cuff you."

Bertrand let out a deep breath and sagged as though deflated. He lowered his head and shambled into the jail. The sheriff ushered him through the door in the rear of the office that led to the cells.

When the sheriff came out of the back room, Sarah tried her best to protest, but the man cut her off and growled, "Get on out of here before I stick you in the lodge too!"

The sheriff's threat made Sarah feel somehow guilty as if she were responsible for everything. She turned, walked outside, and saw the wagon and the bedraggled horse. When the sheriff emerged, she said, "I don't think I can manage the wagon, but I'd be willing to walk the horse back to Mr. Scott's farm."

"I'll put him up in the livery. You get yourself on

back to school where you belong."

"Yes, sir," said Sarah and walked away, but instead of school, she returned to Mr. Scott's farm and tended to the animals.

In fact, she continued looking after them while Molly's father sat in jail.

Sarah needed to testify at the court hearing the following week. Her parents accompanied her, and all three sat in the gallery. When the bailiff called her name, Sarah squeezed past her folks and the other people on the bench until she got to the center aisle. The bailiff led her to the witness box and there he told her to place her right hand on the Bible he held before her. The man recited the pledge to tell the truth. Sarah nodded.

"Say, I do," Judge Phineus Newbold said with a kind smile as he looked down from his seat at the thin red-headed girl.

Sarah recited the two words with all the solemnity she could muster. When asked, she told the court about the apparition of Molly—to the titters and guffaws of many.

"And how did Miss Scott's body get into the woods?" asked Albert Schmidt as he waved his right hand in a little flourish. The man oiled his hair so that it shone and his huge waistline made him an imposing figure.

"I don't know," said Sarah "but you can ask Molly yourself. I've had the feeling all week she wants to speak."

This time Albert led the guffaws until the judge gaveled the room back to order.

"Well," the prosecutor said with a snide grin, "let's

hear from her."

Sarah closed her eyes and took deep breaths for several moments. Her breathing became labored, and she sat back on the chair and moaned.

The judge pounded his gavel several times. "That's enough of this," he proclaimed.

Hugh Marsten, the defense attorney, stood up. "Begging the court's indulgence, sir. If her story is true, it could exonerate my client."

Judge Newbold looked over at Schmidt, who still chuckled. "No objections, your honor," said Schmidt. "I enjoy a good performance as much as anyone."

"I'll let this go on for a minute or two, provided it doesn't turn into a sideshow," grumbled the judge.

Sarah opened her eyes with a start. She looked at Bertrand Scott. "Father," she said in Molly's voice, "what are you doing here?" She looked around with panic. "What? Where am I?"

"You're in a court of law," said Judge Newbold, "and may I remind you, Sarah Bradbury, you are under oath. Are we to believe you are now Molly Scott?"

Sarah looked at the judge with shock. "What are you talking about? Wait—I remember…" Sarah turned to face the people in the gallery. "I snuck out of my house for a buggy ride with John Hyler. I'd never done anything like that before, but I thought with the sheriff's son, there would be nothing to fear."

John Hyler bounded to his feet from where he sat in the rear of the courtroom. "This is crazy!" shouted the young man. "The girl's a lunatic!"

The judge pounded his gavel. "Bailiff, please help the junior Mr. Hyler find his seat. I'm starting to take some interest in this testimony after all."

The sheriff, John's father, moved down the center aisle in the courtroom, adding his protests to his son's. "You can't be serious, Phineas. The girl is clearly disturbed."

The judge held his gavel out toward the sheriff. "Quiet, Charley, and be seated before I have you arrested for contempt."

He turned back to Sarah. "Please continue."

"It was a warm May night, and I wore my favorite blue dress and my late mother's brooch. I crawled out my window and met John in his surrey. We drove off, not saying much, but enjoying the beautiful evening. After a while, John stopped the carriage. We were on Old Mill Road. He grabbed me and started kissing me, putting his hands all over."

Sarah became more distressed as she relived the event. Her arms beat at the air before her, attempting to drive the man away.

"He said everyone knew I was loose, and he wanted his turn. I fought him off as best I could. In the process, Mother's brooch got torn off and rolled beneath the seat. I screamed and cried as he had his way.

"When he finished, he climbed off me and turned the carriage around. We headed back, but I couldn't stop crying. He hit me while he drove the horse on faster and faster. Finally, I said I was going to tell his father and he went berserk. He swore and threw me from the racing carriage. My head struck the ground first, breaking my neck.

"John stopped and went back to where I lay on the road. He dragged me out of sight, through some bushes, and left me there to rot."

Sarah stood up and pointed to the sheriff's son. "John Hyler, you're a rapist, a murderer, and a coward. My mother's brooch is still beneath the carriage seat where it fell."

****

Judge Newbold raised his gavel to stop the proceedings then saw Sarah collapse to the floor of the witness box. The courtroom erupted in pandemonium.

John Hyler started to push his way past the other people in his row of benches, but they stood up and blocked his way. Several men grabbed him from behind.

"It isn't true!" he shouted. He wrenched himself around to face the judge. "It isn't true!"

Sheriff Hyler stood up, crimson-faced and teeth clenched, and charged toward the exit.

The judge sprang from his bench and shouted over the crowd. "Charley, I can't let you go! Deputies, bar his way!"

Two deputies stood before the door. The sheriff turned sideways and drew a fist back for a punch, but the younger of the two deputies put a hand on the sheriff's chest to stop him. "Don't do it, boss," he said.

The sheriff froze then lowered his arm. He turned around and faced the judge, an imploring look on his face.

"You can go with them, Charley," the judge said soberly, as he stared down the sheriff, "but the deputies will check the carriage."

After a few moments, the sheriff nodded in agreement.

Judge Newbold exhaled audibly and set down his gavel. The two deputies turned and pushed open the double doors at the rear of the courtroom. They held them open for the sheriff, who left the court with his eyes downcast.

The judge looked at the forgotten young girl, who still lay on the floor of the witness box. "My God!" he exclaimed and moved to assist her. He pushed the chair aside and bent down to scoop up the child. Moisture beneath his left hand revealed she wet herself. The judge stood and looked across the room at the girl's parents. The two chatted and laughed amongst the others but made no move to help their daughter.

Shaking his head in disbelief, the judge took her into his chambers. He did not have a sofa, but he did have an adjustable parlor chair. He set the girl on the black leather upholstery and reclined the back as far as it would go. He took his light summer suit jacket off the hook by the door and draped it over the unconscious girl.

The judge marched out of his chambers and crossed the courtroom to the gallery, which still buzzed. John Hyler continued his protests to anyone who would listen, but every time he attempted to stand, several men shoved him back down. It didn't appear anyone else was anxious to leave.

The judge yelled and pointed at the girl's parents until he got their attention. He demanded they approach him. Both parents looked scrubby.

"What the hell do you think you're doing?" the judge yelled. "Your daughter is unconscious and you two are standing there with the rest, yammering away."

The mother spoke first. "Oh, she's always doing this sort of thing to avoid doing some chore. We find it best to ignore her until a switch can be found."

"She'll come around," chimed in the father.

"I don't know what to make of her accusations," said the judge, "but the girl is not faking unconsciousness. I recommend you get her to Doc Twining."

"And who's gonna pay for that?" asked the mother.

"I will," said Judge Newbold without a second thought.

The father eyed the judge. "Give us the money. We'll see she gets the treatment she deserves." He grinned.

The judge balked. "I'll fetch the doctor myself."

****

The two deputies and Sheriff Hyler headed for the sheriff's house as the June sunshine bore down on them. All three removed their coats, but large wet spots still emerged on their shirt-backs and beneath their arms.

When they arrived, the sheriff led them around the well-kept home to the carriage house in back. The sheriff threw the bolt on the double doors and swung them open. Sunlight shone in upon the black surrey. Sheriff Hyler stepped toward the carriage, but Deputy Shema grabbed his shoulder.

"The judge said for us to do the lookin'."

The sheriff took a moment to consider his options and moved away. Deputies Shema and McCann climbed up on either side of the surrey and searched every nook and cranny.

"Hold on," McCann announced, "I've got something." He held the object in the light to examine it. The ivory cameo brooch depicted the Virgin Mary and baby Jesus.

"Christ almighty," said Shema. "What the girl said was true."

"That belonged to Gertie," said the sheriff. His wife died three years earlier.

"You willing to swear to that in court?" asked McCann.

The sheriff took a deep breath and kicked at a rock protruding from the soil. "No," he said, almost inaudibly.

When the three of them entered the courtroom, the sheriff glared at his son and shook his head. "You little shit."

****

Sheriff Charlie Hyler came to the jail the next day still wearing his uniform and sidearm, despite being suspended after his son's arrest. When he walked in, he saw Shema's feet were propped up on his desk. Shema was reading *Harper's Weekly*. The deputy awkwardly sprang up and apologized.

"Sorry, boss. I didn't have my feet on anything important."

The sheriff grunted a response and moved around the desk. He headed for the cells. Shema ducked in front of him and stammered. "M-Mayor said you're on leave until further notice. I can't let you in there."

Sheriff Hyler raised his head and glared at Shema. Hyler knew he looked a sight, unshaven and with bloodshot eyes from lack of sleep. He didn't care.

"Get the hell out of my way, Shema. There ain't no power on Earth going to stop me seeing my boy."

Shema studied his boss's face for a few moments, then yielded. Shema stepped to the side and the sheriff opened the door leading to the holding cells. Hyler slammed the door shut behind him.

The sheriff walked past the first two empty cells, each separated by a brick wall, and stopped at the third, where his son sat on the side of a cot with his head in his hands. The younger Hyler raised his head and saw his father.

"Get me out of here!"

Charlie shook his head and scowled. "You're where you belong."

"I didn't do it!" John Hyler came up and grabbed the bars. He put his face to the iron rods and spoke with increasing desperation. "Th-that girl is crazy. I never touched Molly, the whore. Don't get me wrong, I'm sorry she's dead, but half the town could tell you she got what was coming to her. I don't know who did it. I'd tell you if I did!"

"You protest too much," Charley said in a grave voice. "I think you should've seen what happened to the girl you left lying in the woods. Then you could tell me if she got what she deserved. I wouldn't be surprised if they leave you on the rope they hang you from for a month. Give you a taste of your own medicine."

John Hyler's left arm shot out between the bars and snatched his father's pistol from the holster. John sprang back from the bars and pointed the gun at his father. "You get me out of here. *Now*!"

The sheriff shook his head. "I have sworn an oath to uphold the law, even at the expense of my own son." He turned and walked from the room.

"Stop!" shouted his son, to no effect.

Sheriff Hyler went back into the office and slowly shut the door behind him.

The deputy moved across the room. "What the hell

was that all about?"

Now the sheriff put his hand on his deputy's chest. "Don't go in there, Shema. It ain't safe. He stole my gun."

The deputy jerked his own gun from his holster and tried to step around the sheriff who continued to block his way.

"What happened?" Shema demanded.

"He reached through the bars and took it. Don't add yourself to his tally. Let him be."

"Are you nuts?"

"Who's he gonna harm in there?" said the sheriff in a low voice.

Shema shoved the sheriff aside so hard, the older man fell to the floor. Shema grabbed the doorknob as a shot sounded from within. He flung open the door and ran inside.

At the first cell, Shema stopped short. He held his gun out before him, inching past the next cell to the third.

John Hyler sat on the floor of his cell with wide eyes, the top half of his head now sprayed all over the wall behind him. Blood ran from the gaping hole in rivulets down his face, but it gushed from the open mouth and spilled off his chin onto what had been a white shirt. His right hand lay on the floor with the pistol, the index finger still stuck in the trigger guard.

The sheriff came up to Shema and surveyed the scene. The older man choked off a sob.

Shema turned to his boss. "You gave him your pistol, you son of a—"

"No," the sheriff cut him off, squeezing his eyes tight to staunch the flow of tears, "but I had hoped he'd be man enough to take it."

****

As news of what happened in court circulated, people began to converge on the Bradbury farm, asking for, or in some cases demanding, Sarah's help. *"What happened to my husband?" "Please find my wedding ring." "My baby died last summer. Is she in heaven?"* Her father drove them all away. But when Dodgerton's Carnival and Traveling Freak Show performed in Hoeksburg the subsequent week, the tall Morris Dodgerton paid a call on the Bradbury farm.

The owner of the carnival spoke in a loud and blustery voice, awakening Sarah. She opened her bedroom door a crack to observe him talk his way into their house. The bottle of Old Crow he brought with him certainly helped.

Dodgerton looked dark and well-groomed. He removed his silk hat and set it and his cane on the dining table. He wore his black hair slicked back and waxed the mustache above his beard so the ends made fanciful curls. His tailored black silk suit jacket, threadbare at the elbows, partially covered the red vest he wore over his white shirt. Across the vest hung a long chain and watch fob of what appeared to be gold.

"I can tell the future too," Dodgerton announced to Sarah's parents as he poured the whiskey. "I foresee you making far more money than you have ever dreamed."

At the end of an evening of drinking, laughing, and haggling, Sarah's parents agreed to Dodgerton's offer to make their daughter a part of the carnival. They were to receive five hundred dollars now and another five hundred each year she remained in his employ.

When Dodgerton counted out the money onto the kitchen table, her parents' eyes went wide with greed.

Her mother snatched up the money and stuffed it into a pocket. As her father and Dodgerton shook hands, Sarah's mother said, "No refunds," and smiled, showing her mouthful of grayish-brown teeth.

Dodgerton withdrew his hand and wiped it on his coat. "I understand."

Sarah already had one leg out her bedroom window, trying to escape, when Dodgerton came into her room to fetch her. Having caught wind of her fate, she'd dressed and packed a small burlap bag with her belongings.

Dodgerton sprinted across the room and yanked her back inside. Sarah kicked, screamed, and flailed her arms. Dodgerton put a hand over her mouth. "Quiet!" he commanded.

Sarah bit him.

Dodgerton yelped with pain and let go.

Sarah fell to the floor. She scrambled for the door, but her grinning parents blocked her escape. Dodgerton picked her up by the scruff of the neck and backhanded her.

Stunned silence.

"Oh, you two will get along nicely," said her mother.

On the way to the fairgrounds, Sarah rode with her hands bound together and a rope around her waist anchored her to the seat. They rode in silence. Every so often Dodgerton would lick the blood from his left hand where she bit him.

Good. I hope he bleeds to death.

When they arrived, the carnival looked closed, as it

was well after midnight. Lanterns hung from posts before a number of tents on the periphery where the performers and carnival roustabouts stayed.

Dodgerton freed her from the rope tying her to the seat but left her hands bound tight. He pulled her off the wagon and grabbed her bag with his injured hand. He dragged her along a straw-covered path to a tent that glowed from a lantern within. Dodgerton lifted the tent flap and threw Sarah inside.

An old woman, with a pipe in one hand and a book in the other, looked up in surprise at Dodgerton. She shifted her gaze to the hapless girl on the straw-strewn ground before her.

"Add her to the act, Tsuritsa," said Dodgerton. "She's the genuine article." He threw Sarah's bag down next to her. "And keep a top eye open. If she runs it'll cost you."

The old woman puffed on her pipe and regarded Sarah for several long moments. She smiled, causing a myriad of wrinkles to migrate around on her face. Her eyes looked kind.

"Pleased to meet you," she said in a Hungarian accent. "My name is Madame Tsuritsa Vodoma. Come here, child, and let me untie you."

Skittish, Sarah hung back for a minute. *Shall I run? Where?* Back at her house, her attempt at escape grew out of blind panic. Now she considered it, where could she go? She crept forward and held out her hands.

The old woman continued to smile while she reached out and held Sarah's bound hands for several moments. Tsuritsa looked into her eyes, and Sarah began to relax.

"I don't think you'll run."

Madame Tsuritsa Vodoma worked on the knots until they loosened and the rope fell free. She sat back in her chair and laughed. "If you're the *genuine article*, did you know this would happen to you? That you'd end up here with me?"

Sarah shook her head.

"What kind of *genuine article* are you?"

Sarah rose to her feet and brushed the straw from her clothes. "I don't know what that means."

"Mr. Fancy Pants must have some reason for bringing you here."

Sarah told her about the ghost, Molly's body, and what happened in court. "People started coming around our house asking for all kinds of help."

"Did you?"

"Did I what?"

The old woman rolled her eyes. "Did you help them that called?"

"My father drove them off, but there was one woman whose husband died without telling her where he buried their savings. I opened my bedroom window and told her where to look. A voice came into my head and told me."

Madame Vodoma reached out and took Sarah by the chin. She craned forward and stared into Sarah's eyes. She smelled of tobacco and Sarah coughed.

"Yes, I think so," she said. "You *are* something special."

She let go and Sarah backed away.

"Don't be afraid, child. I won't hurt you. Dodgerton won't either, at least for a while. He'll want to protect his investment. It's time you got some sleep. You take the cot tonight. I don't seem to need much sleep these days, and my chair suits me. Tomorrow will be a busy day."

"What will I do?"

"You'll learn. Perhaps you will see or hear things like you did for the woman you helped. What you don't, you will make up."

****

The next day Madame Vodoma dressed her in a Hungarian peasant dress and coached her on what to say and how to behave with customers. Most of the day, Sarah sat in the corner of the stuffy sideshow tent studying the fortuneteller, while the old woman read Tarot cards or palms, or gazed into a crystal. However, whenever anyone asked about the dead, Madame Vodoma gestured to Sarah. She'd move to the table, fake a trance and repeat the lines Madame Vodoma taught her. This happened numerous times until the end of the evening when a black-clad woman came in unbidden.

The woman's mousy brown hair crept out from beneath her black bonnet and hung down in ringlets on either side of her earnest-looking face. The woman held a black kerchief and knotted it between her fingers as she spoke.

"I need your help," she said.

The old mystic motioned her to a folding wooden chair and indicated she should sit.

"I sense you are deeply troubled by the passing of someone you loved," said the fortuneteller, based on the woman's appearance alone. "A child?"

The woman in black looked surprised. "Why, yes."

Madame Vodoma reached over the small table and took the woman's hand. "I am glad you came. We can help."

"We?"

"My daughter here"—she motioned Sarah forward—"is especially attuned to those who have passed on."

"Well, I suppose it's fine, but she's so young. Albert was about her age…"

"All the better," said Madame Vodoma with practiced sympathy.

"Is she all right?" the woman asked.

The fortune-teller looked over at Sarah and gave a start. The young girl acted differently from other performances that night. Sarah's breathing turned ragged and her eyes rolled up into her head so the whites showed between her lids.

"Mother?" said Sarah in a voice not her own.

"Albert?" asked the startled woman. *"Can it be?"*

"Oma and Opa are waiting for me."

The woman's face flushed and tears burst from her eyes. Mucus ran from her nose. The woman's little handkerchief, not up to the task, soon looked soaked. "I miss you so." She snuffled.

"Let me go," her son's voice pleaded. "Elizabeth and Martin need their mamma. Dadda needs you too."

"I can't! I'll lose you forever!"

"Let me go…"

Sarah pitched forward and Madame Vodoma caught the girl before her head smashed onto the table.

The client stood, still crying, but now looking stunned. "Of course," she said in a low voice, as she stepped away, "I have been selfish…"

"Wait!" The fortune-teller shouted, almost too late.

The woman in black froze at the tent flap.

"Please, help us to help others. Offer what you can."

"Oh," the woman sniffed, "Of course…" She came forward and dumped the entire contents of her purse onto the table. She retrieved her keys then smiled and stepped back.

Sarah regained consciousness as the bereaved woman, who now smiled through her tears, backed out of the tent.

"Thank you," said the woman in black as she left.

Madame Vodoma looked at Sarah in her arms, smiled, and gave a little nod of encouragement.

****

When Dodgerton saw the take for the day he grinned. "My investment's already paying off," he said as he took half the money. He turned to Sarah. "I expect you're going to make me very happy over the years." He winked.

Sarah cringed.

Back at their tent, the old woman divided the remaining money into three piles. "This one is for expenses," she said. "This one is for me, and the last pile is for you."

"You keep it for me," said Sarah.

The old woman sat back with her eyes wide. "Does being a fool come with being the genuine article?"

Sarah smiled and said, "I trust you." Her smile evaporated. "I don't trust Dodgerton."

The old woman laughed. "As well you shouldn't, but not to worry, he likes 'em a bit older. Let's go to supper. There are folks I want you to meet."

They stashed the money and left the tent.

"Most everyone congregates here after the day,"

explained Madame Vodoma, as they walked toward the supper tent, "especially the freaks, who are not welcome in towns."

They entered the tent and Sarah saw people crowded on benches next to long planked tables. Lanterns hung from the frame on the inside. Tsuritsa Vodoma introduced Sarah to everyone she had not yet met.

Raymond Henderson, the thin man, paused to say hello while feeding stew to his wife, Angelica. The woman had flippers instead of arms and legs. Angelica, mouth full of stew, smiled and nodded her greeting.

Matilda Van Buren, the bearded lady, wore an evening dress covered in spangles, while the rest of those assembled were either dressed casually, wearing a robe or still in their costumes. Matilda argued politics with Joseph Kerensky, the strong man. They stopped bickering to shake Sarah's hand.

"Welcome, dear," Matilda said in a sweet voice and smiled. A moment earlier she had been screaming at the strong man to make her point.

Joseph stood and made a deep bow. He took her small hand in his huge one and kissed it. "I am honored beyond all measure," he said in a thick Russian accent.

Sarah blushed and curtsied. "Pleased to meet you both," she said in a meek voice.

A diminutive man held the good hand of a normal-sized woman with a gray scaly tumorous condition on the left side of her body. Her left hand looked more like a claw covered in a thick gray hide. The left side of her face was also marred by the scaly growth that ran up into her hair, making it thin and patchy. The right side of her face, however, was quite beautiful. She smiled at

Sarah, and the Lilliputian man swung around on the bench to see them. He hopped down and stuck out a hand.

"Barnaby Potts, the human cannonball," he said with a British accent. "Any friend of Tsuritsa is a friend of mine. This here's me wife, Charisa."

"The Rhinowoman," Charisa said, smiling.

Sarah shook Charisa's good hand and smiled with some trepidation.

"Don't worry, Luv," Barnaby chided, "It's not catchy. I've been *very* close to Charisa for seven years."

Everyone around them laughed, except Sarah, who smiled but didn't know what he meant.

There were many others—laborers and performers. The laborers, all men, seemed to keep to themselves. They laughed and told off-color jokes as a jug of wine passed between them. They stopped their chatter to greet the two. The old woman knew everyone's name and they hers.

On the end of a bench, away from all the others, sat a big man with a large black pin running in and out of one cheek.

"Hello, my friend," Tsuritsa called out to him. "This is Sarah, my young apprentice."

The man gave a sullen shake of his head and continued to eat.

In a low voice, Tsuritsa Vodoma said to Sarah, "You stay away from him. He likes to stick things where they don't belong."

After being introduced to the cook, Sarah and the fortuneteller received plates of thick stew and cornbread biscuits. She and Tsuritsa took a space next to Barnaby and his wife.

Sarah and Madame Vodoma returned to their personal tent after dinner. The old woman sat in her rocker and filled her pipe. She struck a lucifer on the wooden crate that held a lamp and the copy of *Middlemarch* she had been reading the night before. She puffed on the pipe a bit and retrieved the book. She looked up at Sarah, who stood across the straw-strewn floor and stared. The old woman lifted her book. "I know you're sharp as a tack, but do you know your letters? Can you read and write?"

Sarah nodded.

"I give you free access to my trunk over there." Tsuritsa cocked her head in the direction of the large wooden box at the foot of the cot. It had broad leather straps and brass buckles, which now hung loose.

Sarah went over to the trunk and lifted the lid. Books filled the container.

"Shakespeare, Hawthorne, Dickens," Tsuritsa continued, "these men, and others will be your teachers. Pick one to read on your own and another for us to read to each other."

****

And so it went. Sarah and Tsuritsa established a routine, replicating itself each day, in spite of changes in locale. As time went on and Sarah cultivated her abilities, the crowds grew. She had no teacher in this. Tsuritsa Vodoma encouraged her, but the old woman's talents lay elsewhere. The old woman mentored her in showmanship and how to navigate the politics of the troupe. Over the months and years, they performed before ever-larger crowds until they moved into one of the featured tents.

At sixteen, Sarah no longer wore a peasant girl's

outfit when performing. Matilda, the bearded lady, made her a sequin-covered dress like her own, and Charisa liked to paint her face and do her auburn hair, which, in spite of this, most often hung loose.

Still, Sarah's part of the show did involve some risk. Sometimes the deceased were malevolent or angry. One time she became conscious of shouting obscenities at a man for his infidelities.

Another time, she accused a man of robbing a bank and the murder of his accomplice.

The bank robber/murderer came to Sarah's performance in a fancy checkered suit and nestled up to a busty woman in a pink dress. His date's corset pressed so tight across her bosom, the breasts looked about to burst.

A trance took hold and Sarah spoke as Giorgio Spinetti, the dead accomplice. She stood up from her chair and walked to the edge of the sawdust-covered ring and called the man out.

"Alfie," she said in a surprisingly low voice for a girl, "why did you shoot me?"

Alfonso fumbled and dropped the bag of peanuts he had been holding out to the woman next to him. The nuts rolled all over the woman's pink dress. One found a perch in her cleavage. Alfonso glanced around and sat up straight. Sarah continued in the deep voice.

"We got clean away and the New Bedford police weren't going to find us." The timbre became hard with contempt. "But you knew that, didn't you? You wanted the money for yourself!"

Alfonso stood and caused his chair to fall back onto the woman behind him, who screamed in pain.

"Hey!" yelled the man next to her, standing to

confront Alfonso and knocking his chair back into the guy behind him. That man stood up and threw a punch at the man in front.

Alfonso's eyes narrowed with baleful intensity as he gazed at Sarah. "You," he said in a low voice, "are dead."

A threat or a statement?

Alfonso looked back at the brawling men behind him and at his prostitute date, now covered in peanuts. He turned to run and stumbled over a number of spectators, despite their protests. By the time he got to an aisle, the bleachers were in chaos. Fists flew with abandon.

****

Furious, Dodgerton marched into the ring and confronted Sarah. "Why the hell did you say that?"

Sarah's eyes rolled upward and she collapsed onto the sawdust.

Dodgerton drew back his right boot, prepared for a kick, but Tsuritsa came between them. She helped Sarah onto a folding chair.

Sarah looked up at him, eyes glassy. Her mouth hung slack and a string of drool ran from her lips, which allowed pieces of sawdust to adhere to her chin. The old woman wiped the girl's face with her hand.

The fortuneteller turned to Dodgerton. "You wanted the genuine article? *This* is what it means!" She added, "Should we go to the police?"

Dodgerton turned away and strode toward the exit. "I'm going out to exhort folks to see the other acts. If they all go home mad, it'll be bad for business. Forget the police," he added. "The word of a freakish girl will not carry any weight."

The crowds eventually returned to the tent, but Sarah did no further performances that night. The old woman helped Sarah back to their tent, the one they still shared and encouraged her to lie on the cot. The girl lay down as directed and went to sleep.

****

Sarah awoke, alone, and saw their clock read almost midnight. *Tsuritsa must've thought I needed more rest.* She felt better and craved something to eat. If she hurried, she might still get some dinner. Sarah rose and went out into the dark.

The carnival site looked deserted. The last patrons left an hour ago. At this time, performers and crew either went into town, retreated into their tents, or headed to dinner. Sarah wended her way through the performers' tents. She approached the dining area when a shotgun blasted behind her. She screamed and jumped, then turned.

Alfonso Gambini lay prone on the straw-covered path a few feet behind her. Blood oozed from a hole in the back of his checkboard suit. In his right hand, he clutched a long sharp knife.

Dodgerton stepped out of the shadows with a shotgun in the crook of his arm.

"Was the knife intended for me?" she asked in a shaky voice.

Dodgerton spat a sluice of tobacco juice onto Gambini's back. "I'd say your ability to foresee your own future is piss-poor."

"I'm in your debt," Sarah stammered as she edged away from the body.

"That you are."

****

Over the next two years, Sarah gradually took on the role of caregiver as Tsuritsa Voldoma's health declined. The old woman, often short of breath and unsteady on her feet, would often rise to the occasion once a show began, acting like her former self.

But one warm October evening, after a large performance, Tsuritsa crumpled to the ground on the way back to their tent.

Joseph Kerensky, the strongman, dropped his weights with a crash and plowed through the crowd standing before his sideshow stage. Kerensky scooped up the old woman and carried her to Sarah's and Tsuritsa's tent. With care, he lay Tsuritsa down on her cot. Other circus folks abandoned their acts, despite the cries of protests from spectators. The performers followed the strong man in a procession of concern. When Kerensky exited through the tent flap he waved them away.

"Let them have some peace," he said, but he himself only moved a few feet. No one else left either until Dodgerton arrived and forced people back to work. Dodgerton poked his head into the tent, surveyed the scene and snorted.

Inside, Sarah knelt next to Tsuritsa and stroked the old woman's wrinkled forehead.

Tsuritsa came to and took Sarah's hand. She raised her head and in a hoarse whisper said, "You must leave." She struggled for breath and swallowed. The wrinkles on her face and neck roiled around with the effort. "Tonight," she croaked. Tsuritsa fell back onto the pillow and shut her eyes.

Sarah looked up. Dodgerton was gone.

Despite the warning, Sarah stayed by Tsuritsa's

side. She knelt on the straw-covered floor and held the old woman's hand. Tsuritsa's breathing became labored, rattled and irregular. The interval between each breath became longer until the old woman stopped breathing altogether. The dead woman's hand became limp and slipped from between Sarah's onto the side of the cot.

Sarah's sobs were intense. One caught in her throat and she could not breathe until her lungs forced her to take in huge wracking gulps of air. *Tsuritsa is gone—* her mentor and surrogate mother. Sarah felt this loss far more acutely than what she'd experienced when taken away by Dodgerton nine years before. The carnival became her home, and Tsuritsa made it so. After a while, Sarah fell asleep next to the cot with her head on top of the old woman's hand.

She awoke sometime later, her knees stiff and sore. With great effort, she moved them around, trying to work out the pain. She struggled to her feet and wiped away the vestiges of tears.

Sarah gathered her things. Tsuritsa and she discussed this event for well over a year. At the old woman's insistence, Sarah kept a bag packed, filled with clothes and her money, of which she'd spent little over the years.

She lifted the strap to the carpetbag and turned to go, but Dodgerton stood in the tent's entryway. *For how long?*

Dodgerton entered and regarded the corpse. He jerked a blanket over the old woman's face and looked over at Sarah. "I started this enterprise with Tsuritsa. I'll miss her." He lowered his head a moment, and Sarah heard him sniff. With some hesitancy, she stepped toward him and put a hand on his back. Dodgerton's head sprang up. He whipped around and snatched Sarah's arm.

"It's time I collected what's due." He worked his way out of his jacket one arm at a time so he could continue to hold her by the wrist. "Tsuritsa put me off long enough. As you once said, you're in my debt. It's time to pay up."

"No!" Sarah screamed. She tried to break free.

Dodgerton twisted Sarah's arm around her back and put his other hand behind her head. He yanked her to him and kissed her with rough intensity. Sarah twisted her face away and started to scream until he clamped a hand over her mouth. His eyes drifted down to the costume she still wore, another one of Matilda's creations. Dodgerton let go of her mouth, grabbed the front of her dress, and tore it to reveal her breasts.

"These have ripened nicely," he said. Dodgerton grabbed her left breast and squeezed hard.

Sarah screamed until Dodgerton slapped her across the face. Sarah fell to the ground, and before she could stand, Dodgerton moved on top of her. He flipped her onto her back and pinned her hands down with his knees. He raised himself, yanked up the bottom of her dress, and fumbled with his belt.

"Stop!" shouted a deep voice.

Dodgerton craned his neck around, still working his belt. The strongman stood in the entryway to the tent. "Mr. Kerensky, I'd thank you to stay the hell out of my affairs," Dodgerton's breathing, heavy with excitement and with the exertion of holding Sarah down, didn't prevent his voice from being firm. He unbuttoned his pants. "That, or you can find yourself another job."

Kerensky held open the tent flap. "You should extend your offer to everyone."

Dodgerton looked back again to see the entryway now filled with people and more outside. Voices shouted.

"Let her go, damn you!"

"Get off!"

"You monster!"

"Leave off," came a voice Sarah recognized as Barnaby's, "or I'll kill you!"

Sarah kicked out and knocked over the box holding the lit kerosene lamp. The glass lamp fell to the floor and shattered. Flames danced to life on the spilled fuel and spread across the straw and up one side of the tent.

Dodgerton sprang up. "You crazy bitch!"

He hiked up his pants, grabbed his jacket, and used it to bat the flames. This made matters worse, as bits of burning straw began to fly around the room and ignite elsewhere. Dodgerton ran up to the strongman and yelled at him and to the others standing outside. "Man the buckets, or everything will be destroyed!" He pushed his way past the on-lookers.

Coughing, Kerensky lifted the body of Madame Vodoma and placed the dead woman over his shoulder. With his other hand, he grabbed the blanket from the cot and draped it over himself and Sarah, who managed to retrieve her bag. The two ran from the tent and Kerensky threw off the smoldering blanket. They escaped without injury.

A bucket brigade started, and pails of water passed along the line.

Both Sarah and Kerensky coughed for some time

until their lungs cleared themselves of smoke, soot, and mucus. Kerensky carried the fortuneteller's body a safe distance away and set her down with reverential care. When he stood up, he took Sarah by the shoulders. Sarah held up the torn front of her dress with one hand and her carpetbag with the other.

"Leave, my young friend, and never come back. We will hold you in our hearts."

Tears filled Sarah's eyes again. She dropped her bag and threw her free hand around Kerensky in a clumsy hug.

The strongman pushed her back a foot or so and regarded her with evident concern.

"I'll be all right," she assured him. She looked back at the bucket brigade, many of whom stopped for a moment to stare at her. Those whose hands were free waved goodbye.

Matilda threw the contents of a bucket on the flames, turned and smiled at Sarah through her beard. "Fly, little bird!" Matilda shouted.

So she did.

Chapter Two

"I'm sorry, but the news is not good." The Reverend William Weston Patton looked at Edgar with sympathetic eyes and bowed his silvery gray head.

"As you know, I have long taken a personal interest in you." He raised his head and gave Edgar a broad smile. "You are a remarkable young man, and when you go out into the world, you are also representing Howard University and your race. It was with our assistance you were able to secure the funds to get your Ph.D. at Yale."

Edgar smiled and thanked him for the hundredth time. The reverend smiled in return and said, "Tut, tut." Still, the reverend had raised the issue of his indebtedness.

"On your behalf," Reverend Patton continued, "I have written many institutions to help you gain a position but without luck. However, given a personal connection I have with Professor Trowbridge at Harvard, and knowing they are completing a new physics laboratory, I thought our, that is, *your* chances were excellent."

Edgar now sat up on the edge of his chair, anxious at news of a real prospect.

"I have sent three personal letters to President Charles William Eliot, on your behalf. The first two went unanswered, the latest, a curt response stating the physics department is fully staffed. Trowbridge tells me that isn't true. Trowbridge's lobbying has also gotten nowhere. I'm afraid we have run out of options."

Edgar heaved a sigh and glanced around the room. A picture of General Howard, the one-armed Civil War general who founded the university, stared down at him. He seemed to say, "Don't give up. By God, I never have."

Edgar looked at his benefactor. "I have an aunt in Shrewsbury, Massachusetts. Perhaps I'll pay her a visit."

Reverend Patton leaned back in his chair, which screeched in protest. "Good idea. Make him tell you "no" to your face. Perhaps he won't be able to. If you can't make any headway, I know a normal school whose administration would feel lucky to have you."

Edgar stood up and shook the reverend's hand. He was grateful for the assistance, in spite of it going nowhere. On an impulse, he asked, "Do you mind if I take Mr. Eliot's letter? It may help strengthen my resolve."

"Of course." The reverend handed it to him. "Good luck."

"I am tremendously grateful." Edgar shook his benefactor's hand and nodded goodbye to the picture of General Howard.

Several days later, Edgar arrived at Harvard and found his way to President Eliot's office. The officious secretary was a gray-haired woman with a gray disposition. Her face featured a sharp beak-like nose, and she would periodically dart her head this way and that, like a hawk. The woman began to bang away at a typewriter as Edgar came up to her neat but crowded desk. Edgar removed his hat and bowed. The secretary froze with her hands poised above typewriter's keys. She brought her head up, then looked away.

"Yes?"

"My name is Dr. Edgar Gilpin. I don't have an appointment, but I would very much like to have a moment with President Eliot. I don't mind waiting."

"President Eliot is extraordinarily busy today. It would be impossible for you to see him."

Edgar smoothed the front of his vest with one hand. "What about tomorrow?"

"The same."

"And the day after?"

She sighed. "He's a very busy man."

"I see." Edgar noticed the three empty chairs against the wall. "I'll wait here and see if he has a moment to spare."

Edgar sat there for an hour before President Eliot arrived. The president opened the door and strode across the room to his office. "Morning, Clarissa," he said in passing.

"Good morning, sir."

Edgar stood, recognizing the man from the photo in the hall, but the president continued into his office and shut the door. Edgar sat down again. In a short while, the secretary stood up and took a stenography notebook plus several sharpened pencils off her desk and retreated into the president's office.

A half-hour later, she emerged, returned to her desk, and resumed typing.

A total of three men came and went on separate occasions before lunch. They were each ushered into the president's office as soon as they arrived. The last walked out of the office around noon, laughing with the president, both smoking cigars. They left together, without so much as a glance toward Edgar. At that, the secretary straightened her desk and walked toward the door.

"I'm afraid you'll need to leave now. I lock up when I go to lunch."

Edgar exhaled audibly and followed her out. After a little searching, he found an eatery near campus that would serve him. He returned to the president's office around one o'clock, as the secretary unlocked the door. She did not acknowledge him and simply went inside, shutting the door in his face. Edgar pounded the flat of his hand hard against the door. The sound and sting of his hand gave him pause. Don't, he said to himself, calming his temper. After a moment, he entered and reclaimed his seat.

The secretary stood with her back against her desk looking frightened. "What was that?" she asked in a shaky voice.

"A student dropped an armload of books out in the hall. I stopped to give him a hand."

The woman now seemed scared of him. She tentatively moved around her desk and resumed her work.

President Eliot returned around two-thirty and emerged from his office again around four. He carried his briefcase, plus his hat and coat. This time, Edgar stood and introduced himself as the president crossed the room. The man simply walked by without acknowledging him.

Edgar became boiling mad. *The pretentious bastard!* He turned toward the secretary as anger rushed through him. The urge rode him to sweep everything off her desk and chuck her typewriter through one of the windows. Instead, he asked in as even a tone as he could manage, "Will he be returning?"

"I'm afraid not," she said, averting her eyes from him as she typed. "He has two receptions this evening."

"I see."

Edgar retrieved his hat from the chair and stormed out of the office, still biting his tongue. Down the hall, he stopped at a drinking fountain. He filled his right hand with water and used it to splash his face, trying to cool off, both figuratively and literally.

"Dr. Gilpin, is it?"

Edgar straightened up as water ran down his face.

"Yes?" The man standing before him surveyed Edgar with intense eyes. He possessed a high forehead, dark hair, and a beard with a few streaks of gray running through.

"Forgive me," said Edgar, running his hands over his face to wipe off most of the water. He pulled a handkerchief from a pocket and pressed it to his cheeks. He lowered the damp cloth and looked at the bearded man before him. "I was feeling a little faint."

The man stuck out his hand toward Edgar. "Dr. William James, professor of psychology and philosophy here at Harvard. I caught wind of Eliot giving you the cold shoulder."

"*What?* Am I the butt of jokes in the faculty dining hall?"

"Well, yes, frankly, but good in the sense I learned of you. I asked the people at my table, and Trowbridge said you came highly recommended. He pushed hard for your candidacy but couldn't get anywhere. So you see, you do have some champions here. I'd like to be one of them."

"Do you have the weight to get me a position?"

"No, not per se."

"I thought not. Perhaps I'll find better luck in Europe."

Professor James held up both his hands before him, as though trying to calm a horse. "Before you desert the motherland, like my famous brother, I'd like to propose a job that would offer you a unique opportunity to use your expertise in both physics and engineering.

"Prior to you making a decision," James continued, "I wonder if you might join me and my family for a light supper and then allow me to take you to a demonstration which I hope may pique your interest."

Surprised at this sudden turn of events, Edgar chuckled in spite of himself and made a little bow. "I would be honored."

Later that evening, after a meal of beef barley soup, fresh bread, cheese, and apples, Edgar, Professor James and his wife enjoyed coffee and small talk.

"Where were you born?" asked Alice James. She took a sip of coffee and then smiled at him. Attractive but serious-looking, Alice seemed to run the house with a firm grip, despite her soft voice and demeanor. Her wide irises made her eyes look dark, and she wore her ebony-colored hair tied up on her head with a blue ribbon. She appeared to be in her early thirties.

Edgar met their two boys when he and the professor entered the kitchen through the rear of the house. The nanny had been feeding the boys—Harry, three years, and Billy, three months.

"I was born into slavery on a plantation in South

Carolina."

"And you have a doctorate in physics," noted the professor. "You have made remarkable strides, young man."

"I have had much help along the way."

Just then, the three-year-old scampered out of the kitchen and sat on his father's lap.

"Harry, please say hello to Dr. Gilpin," said the professor.

Edgar smiled and offered his hand for the boy to shake. Instead, the child swiped his fingers along the darker skin on the back of Edgar's hand. The boy studied his fingers. "Does it come off?" he asked.

"Harry!" shouted Alice, clearly mortified. The boy looked surprised at his mother's reaction and began to wail. He jumped from his father's lap and ran into the arms of his nanny, who emerged from the kitchen.

"It's all right. The boy didn't mean any harm," said Edgar.

"It's not all right," said Alice. She turned to the nanny, who held the crying boy in her arms. Alice softened her voice. "Please take Harry back to the kitchen. I shall speak to him later."

"Harry, our first child, is my domestic catastrophe," continued the professor. "I should have learned my lesson, but it seems Alice and I are producing a litter."

Alice flushed and lowered her gaze. "William!"

"Right." The professor grinned and changed the subject. "It's time we should be about our evening's business." He stood.

"Will you be staying with us, Mr. Gilpin?" asked Alice. As she rose from the table, Edgar noticed for the first time her bump of pregnancy.

"I wouldn't presume—" Edgar started to say, but Alice cut him off.

"Nonsense. We'd love to have you, right, William?"

"Right. So long as you don't mind sleeping on the sofa. Our guest room is currently occupied."

"I would be more than happy with such accommodations."

"Then it's settled." The professor fetched his hat from the stand near the front door. "We won't be late, Alice. A couple of hours at most."

When they arrived at their destination, a row house in Cambridge, Edgar and the professor were ushered into the room by Annabelle Douglas, who introduced herself as the professor's assistant. The woman wore her dark brunette hair pulled back over her ears into a bun, and her navy-blue dress lacked lace or ornamentation. Despite the effort to appear prim and businesslike, she looked quite beautiful. Edgar stuffed those thoughts aside. Not only were they taboo, but he had no time for women.

They walked into a drawing room and Edgar saw a small dark-haired woman being tied to a chair by two men.

Edgar stopped in his tracks and backed out of the room. "What in God's name is going on here?" he demanded.

The professor followed him out into the hall.

"This may appear a little untoward," Professor James admitted in a low voice, as he shut the door, "but I assure you everything is being done in the name of science. The woman is Eusapia Palladino. An associate of mine, Cesare Lombroso, recently sent her to America from Italy. She is currently staying in my home as a guest of our family."

Edgar continued down the hall toward the front door. *Could this man's hospitality be designed to dupe me?* He looked back over his shoulder at the professor who trailed him. "Is this how you treat your house guests? No thank you!"

The professor grabbed Edgar's arm and swung him around. Edgar prepared to break free, but the older man's face appeared earnest. Edgar took a deep breath. The professor's kindness necessitated he at least hear him out. He decided to give the man a chance to explain himself.

"Back in Italy," the professor continued, "Eusapia is a famous medium. Lombroso, a natural cynic decided to investigate her on behalf of the Society for Psychical Research. He and his assistants traveled to Sicily and sought her out. There, they insisted she conduct a demonstration in a well-lit room of Lombroso's choosing. She agreed to the room but insisted the room be darkened. When he protested, she screamed at him.

"I'm afraid this is a regular and colorful aspect to Miss Palladino's personality. Needless to say, she got her wish. However, Lombroso insisted she be tied to her chair.

"So there she was, tied up like a hog, and seething mad. She glared at Lombroso for ten minutes and nothing happened. Impatient and disgusted, Lombroso rose to end the session. He turned up the lamps, and froze, dumbfounded.

"Eusapia Palladino sat in the chair with her eyes shut, oddly pale. Several feet away, the heavy curtains covering the windows billowed as though blowing in the wind.

"Lombroso's two assistants dove for the curtains to catch whoever lurked behind them but found no one and the windows latched tight. A small table in the center of the room began to slide across the floor. Lombroso and his two men checked everywhere for any wires or other devices but could find none. They were forced to conclude Eusapia Pallidino possessed certain powers.

"The SPR decided she should come to America so I might conduct further tests along with Fredrick Meyers and Oliver Lodge—other members of our organization. Fred's family initially decided to take her in, but it became a debacle.

"First of all, it seems Eusapia hates Cambridge. She always complains of being cold, even in summer. Evie, Fred's wife, attempted to be very accommodating at first, taking Eusapia shopping, cooking Italian meals, and allowing Eusapia to dominate the table conversation. However, only Fred speaks Italian and Eusapia speaks hardly any English.

"Eusapia would shout down anyone else at the table and would chatter on incessantly. She would often reenact scenes from her life, including when brigands invaded her childhood village. She'd even grab steak knives and jab them at members of Meyer's family for effect. In the end, Evie became fed up and insisted Eusapia go, which is why the medium is currently a guest in our home.

"We were not having much success with our testing of her. We held a number of sessions in the Meyer's home, Eusapia remained sullen and uncooperative. A few things would rattle on the mantel, but nothing more. Most troubling for our work occurred when Richard Hodgson, head of the American branch of the SPR, came to a session. He told me to avoid any safeguards, and he would play a gullible fool. In doing so, he caught Eusapia cheating.

"Hodgson, who in reality is brilliant, acted dim-witted and enthralled with anything Eusapia said. At the session we all sat around a table with our hands joined on top—the tips of our little fingers touching. In the near-darkness, Eusapia manipulated her hands so Hodgson's soon touched the tip of the finger of the man on the other side of her. With her hands free, she began moving things around in the center of the table. Likewise, he caught her moving her legs, knocking and moving things with her foot. He bounded to his feet and accused her of being a fraud and a cheat. Which she clearly is, when given the opportunity.

"I confess to being similarly disgusted with her, but I had already arranged another session with two visiting British physicists, Lord Raleigh and Joseph John Thomson, also known as J.J."

"*Really*?" said Edgar. He shook his head in amazement. "Raleigh and Thomson would actually subject themselves to parlor room trickery?"

"I told them she was a cheat, but they insisted on the session nonetheless. J.J. told me, legitimate or no, it sounded like a good deal of fun. I let them know I planned to make every effort to prevent a recurrence of cheating.

"Like tonight, we bound Eusapia to a chair and checked everywhere for wires or any other form of subterfuge. Eusapia sat apart from everyone, and our only concession being to darken the room somewhat. As with Lombroso, nothing happened at first. In fact, twenty minutes went by and I looked at Lord Raleigh and J.J. for guidance on whether or not we should continue. J.J. made a little motion with his hand to relax and sit tight.

A moment or two later, the curtains began to billow, exactly as Lombroso witnessed. J.J. and Lord Raleigh went to the draperies and pushed on them. They would not move, except by their own accord. As before, we checked behind the curtains and saw no one and the window latched tight. By Lord Raleigh's estimate, the curtains billowed out at least three feet. We checked all around Eusapia for any threads or wires. None. Lord Raleigh pronounced the occurrence *odd.*

"Odd indeed, but I could not interest them in further research. Thus I have asked you, Dr. Gilpin, to join us here tonight. I dare say, you are every bit as bright as Lord Raleigh and J.J., and I hope your curiosity extends beyond simply pronouncing things "odd," and moving on."

Edgar looked at the professor wide-eyed. "So this is why you brought me here? Am I to lend some legitimacy to her little stunts?"

"Hardly. While admittedly, the field is riddled with fakery, we have determined approximately five percent of reported paranormal occurrences cannot be dismissed as fraud. These deserve scientific investigation. Lodge is also a physicist, visiting from Liverpool where he is a professor. I ask you to approach this with an open mind. Before the invention of the microscope, people could not believe a whole other world existed beyond the view of the naked eye."

Edgar looked down the hall at the door to the parlor. He looked directly at James. "Your kindness today compels me to indulge you in this, so long as you can assure me the woman is not being held against her will?"

"Indeed! But let's return before Eusapia finds a way out of her restraints.

"This house belongs to a friend of ours, and Eusapia has never been here before. We have checked the room for wires and threads and have sealed the windows. My assistant in these matters, Miss Douglas, has monitored her all day. These precautions, together with binding Eusapia's hands and legs, can assure us if something happens, it will not be due to underhanded trickery."

"If *what* happens?" asked Edgar.

"Let's wait and see."

James opened the door and they rejoined the others.

The professor introduced Edgar, Meyers, Lodge, and Eusapia, the latter of whom simply gave her head a curt nod. James insisted they all take their seats. In perfect Italian, which Edgar understood, the professor said, "You may begin, Miss Palladino."

At first, the bound woman just stared at them, seeming to focus her attention on each, one at a time from across the room. Edgar studied the woman as best as he could manage in the dim light. She looked short and sturdy-looking but not fat. She wore her mass of black hair drawn back from her face in a careless tail, and bangs hung down to her dark eyebrows. She had olive skin and intense-looking eyes. Her nose appeared a little larger than average and her lips were thin. Still, she projected a forcefulness about her he found attractive.

From across the room, it seemed as though her eyes locked on Edgar's. He stared back, fascinated by the intensity of the diminutive woman. He felt himself being drawn into her gaze and could not look away.

"He doubts!" She screamed the words again, "*He doubts*!" She suddenly broke out in a loud hysterical laugh. This trailed away as the color seemed to go out of her face. Eusapia closed her eyes.

Just like before, the drapes billowed and undulated as if from some breeze. In the corner of the room, a music box began to play.

The group watched as the music box rose into the air and flew toward Edgar, who caught it. He closed the lid, but the music kept playing. He turned it over in his hands, trying to find some sort of switch.

"Curious," Edgar muttered and tried to remove the key, but it would not come free. The music box fell from his hands and clattered onto the wooden floor. Edgar bent to retrieve it, but as he did so, something slapped him from behind and knocked him to the floor.

"Hey!" yelled Edgar.

The rest of the group seemed stuck to their seats. Edgar pleaded with them for help while some unseen force dragged him beneath the heavy-looking table in the center of the room. As he watched, unable to get up, the table rose into the air above him.

"What the hell? Help me!" he screamed.

Annabelle shouted, "Look at Eusapia!" Edgar craned his neck around to see a spectral white substance emerge from the top of the medium's head. He returned his gaze to the table above him and stared in disbelief.

The heavy table, hovering five feet in the air, upended itself, so its thick spiraled legs stuck up toward the ceiling.

"Good God, help me!" shouted Edgar.

Annabelle screamed.

With incredible speed, the white excretion extending from Eusapia darted across the room and shoved Edgar back toward his seat, just as the table crashed down onto the floor. The moment the table hit, the white substance vanished.

"Merciful heaven!" cried Meyers.

Edgar, now free to move, rolled over, pushed himself up on all fours, and sobbed with relief. The professor and the rest of the group surrounded Edgar who looked up with sudden anger. "*Why didn't you help me*?" he shouted.

"We couldn't move!" Annabelle said in their defense.

"Frozen to our chairs," said Lodge in his British accent.

"Are you all right?" the professor asked.

"Yes, I think so." Edgar stood and patted his body. "Yes, I'm fine." He looked over at the professor and shook his head. "I didn't realize I was risking my life in being here."

"We're so sorry," said Annabelle.

"This has never happened before," Lodge added.

"Could it have been her doing?" the professor wondered, as he looked at the bound woman.

Eusapia sat drenched in sweat, head bowed down to her chest.

"Or could she be some sort of catalyst for things

not entirely in her control?" he added.

Lodge and Meyers went to Eusapia and began untying the medium. Having freed her constraints, Meyers bent down on one knee before her and lifted her head in his hands. Eusapia's eyes flew open, and she grabbed Meyers' head and kissed him passionately.

When she released him, Meyers stood, looking embarrassed, and wiped his mouth with a handkerchief.

"She appears to be fine," said Edgar in a frosty voice.

Professor James coughed and shook his head in dismay. "Seems to be a side effect of these sessions. She is—how shall I put it?—aroused."

Eusapia stood, unsteady, and nearly fell. Lodge held her up. She looked at Edgar and said in English, "I save you."

"I dare say, you almost killed him!" said Lodge.

After conferring, they agreed the professor would take Edgar in his carriage, and Annabelle would follow behind with Eusapia. Lodge and Meyers would try to put the room back in order, and before the others left, they started to right the heavy table.

"This must weigh over a hundred pounds," Lodge said, grunting.

Later, as the horse clomped along on Cambridge's cobblestone streets, the professor shot a glance at Edgar, then smiled. "So, my friend, were you intrigued?"

"Afraid would be more apt."

"There are sometimes dangers when dealing with the unknown. I sought you out today because I am putting together my own team of researchers. I would like you to be a part of it. I'm calling the group the

"Eidola Project." Eidola is an ancient Greek word for ghosts, but I envision us investigating all things supernatural. At the very least, you'll never be bored."

"You already have a physicist," said Edgar.

"Lodge? He is heading back to England in a few days. In addition to me, it would be you, Annabelle Douglas and possibly Meyers—if I can convince his wife to loosen the reins."

"I don't know… According to you, much of what is purported to be supernatural is faked."

"Debunking those frauds would be of service to many people who would be taken in by charlatans."

"I hoped to do research, perhaps invent things."

"Wonderful. I would gladly provide you with space in my lab at Harvard and with what funding I can manage."

"This is not at all what I expected when coming to Boston."

The professor brought the horse to a stop. "Opportunity knocks, Dr. Gilpin. A man of your intelligence should be at the forefront of human knowledge. What say you?"

They stopped just outside of the city proper, where the road changed from stone to packed earth. Without street lights, it was difficult for Edgar to see. However, there was faint illumination from the widely spaced homes, and from the lanterns on each side of the carriage. After a few moments of silence, he realized the professor had extended a hand to him. Edgar stared awkwardly at it in the dim light.

"I'm afraid I need some time to think on this. May I give you my answer in the morning?"

Annabelle's and Eusapia's carriage came to a stop

behind them. He heard their horse whinny.

"Quite all right, but realize you have a chance to build a life and a career free of racial impediments. It would be an honor to work with you."

"I appreciate that."

The professor shook the reins and they started up again. The two rode in silence the rest of the way to the James' home.

In front of the house, the professor stopped the carriage and let Edgar get out. He hopped down and went to Annabelle's carriage as it came up behind. The front door to the house opened and Alice James appeared and ran across the drive to her husband. She kissed his cheek and put her arm through his. She gave Annabelle, what Edgar assumed to be, a quick proprietary glance and then turned her attention back to her husband.

"I'm so glad you're back," said Alice. "The kids are abed. I'll draw you a bath."

Eusapia jumped down from her carriage and looked at the professor and his wife. "Bath? Yes!" Eusapia spoke with conviction and strode into the house.

Incredulous, Alice looked at her husband. The professor let go of the bridle on Annabelle's horse long enough to pat Alice's hand. "Don't trouble yourself. I need to put the horse in the stable. I'll be in directly. Perhaps you can see that Dr. Gilpin is well situated for the night."

Alice looked crestfallen but complied. She went over to Edgar and gave a strained smile. "I trust you enjoyed a pleasant evening?"

Sensing the tension, Edgar cocked his head. "Are

you sure this is not putting you out? Perhaps the professor's assistant, Miss Douglas, could give me a lift somewhere I might find lodging."

Alice visibly recovered herself. She smiled now with real warmth. "No, I wouldn't hear of it. You are no trouble at all, Mr. Gilpin." She put her arm in his and led him into the house. Alice looked over her shoulder at her husband and Miss Douglas. "Don't be long, dear."

****

The professor turned toward Annabelle once Alice and Edgar went into the house.

"So?" asked Annabelle. "Did he agree?"

"He wants to sleep on it."

"Well, that's something," she said. Annabelle took in a deep breath and exhaled. "I don't mind telling you, tonight frightened me. Were you not there, I don't know what I would've done." Annabelle surprised herself at these remarks. She never before projected weakness and hoped, if he didn't take the bait—flirting with him by feigning to be the weaker sex—he wouldn't think any less of her.

The professor, lost in his thoughts, seemed oblivious to her flirtation. After a few moments of silence, he said, "Yes, quite an eventful session. I can't see how any of it was faked."

Annabelle, rebuffed, composed herself and picked up the reins. "I do hope Mr. Gilpin joins our little company. I expect I shall see you tomorrow in any case. Sweet dreams."

The professor let go of the bridle and stepped back. "And to you, Miss Douglas."

****

Alice brought Edgar into her husband's study. A small lamp lit the room from the desk, a workspace crowded with research materials and stacks of manuscript papers.

"My husband's book project on psychology," she said, indicating the manuscript. "He's been working on it for years and admits he's nowhere near done."

Behind the desk and on another wall were tall bookshelves, filled with numerous volumes. Above the fireplace, among the many other pictures, stood a framed portrait of a pretty Alice as a teenager. A sofa, already made up as a bed, stood between two sets of draped windows.

"I thought you'd be more comfortable in here than in the living room. Our son, Harry, whom you met at dinner, knows not to enter this room. Otherwise, he would probably roust you from your slumber at the crack of dawn. Besides, with you in here, odds are William will spend the rest of the evening with me, rather than with his tome." She pointed to the manuscript again with a wry little smile.

Edgar bowed. "I am happy to oblige you in your domestic machinations. Thank you again for your hospitality."

Alice turned with a rustle of her long skirt and shut the door on her way out.

Edgar strolled over to the desk and studied the items without disturbing things. Some manuscript pages were in longhand, others typed. He turned up the desk lamp and lifted one page to catch the light.

Sensations, once experienced, modify the nervous organism, so that copies of them arise again in the mind after the original outward stimulus is gone. No mental copy, however, can arise in the mind, of any kind of sensation which has never been directly excited from without.

Edgar set the page down. If the professor was right, the frightful situation he experienced a few hours ago may well arise again in his mind. He turned to the bookshelves for distraction.

The extensive library contained volumes representing numerous religions—an old Bible, a Koran, the Torah, the Bhagavad Gita and texts on Buddhism—to modern scientific texts, including Darwin's *The Descent of Man*, and Lyell's *Principles of Geology.* There were also classics: Shakespeare, Chaucer, Ovid, Aristotle. One portion of a shelf was reserved for volumes by Henry James.

"The proud brother," Edgar said under his breath.

Never having read Henry James, he decided on a volume entitled, *The Portrait of a Lady.* Edgar set the book on the sofa and lit a nearby lamp. He went back and blew out the one across the room.

After reading for an hour, Edgar set the book on the little table behind him and turned the lamp down. He drifted off to sleep, hoping the trials of Isabel Archer would dominate his dreams, rather than the evening's proceedings.

He dreamt being dragged across a wooden floor again, screaming for help. Though bound, Eusapia stared at him with her intense eyes and laughed. A weight settled on his midsection, and for a second, he wondered if the heavy table had crashed down upon him.

Edgar awoke and stared into Eusapia's eyes.

Eusapia was pulling down his pants while

straddling him and continuing to hold his stare. Her nest of black hair hung loose about her face and onto the white of her gown, which she'd hiked up to her hips. She reached down and clutched him as she continued to stare into his face. "I save you," she said with a smile.

Edgar's member hardened, in spite of himself. When she guided him into her, Edgar gasped.

In his twenty-six years, he'd never been with a woman, devoting himself to his studies and advancing his career. And he became awkward around the ladies. Opportunities were ignored or turned away, fearful of entanglements. Now…

What am I doing? But he couldn't stop.

Eusapia began to rock back and forth, as she pressed down upon his chest. She stared at him all the while, and he could not look away. His eyes began to water with the strain. At last, she shut her eyes and shuddered and Edgar did the same, climaxing together.

Eusapia began to laugh hysterically.

"You'll wake them!" Edgar said in alarm.

Eusapia put two fingers on his lips and hushed him. "I save you," she whispered. She bent over and kissed him on the mouth.

Her breath, more pungent than a dirty sock, caused him to turn his head away. A moment later, reconsidering this, he turned back and kissed her.

In the morning, when Edgar emerged from the study, he found Alice and the maid setting the table. Edgar could hear the children in the kitchen with the nanny.

Alice smiled. "Good morning, Dr. Gilpin. Did you sleep well?"

Edgar smiled in return. "All things considered,

remarkably so."

"I'm glad. Would you like some coffee?"

"Yes, please."

"It should be ready in a moment. Please sit down."

Edgar sat and idly played with the silver fork at his place setting. He heard footfalls on the steps and saw Professor James descending the stairs while he tied his tie. It seemed dangerous the man should be doing so on the stairs; however, certainly less dangerous than what he experienced the previous evening.

Edgar grinned and shook his head, amazed at everything in the preceding twenty-four hours.

"What?" said the professor. "Does my tie clash with my jacket?"

"Forgive me, I was recalling last night."

"Well, if you're smiling, can I take that as a good sign?"

Before Edgar could answer, a thunderous clamor occurred as a suitcase tumbled down the stairs, followed by a string of Italian profanity. Eusapia continued to swear as she struggled down the stairs with a second piece of luggage. She retrieved the fallen bag and moved to the front door. She turned and announced, "I go now."

Alice burst out of the kitchen. "Did someone fall? Is everyone all right?"

The professor went to his wife, took her hand, and patted it. "We're fine. It seems Eusapia wishes to go back to Italy."

Alice rolled her eyes. "And not a moment too soon," she muttered loud enough for Edgar to hear. Edgar wondered if Eusapia heard and understood the words.

As if on cue, Eusapia began to scream in a high ear-piercing howl.

Alice's mouth dropped open. She turned to her husband and back to Eusapia.

Professor James patted his wife's hand again. He looked at Eusapia and shouted in Italian over the din, "I understand your desire to leave."

Eusapia stopped screaming.

The professor lowered his voice and continued. "We were about to eat, and you have a long trip ahead of you. Please join us at the table before I take you to Boston."

Eusapia gave her head a curt nod and dropped her bags to the floor with a crash. She went to the head of the table and sat. "I eat!" she announced in English.

Edgar took this all in, wide-eyed.

"So, Dr. Gilpin," said the professor as he took a seat opposite Eusapia, "are you preparing to abandon ship as well?"

Edgar looked at Professor James and smiled. He shook his head. "I've decided to accept your offer. As you indicated yesterday, I shall never be bored."

Chapter Three

Sarah emerged from the bushes, dressed in one of Tsuritsa's old outfits. She put her torn dress in her bag and now wished she packed another outfit instead of so many books. Perhaps she would stop somewhere for a needle and thread. She could also buy another outfit, but with the travel ahead of her, it didn't make sense to soil a new set of clothes. She would deal with that later.

Where to go? Sarah and Tsuritsa considered this event for some time, ever since the old woman's health began to decline. Tsuritsa broached the subject and encouraged Sarah to decide her next step, but Sarah couldn't manage to come up with any plan so chose inaction. Denial could be a powerful force, but it no longer held sway. It couldn't.

Sarah already missed her carnival family, except for Dodgerton, but because of him, she could not return. She rejected the option of her parents, not seen in nine years. She felt as though she no longer belonged to a family.

She could work for another carnival, but she hated the need to fabricate responses when she could not establish contact with the world beyond. Employment elsewhere or trying to settle into a normal life seemed risky. What would people say when she spoke to spirits or went into a trance and spirits spoke through her? Hardly apropos for a typical job or a sewing circle.

Where did she belong?

In the back of her mind, she recalled a client who once mentioned a professor at Harvard, William James, who studied the supernatural. If anyone, she felt, he would understand. He would not treat her like a freak. Perhaps she could build a new life around that.

Sarah looked back and forth on the empty road. The sun poked above the horizon, and the sky was filled with beautiful hues of red, pink, and orange. *An omen?*

****

"The way we perceive the world and order our thoughts conforms to a specific structure, that which we call our consciousness." Professor James stood in front of a blackboard on which he wrote the name Wilhelm Wundt in white chalk.

The professor wore a three-piece charcoal suit and noticed considerable chalk dust down his right side, where he unconsciously wiped his hand when lecturing. *Perhaps this merits a chapter in my book.*

His students, all young men, began to whisper amongst themselves. The professor turned and saw an attractive young woman by the door, dressed in old clothes. She looked like a gypsy.

"Well, what have we here?" he asked as he crossed the room.

"May we speak for a moment, sir?" said the young woman.

Her effrontery took him aback. He considered ordering her out of his classroom but held off as he studied her face. She smiled back at him with equanimity.

The students in the room were abuzz with

speculation. The professor shot them an annoyed look and turned back to the young woman. He took her by the elbow and steered her through the door and out into the hall.

"You have one minute, young lady, then I need to reclaim some order in my classroom."

The woman looked him in the eyes and spoke in a low voice, as though making a confession. "I speak to the dead."

Professor James did a double-take and cocked his head. "Come again?"

"I hear spirits and often let them speak through me. I was part of a carnival act, but I assure you it's true."

The professor assessed the woman before him. *Another fraud?* She seemed sincere. He wanted to maintain critical detachment but felt like jumping out of his suit with excitement. "Young lady, what is your name?"

"Sarah Bradbury."

He reached down, took her hand, and pumped it. "Professor William James."

"Yes, I know."

"D-did spirits tell you?"

"No." Sarah chuckled. "A woman after one of my shows told me you were making a scientific study of the afterlife. I would like to join you."

"Miss Bradbury, do not, under any circumstances, go away."

The professor threw open his classroom door and ran inside. "That's it for today, gentlemen. Please read the next fifty pages in Wundt, and I'll see you all on Wednesday."

Professor James stopped at his desk and scratched

a note. He folded the sheet and wrote Annabelle Douglas on the outside. Searching the stragglers, he spotted awkward Walter Shoemaker, often the last to leave, attempting to pack his book bag.

"Walter, would you mind doing me a favor?"

Walter perked up like a dog at the prospect of a walk. "Sure, Professor! Anything."

The professor told him to deliver the note to the young woman at work in his office.

"Right away, sir," said Walter and scampered out the door.

Professor James went back into the hall and beamed with relief to see Sarah waiting for him, worried she had been some sort of apparition who would dissolve the moment he stepped away. He took her again by the elbow and moved her at a quick pace down the hall. He politely put off any student who approached them.

They left the building and made their way to Harvard Yard. The two sat on a marble bench. Above them, the leaves on the maple trees displayed variegated hues of red, yellow, and orange, as they rustled in the October breeze.

A moment later, Annabelle arrived and Professor James made hasty introductions and bade her sit on the bench as well. "I have another associate, Dr. Gilpin, who I'd like you to meet, but he is unable to join us at the moment.

"Now, Miss Bradbury," his voice betraying his excitement, "I would like you to begin at the moment you first realized you possessed these abilities."

****

After several days of interviews, to see if Sarah's

stories stayed consistent, the professor and Edgar wanted to begin a series of tests they designed. They decided to use the lecture hall after hours, instead of the lab, because it remained unoccupied following classes. Several storage rooms on one side of the hall provided space for Edgar to keep the machines he assembled or acquired. Indeed, when Sarah and Annabelle arrived, the floor before the amphitheater seats looked crowded with Edgar's devices.

In the midst of it all sat a plain wooden chair.

Professor James hurried over to greet them. "Good evening to you both. I hope you will indulge us, Miss Bradbury—"

"Please call me Sarah," she said. "After hearing my life story several times over the past three days, I think we can be less formal."

"Right," said the professor. "Sarah it shall be." He offered no familiar name in return. The professor turned toward the center of the room and ushered her forward.

"If you would be so kind as to have a seat," Professor James continued, "we will get started. I hope you are not disturbed by Dr. Gilpin's—I mean Edgar's since we now know each other so well—machinery. We are doing this all in the name of science."

The professor held the chair for Sarah. She sat and looked around at the devices surrounding her. A camera stood perched on a tripod with a flash-pan above. Before her stood a table on which lay a large black box with a glass portal on top. From this box ran two insulated wires with six inches of exposed copper at the end of each. Another table held one of Edison's tin drum phonographs with a large megaphone aimed right at her.

Edgar smiled to reassure her and handed her a wire for each hand, the bare copper to be squeezed.

"Is this safe?" she asked.

"Not to worry, there's no electricity in the lines. Yet. In fact, my device is designed to measure electricity flowing from you. The Society for Psychical Research has published several tracts about electromagnetic charges generated by true mediums. We want to see if these can be measured."

Annabelle stood by the phonograph, with her hand on its crank, prepared to record. Professor James held a board with paper clipped to it and a pen at the ready.

"Okay, Miss Bradbury," said the professor, "you may begin."

Sarah looked at them with amazement. "I'm not sure I can perform like a trained monkey."

"I understand, but I ask you to try. You worked in a carnival, surely you needed to perform on demand?"

"In which case, I was often forced to lie."

"Heaven forbid." The professor tried anew. "Please be assured, we don't want you to fabricate anything. We'll all just sit here. If nothing happens, we'll try again tomorrow evening and the next."

Sarah closed her eyes and took several deep breaths. After she sat for quite some time, she cracked open one eye. They stared in expectation. She repeated the breathing regimen and tried to call up any psychic impressions.

Nothing.

Sarah opened both eyes and shrugged. She saw their disappointment.

Professor James set the pen, board, and paper on the podium and took out his pocket watch. He and

Edgar made eye contact and the professor signaled to continue. “We’ll give it another fifteen minutes,” he said.

Edgar’s audible sigh marked the passage of another quarter of an hour.

“I’m sorry,” said Sarah

“No,” the professor responded, “It’s you who’s owed an apology. We did not intend to treat you as a circus animal. The question is, how do we proceed? If we sat here for several hours more would it be a good use of our time?”

Sarah shrugged. “I couldn’t tell you.”

The professor scratched his head and looked over at Sarah. “What do you need in order to have the insights you described?”

“I’m not sure. Sometimes they wash over me unbidden, leaving me with knowledge I could not otherwise have known. Other times I pass into a trance. Upon awakening, I sometimes need to be told what I said.”

“Can we get you something so you are more comfortable?” asked Annabelle.

“A crystal ball?” asked Edgar.

“No.” Sarah chuckled. “That’s just a prop. However, these two wires *are* distracting.”

“Let me give this some thought. I’ll try to have a different setup tomorrow.”

The professor sighed as well and snapped his watch shut. “Not a very promising start. Let’s see what tomorrow brings.”

****

The two women left campus and caught a cab to their rooming house. The professor billeted Sarah in the same place as Annabelle, a rooming house catering exclusively to women. The boarders would share meals together, and the proprietor, Mrs. Flanders, served as not only as a surrogate mother for the chicks who nested in her house but as an excellent cook.

Sarah stared out the cab's window. They rode in silence. At first, Annabelle didn't intrude, but after several minutes, she decided to press the issue.

"So," Annabelle said, "what do you suppose is the problem?"

Sarah turned to look at her, just visible in the light cast by the small oil lamp inside the cab. "I don't know. Perhaps all the apparatus? I've done legitimate channeling before crowds for years. I'm not sure why it sometimes deserts me. Did I embarrass you?"

Annabelle looked incredulous. "I should think it would be you who'd be feeling embarrassed."

Sarah lowered her eyes and smiled. "I can tell you are in love with the professor—"

"Stop right there!"

The cab jerked to a stop and they could hear the horses' hooves scrambling upon the cobblestones.

Annoyed, Annabelle, pulled down the hatch in the ceiling so she could see the cabbie outside. "I'm sorry, driver. I did not mean you. Please proceed with my apologies." She let go of the cord and the small hatch sprung back into place.

Annabelle looked back at Sarah, "Of all the nerve!" Her indignation evaporated as a sudden thought caused her heart to drop down to her abdomen. "Did you—did something tell you?"

Sarah reached out and took Annabelle's hand. "I could see it with my own eyes. I could also see he is oblivious to your affection and by his ring that he is married."

Annabelle used her free hand to cover her mouth. "Oh, my."

"Don't worry," said Sarah, "I won't tell a soul."

Now Annabelle stared out the window.

They traveled in silence for several more minutes until the cab pulled up before their red brick rooming house. Annabelle got out and paid their fare. She ascended the steps, unlocked the door, and held it open for Sarah, who thanked her.

"Would you like a cup of tea?" Annabelle offered.

Sarah said she would, and the two went up the stairs to where all the boarders stayed.

Anabelle opened her room and encouraged Sarah to take a seat while she left with the kettle to fill it in the bathroom down the hall. When she returned, she set the pot on a small gas fire she ignited in the grate, then offered Sarah some biscuits from a tin. They both sat at the little table in her room and began to nibble.

"I'll trust your discretion," Annabelle said at last. "You were right, but I've told no one."

"Of course."

Sarah scanned the apartment.

It mirrored Sarah's, but Annabelle added homey touches. A bouquet sat in a vase between them and several bucolic prints hung from the striped wallpaper-covered walls. Next to the bed stood a small table, crowded with a lamp, a picture frame, and a stack of books. Two piles of books rose in one corner, next to a bureau. On top of the bureau sat a blue and white ceramic washbasin and a matching pitcher.

"You've been here long?" asked Sarah.

"Ever since I came to Harvard, well, Harvard Annex—it's where the women are for the time being. Someday soon I'm confident they will admit women on an equal footing." Annabelle got up and retrieved the folding picture frame from beside the bed. The gilt frame contained sepia-colored photos of a middle-aged man and woman, the man on the left side and the woman on the right.

"Your parents?" Sarah asked, reaching for the frame. The moment Sarah touched the picture of Annabelle's mother, she collapsed onto the floor and began to shake, as though having a seizure.

Annabelle dropped down beside her and put her hands beneath Sarah's head, to keep it from banging on the floor. A moment later, Sarah's eyes flew open.

"I miss you, dear," said Sarah, in the voice of Annabelle's mother. Sarah smiled as she looked at Annabelle, but her expression darkened.

Sarah reached up and grabbed Annabelle's forearm in a vice-like grip. "There's danger ahead! Take care!" Annabelle's mother said. "Promise!"

"Yes, Mother, I promise!" Annabelle cried.

The kettle began to whistle and Sarah went limp. Her eyes closed and she lapsed into unconsciousness.

Chapter Four

Annabelle could not sleep. She lay on her bed wrapped in her comforter and looked at the form of the strange young woman who collapsed onto her apartment floor. Unable to rouse her, Annabelle covered Sarah with a blanket and placed a pillow beneath her head.

The words from her deceased mother ran through Annabelle's mind. As she thought about the course of the last few years, she realized her mother still had a hand in most of it, despite being dead.

Annabelle excelled in school, but it was at her mother's insistence Annabelle submitted an application to the Harvard Annex. Her mother read in the newspaper Harvard supported a new program for the higher education of women. She wanted Annabelle to be among the vanguard, and she got her wish.

Admitted into the first class of women in the program, nicknamed the "Harvard Annex," they attended classes taught by the main campus faculty. On the first day, one of the program's directors, Elizabeth Cary Agassiz, stated in an assembly her hope the Annex would soon be part of Harvard proper. Unfortunately, this had yet to occur.

When Professor James entered the classroom, he strode to the podium and set down his books and papers. He tapped his fountain pen on the podium, gaveling the class to order and surveyed the room full of women. "Well, what have we here?"

The professor smiled and Annabelle felt he directed it at her, especially since she chose a seat in the center of the front row.

"Well, I say it's high time we did not ignore the potential of half the human race!" proclaimed the professor.

Annabelle chose the same seat thereafter in all Professor James's classes, which became often since she decided to major in the new field of psychology. She swore something extra existed in his smile, and a twinkle in his eye, whenever he greeted her or looked at her during class. There must've been, because he noticed when she became despondent after her mother's death—of course, being in the front row may have helped.

Lilly, her mother, simply dropped to the floor of the kitchen one day after supper. No warnings, no sign of ill health, and no opportunity to say goodbye. In fact, Annabelle's father already returned to the harvest and didn't know she passed until he came home many hours later to find the house dark and Lilly sprawled on the floor, a broken china soup tureen and left-over tomato soup pooled on the floor around her.

Two days later, after her father conveyed the news via telegram, Annabelle returned home to find the house crowded with neighbors and relations. Her mother's body lay in an open casket in the parlor. Annabelle dropped her bags amid the guests and walked straight to her mother. She lifted the woman's cold, unresponsive hand, then let go.

Annabelle studied the figure in the coffin. She

touched the woman's face and bent closer. She smelled the familiar rose water her mother used, mingled with a faint scent of decay. Annabelle told herself this wasn't the woman who loved her and she loved in return. This must be an imposter. A resemblance existed, to be sure, but she *knew* her own mother. "It's not her!" she shouted.

She turned and saw everyone in the next room stop their conversations. They stared at her through the arched opening between the two rooms, silent, frozen, as they held their cups of tea or coffee and small plates of food. She couldn't ascertain the looks. Pity in their eyes? Concern? Whatever their intent, upon seeing them, Annabelle froze.

Her father broke free of the crowd. He came up and grabbed her upper arm so firmly it hurt. "Come, Annabelle, get ahold of yourself. Let's not make a scene." He steered her into the aptly named living room where everyone else stood. He found her a wooden chair in a corner with its back against the wall. "Would you like some coffee?"

Annabelle didn't respond and her father moved away.

He returned with the coffee, but the cup and saucer sat in her lap. She hung her head and studied the traces of milk running through the dark fluid. It needed to be stirred, but she made no effort to do so.

Throughout the evening, people approached her to express condolences but soon moved away when Annabelle did not raise her head, even when addressed. After everyone left, her father led her upstairs. He sat her on her old bed and told her to get some rest before the funeral the next morning.

Annabelle forced herself up to relieve herself in the chamber pot. But she did not replace the cover, nor slide it back beneath the bed. She lay on top of the bedspread and went to sleep with the smell of her own urine filling the room.

At the funeral and the subsequent burial, people continued to stare. They seemed to look to her for a signal on how to express grief, but their expectations were misdirected. Annabelle could not express anything for the imposter being lowered into the ground.

After they returned to the farmhouse, Annabelle, walked out into the fields. Stubble covered their acreage from the harvested corn, barley, and rye. Death could not deter her father from bringing in the crops. The brown, withered stubs of stalks covered the same bitter earth in which they placed the coffin. Somehow, it seemed fitting. She stayed out until nearly dark. Finally, she headed back to the house. The main floor remained crowded with folks, eating and drinking their choice of hard cider, beer or wine. Some laughed.

Without a word, Annabelle went up to her room and grabbed her bag. She descended the stairs, pushed her way through the crowded living room, and walked out the front door.

A quarter moon and stars hung in the sky—providing enough light for her to stay on the road the six miles into town. Several wagons and carriages of people stopped on the way with offers of a ride, but she remained unresponsive and simply continued to walk.

The station was closed, so she sat on an outside bench and shivered until morning. Annabelle boarded the first train back to Boston.

When she sat down on the train she could deny it

no longer; her mother was really gone. First came one tear, a trickle, and then a deluge. She'd wept so loud the conductor told her she needed to be quiet, or she'd be put off at the next stop. Instead, a woman in black, also in mourning, came and sat beside her. She first held Annabelle's hand. When Annabelle turned and began to sob onto the woman's shoulder, the lady hugged Annabelle and begun to cry too. She stroked Annabelle's hair and softly repeated, "I know. I know."

Back at school, the cloud which followed her did not lift. Several days passed before she could face classes again, but once there, she could not concentrate on the material.

A day or two later, after one of his lectures, Professor James ushered the other students out the door. He came over and stood in front of Annabelle, then crouched down so their eyes met.

"Your father contacted the dean of students. I'm sorry for your loss. I know how hard it can be to lose a parent. Your father is worried about you."

"He doesn't want me to make a scene." She looked into the professor's eyes.

"Do you want to make a scene?"

"Will it bring my mother back?"

The professor scratched his beard and smiled ruefully. "I doubt it, but if you think it will help, be my guest. Professor Smith, a rather detestable classics professor, has this room next. If anyone deserves a scene it's him. I'm sure his students will appreciate it."

Annabelle smiled for the first time in days.

"Come," he held out his hand, "let's go get a cup of whatever at Taylor's."

Annabelle took the hand. She stood and continued

to stare at him. He smiled at her. The two made their way off campus to Taylor's Coffee House, where instead of coffee they each ordered cocoa. The weather had become unusually cold for October, and they sat opposite each other at a wooden booth, warming their hands around their large cups.

"I've been considering leaving school," she confessed.

The professor groaned under his breath and said, "I understand depression more than you may suspect. I speak from personal experience. It can hit some of us quite hard. In such cases, it has been helpful for me to outline what is truly important in my life. For myself, it is my family and my work—all of it—which includes helping students like you."

"I feel I am beyond help. Nothing seems important to me."

Professor James picked up a spoon and stirred the thick cocoa. "What held importance to you before this?" he asked.

Annabelle heaved her shoulders and looked out the window. A wind blew colored leaves down the brick and cobblestone street. At last, she said in a low voice, "My mother and school. I feel guilty for not including Father. He cares, I know, and I care for him, but there has always been a distance. Mother and I were close. She insisted I apply to the Annex."

"Would she want you to leave school without your certificate?"

Annabelle looked back at him. The professor smiled through his beard.

"No," she said in a soft voice.

"You are an exceptionally bright young lady.

Psychology needs fine minds like yours, so we can leave Medieval superstitions and popular misconceptions behind. It needs *you.* You have seven months to go. This is no time to quit."

Annabelle stared down at the scarred tabletop. She dreamed of the chance to be alone with Professor James, but the circumstance was very different than she ever imagined. Still, he said she had a fine mind! While she always felt this, to have it voiced by the professor meant the world to her. The weight of the past few days seemed to lift from her bosom, and she breathed more easily.

"There is one more thing," Professor James said after he took a drink from his mug. "It may also be possible to bring your mother back."

Annabelle looked up in shock and slammed her cup down. "What?"

"A passionate sideline of mine has to do with an organization out of London, The Society for Psychical Research. Their investigations are providing tantalizing clues about life after death. If you are up for it, on top of your senior-level coursework, I would be happy to share some of their monographs with you."

Annabelle, let go of her mug and impulsively took the professor's hands. "Do you really think it's possible?"

William James squeezed her hands in excitement. He smiled again and nodded. "They apply the scientific method to their research. Like psychology, this is the only way to escape the baggage of the past, plus it's a way to finally discredit the people who prey on the bereaved. I and some like-minded folks have considered establishing a chapter in the U.S. Come graduation, this might be a project worthy of one such as you."

And so it began. Annabelle applied herself with renewed commitment to her studies and graduated magna cum laude. Upon graduation, she took the professor up on his offer. During the summer she read all she could get her hands on published by or about the Society for Psychical Research, including their recent book, *Phantasms of the Living*. The society had determined about five percent of all reported cases seem to be credible. The rest were largely a question of fraud or misinterpretation of natural events. This five percent was tantalizing.

Professor James did not teach that summer. He and she met often to confer and plan their next steps—when the professor wasn't otherwise engaged in his massive volume on psychology or distracted by the demands of domestic life. On those occasions when invited to the James' house for dinner, Alice James would hardly speak to her. Annabelle assumed the woman's decidedly cool disposition toward her originated in her sensing a potential rival. Nevertheless, Annabelle kept her behavior above reproach, though she yearned for more.

Eventually, the SPR established an American branch, but the professor declined the offer to lead it. He claimed the demands of teaching and research at Harvard necessitated he defer to someone else. Unfortunately, the London branch, which headed the organization worldwide, appointed Richard Hodgson, to direct its activities in America. Hodgson's profound skepticism hindered the research. In the face of this, the professor and she created the Eidola Project—what the professor dubbed their own investigations into the supernatural—Eidola being an ancient Greek word for ghosts. Eventually, they welcomed Dr. Edgar Gilpin into their group, who brought his expertise in physics and his penchant for invention.

Now, in Sarah Bradbury, they may have found their fourth member…

****

Sarah awakened and stirred uncomfortably on the floor where she obviously spent the night.

"Oh, dear," she said, as she threw off the blanket and struggled to her feet, still dressed from the night before.

Annabelle, also dressed, pushed back the half of the quilted comforter she pulled over herself that night and sat up on the side of the bed. "You all right?" she asked.

"I've wet myself," Sarah admitted. Unsteady, she grabbed the back of a wooden chair by the table.

Annabelle came up and braced her.

"I'm so embarrassed," Sarah said as she began to cry.

Annabelle hugged her tighter. "There's no reason to be ashamed."

"I just want a place where I belong," sobbed Sarah. She reached into a small pocket for her handkerchief but finding it wet, withdrew her hand. "After failing your test and now with this spectacle, I'm sure you've had your fill of me."

"On the contrary," said Annabelle. She drew out her own handkerchief and dabbed Sarah's cheeks. "After last night, I am convinced."

"Last night?"

"You don't recall?"

"No."

"I'll tell you later. First, let's get you to your room, so you may clean up."

As they went out into the hall, Sarah leaned against Annabelle for support. There were a number of young women already in line for the bathroom. They all turned to stare, but one frowned with disapproval.

"I hope you kept your drinking elsewhere."

"Be a little charitable, Penelope, Miss Bradbury is ill." Annabelle, helped Sarah unlock her room.

"That's what happens when you imbibe." Penelope would not let it go.

Sarah and Annabelle entered Sarah's room and Annabelle kicked the door shut behind them.

"Don't be troubled by her," said Sarah. "Her fiancé abandoned her at the altar last year and she's had no suitors since."

"How…?"

"I haven't a clue. But I know it's true."

Annabelle helped her to a wooden chair and Sarah sat. Annabelle checked the pitcher and washbasin. Empty.

"I'll get you some water," said Annabelle. "Will you be okay on your own for a moment?"

Sarah nodded and began to unlace her shoes.

****

In the hall, Annabelle carried the pitcher from Sarah's room to the front of the line. "Sarah *is* ill," she explained. "I just wish to get some water." Eunice and Jeri, the two other girls in the hall said it was okay, but not Penelope.

"Too bad," said Penelope without sympathy. "Get

to the back and wait your turn. She can suffer and meditate on being a reprobate. Perhaps, then, you and she will change your ways."

"Penelope, what makes you the arbiter of all goodness and right?" Annabelle's voice sounded testy, in spite of Sarah's admonition.

"I know a sinner when I see one," hissed Penelope.

"No doubt. When you put your kindness in a hole along with your broken heart, you can only find fault with the world."

Penelope's mouth fell open and her towel and toiletries dropped from her hands to the floor. She looked about to cry and ran to her room.

Annabelle turned to Eunice and Jeri, "I can't believe what I just said. I'll go apologize."

Eunice stopped her. "Perhaps, a little later. The comeuppance might do her good."

Jeri nodded in agreement.

When Annabelle returned, Sarah had stripped down to her petticoat.

Annabelle poured water into the ceramic basin, turned, and said. "Let's go out to breakfast. The professor has given me a stipend to look after you, and I don't want to run into Penelope downstairs."

Annabelle returned to her room where she washed and changed clothes as well. While lacing her boots, a knock came at the door.

"Enter."

Sarah came in and sat on the side of the bed. Annabelle looked over at her as she used the hook to fasten the last of the laces.

"I recall a little about last night," said Sarah, "I'm sorry about the loss of your mother."

"Again, how did you know?"

Sarah shrugged. "I'm hoping your group will help me to understand myself."

"Well, like you, I'm dying to know."

After an awkward pause due to Annabelle's word choice, they both laughed.

****

Following breakfast, Sarah and Annabelle made their way to the professor's office and spent the day doing clerical work for the Eidola Project.

When Professor James whisked into the office between two classes, Annabelle recounted what happened with the photo of her mother.

"Capital! Edgar and I shall assemble objects which may evoke other visions." He spun around to Sarah. "Is this your modus operandi? Do objects help your channeling?"

"On occasion. Other times, visions or knowledge just comes to me. At times I hear voices."

"Voices? Hmm…" The professor scratched his beard and scrutinized her with a worried expression. "Hearing voices can be a sign of instability."

He's doubting my sanity. Nevertheless, what choice did she have but to trust this man and his group with the truth—she did not want to return to a carnival.

"What or who speaks to you?"

"It varies. Sometimes it's who I want to reach. Other times it's someone altogether different. Once in a while, I'm afraid of who I've let in."

"I can imagine how disconcerting that would be." The professor reached out and touched Sarah's elbow. "I need to head to class, but I look forward to seeing you and Miss Douglas this evening." The professor swept up a stack of books and papers from his desk and hustled from the room.

Annabelle looked at Sarah. “He’s like a small tornado.”

“It’s how he keeps from sliding into melancholia,” said Sarah. “He’s kept it at bay for several years now.”

Annabelle looked at Sarah and shook her head. “You’re more than a bit scary.”

“The professor agrees with you. He implied I might be insane.” Sarah looked downcast.

Annabelle came up and gave her a hug. “Forgive me, I didn’t mean that, and I don’t believe the professor did either. However, it is unsettling how you know things.”

“If it’s any consolation,” Sarah said, as she brushed some strands of hair from her face, “as soon as I get attached to people, my insights about them fade. It seems the more I know them in one sense, the less I know them in another. My ability to see my own future was once described as *piss-poor*.”

“Very reassuring.”

When Annabelle and Sarah arrived at the lecture hall that evening, it looked as before, with one significant change. Two metal plates were set a couple of inches apart on the seat of Sarah’s chair and a wire ran from each into the monitoring box.

Edgar sat in the chair first to prove its safety. “When you sit, you will complete a circuit,” he said, “so there’s no need to hold the wires.” He rose and motioned for her to be seated.

Sarah hesitated.

“Don’t worry. I’m looking for changes in your own electric field.”

Sarah studied his sincere face as he smiled. She sat down as directed.

Professor James approached with a small satchel. “Based on what Annabelle stated about last night, we are going to see if you might have a similar response with a variety of objects.”

“All right,” said Sarah. “Give me a moment to clear my thoughts.”

Sarah closed her eyes and took a number of deep breaths. She held each breath for several seconds and exhaled. Despite her best efforts, the negative thoughts troubling her all day still intruded. *If I fail again, will they still be interested in me? Where will I go if they don’t want me? Am I only fit to be a carnival entertainer? Aaagggh!*

After a time, she managed to quiet her mind. Sarah opened her eyes and gave a nod. Annabelle turned the handle on the recording device as the professor reached into the satchel and handed Sarah the folded picture frame containing the photos of Annabelle’s parents.

Sarah took the gilded frame in her hands and opened it. On the left, Annabelle’s father in his Sunday best stood next to a short pillar with a fern on top. Annabelle had mentioned he still tended the family farm in Braintree. On the right, the picture showed Annabelle’s mother in a dark dress. She sat in a rocker with her hands folded on her lap. Sarah put her right palm over the deceased woman’s image and closed her eyes. “I only sense what Annabelle told me from last night. I can’t be sure if I’m recalling what she said, or it is the same message being repeated.”

The professor reached for the picture frame, but Sarah sat back with wide eyes. “Wait, there’s more.”

Sarah looked at Annabelle. "Your mother says to be patient the next time you see your father. She always found him to be a difficult man."

Annabelle stopped turning the crank as both Edgar and the professor laughed.

The professor turned to Annabelle. "Is this true?"

"I've always felt so." Annabelle blushed.

The professor turned to Sarah. "Anything further?"

Sarah shook her head and handed back the pictures.

Next, the professor reached into the satchel and removed a scorched piece of wood in the shape of an oval. On the other side was a clump of burnt animal hair. He handed it to Sarah, who, as she touched it, took a sharp intake of air. Her eyes rolled back into her head. "Edgar!" she said in a deep voice, not her own.

Edgar looked up from monitoring the machine to regard Sarah.

She continued, "Son, you've made me proud."

Annabelle ran to Sarah and yanked her from the chair. The two fell together onto the floor.

"What in blazes?" said Edgar.

Sarah regained consciousness, blinked her eyes, and looked surprised.

Annabelle stood and explained, "When Sarah went into a trance last night, she wet herself. I feared she would be electrocuted."

"No, no," said Edgar. "The galvanic cell in this box is producing a very small current. Too small to notice—wet or not."

"I see nothing much is to be kept private in this group," said Sarah from the floor, "including my incontinence."

"We are all scientists," said the professor. "No one

thinks any less of you. And you, it seems, know many secrets about us."

Sarah rose from the floor and composed herself. "Fortunately, I am dry."

"Does wetting yourself often occur when in a trance?"

"No. Last night was the first time since childhood. I'm not sure why. Perhaps the intensity of the vision."

The professor looked at Edgar. "Did you get a reading?"

"It spiked to seventy-eight point four—both with Annabelle's photo and with my father's hairbrush. It's remarkable." Edgar looked at Sarah. "Of all the spiritualists I've tested this year, you, Miss Bradbury, are the only one who caused this to register a change."

"We doubted the legitimacy of the others, except for Miss Pallidino, who left before you developed your device." Professor James smiled at Sarah. "It seems you are the first medium we'll be able to document as bona fide."

Sarah smiled in spite of herself. Embarrassed, she lowered her eyes. "Thank you. But I need to tell you—I've given this a great deal of thought—as much as I want to be a member of your group, I wish to remain anonymous. I've lived as a public spectacle for half my life. I no longer wish to do so."

The professor appeared both shocked and disappointed. "Are you saying we won't be able to share our findings?"

"If you can't guarantee my anonymity, then no. I'm sorry."

Annabelle voiced her own concerns. "This will cripple our reporting. Without substantiation, people will doubt its veracity."

"Again, I can't express how sorry I am, but I insist. I hope there might still be a place for me in your organization."

Both Edgar and Annabelle turned to the professor for an answer.

The professor still looked taken aback, but a moment later he took a deep breath and straightened up. "Well, this seems to be a matter for further discussion. In the meantime, we will, of course, honor your wishes. Are you game for one more item?"

Sarah said yes and retook her seat. She held up a hand to indicate she needed a moment and repeated her breathing regimen. When ready, she opened her eyes and nodded as before.

The professor reached into his satchel and removed another small sepia-colored portrait. This one in a silver frame, depicting a middle-aged woman, with a rather severe expression. Sarah took the photo and regarded it for a moment. She shook her head and handed it back.

"Your sister. She's not dead."

The professor grinned at his subterfuge. "Very good."

"She won't be for another seven years," Sarah added.

The professor's smile disappeared. *"What?"*

Annabelle covered her mouth. "Oh dear."

"I… That just came to me—I'm not sure it's true."

The professor looked over at the others and back at Sarah. His face blanched. He reclaimed the photo of his sister and stood it up on top of the lectern, where it toppled over. He rescued it from falling and stared at Sarah. "How?"

"I'm sorry…"

Edgar looked up from his device and announced, "Seventy-eight point four, the same as before."

"I think we should adjourn for the evening," said the professor. Without another word, he walked from the room, carrying the framed portrait of his sister.

The next morning Sarah and Annabelle worked in the professor's office, as on the previous day, but now with Edgar present. While the women busied themselves with clerical matters, the physicist pulled books from the shelves and glanced at them with distracted indifference. Eventually, Professor James opened the door and all three stared at him.

"Well, good morning to you all," said the professor. "I confess to having been discombobulated by our work last night. I went home and wrote my sister a long letter, expressing my very great affection for her. Needless to say, I left out Sarah's prediction." He set his books and papers down on the desk and grabbed another pile in preparation for the next class.

"It looks as though we have found a legitimate medium and clairvoyant in you, Sarah," the professor continued. "We would like to do further tests to help us understand the scope of your abilities, but those will have to wait. The Society for Psychical Research has requested we investigate another purported medium this evening. I have made arrangements for us all to attend her séance tonight. Is that agreeable?"

Edgar and Annabelle both nodded.

"Sarah?" he asked as he looked at her.

Sarah blushed. "I would be honored."

"Fine! Why don't we all meet at my place for supper beforehand?" said the professor. "I'm sure Alice won't mind."

****

In fact, Alice did mind, but she seemed stoic by nature and made every effort to appear the perfect hostess. Following the meal, the group headed back to Cambridge in the professor's surrey. Annabelle and Sarah sat in the rear, with Edgar next to the professor, who held the reins.

After they were underway, the professor craned his neck around to glance at Sarah. "What do you think of our little troop?"

"You all seem very nice. Again, I am honored I may accompany you." Sarah became circumspect for a moment then decided to speak her mind. "But are you sure about tonight? What you've planned will not soften anyone's heart toward the group."

"So you know what we're up against?" The professor nodded and gave the reins a little shake. "Richard Hodgson, who heads the American branch of our parent organization, is so critical of paranormal research, it's a wonder the Society appointed him as head. Nevertheless, he has become convinced Charlotte Rogers is legitimate. He and Meyers have conducted a dozen tests on her and can find no evidence of cheating. Hodgson often keeps me at arm's length and is decidedly cool toward the Eidola Project.

"At any rate," the professor continued, "Hodgson wants to publish his findings about Mrs. Rogers but agreed to hold off, with considerable arm-twisting on my part, until we could also substantiate this woman's legitimacy. She refuses to come into the lab, so we are going to her. We shall see."

The carriage drove through Cambridge and onto

the ferry dock. They got out and led the horse and carriage onto the ferry for the trip across the Charles River.

Once docked in Boston, it was a short ride to the North End and the Roger's Home on Prince Street. They saw to the horses and then knocked at the door.

A squat man wearing a bright green suit and a gold-colored vest opened the door part-way. Bald, except for red hair growing out in tufts from above his ears, he also sported a paintbrush mustache. Sarah thought he resembled a leprechaun.

"Mr. Rogers?" asked the professor. Before he could answer, the door swung wide and a tall stout man with a grayish beard pushed past the first man and came outside. He greeted the professor with a bear hug. "Great to see you, Bill!"

When released from the affectionate hug, the professor stepped back and gestured toward the others. "Mr. Fredrick Meyers, may I present Sarah Bradbury, the newest member of our team. And, of course, you know Anabelle and Edgar."

Hearing him introduce her as a member, Sarah beamed.

"Well, well, you're the young lady Bill has been so excited about!" Meyers stepped forward and kissed Sarah's hand.

"And I am Ernest Rogers," said the short man with annoyance. He still stood in the doorway. Mr. Rogers moved away from the entry. "Come in and we'll get started."

As they entered and went down the hall, Meyers hung back and spoke to the professor. "I apologize once again for having to turn down the offer of membership in your little splinter group. Mrs. Myers was not the least bit keen on me traipsing around the country in search of spooks. She'd rather I stick closer to the home fires."

Annabelle leaned over to Sarah and whispered, "Do you sense anything here?"

Sarah wrinkled her nose. "Other than incense, no."

Mr. Rogers opened a door at the end of a hallway and they entered a parlor where the smell of sandalwood incense became overpowering. Another large man and a rail-thin woman sat at a table in the center of the room. Instead of greeting them, the man continued writing in a leather-clad journal, while the taciturn woman stared straight ahead. Fred made the introductions.

Large and strong-looking, Richard Hodgson had a ruddy complexion and reddish-brown hair. Mrs. Charlotte Rogers' two large front teeth and thin gray hair complemented her rat-like features. Her plain black dress hung over her skeletal frame.

Hodgson set down his pencil and rose from his chair. "William," he now said in greeting. "I'm glad you brought your entire entourage. I want the ladies to do a thorough examination before we begin."

Mr. Rogers, who sat at the table, rose up and began to bluster. "Now, just hold on a minute! My wife will do no such thing. It will not be that kind of a demonstration. No sir!"

Hodgson dismissed him with a wave of his hand. "The men shall leave the room, Mr. Rogers. The examination is necessary to prove your wife's authenticity. You and she are on the verge of becoming quite famous, but we need to assure ourselves of no deceit. Take it or leave it."

Mr. Rogers fumbled with the shirttails hanging below his vest. He looked at his wife. "What say you? This acceptable?"

Mrs. Rogers sat still for several moments. She tilted her chin up then down once, indicating her assent.

Hodgson turned to Annabelle and Sarah. "I want you to search every part of her. I mean *every part*. Every orifice and every stitch of her clothing." He turned to William James. "I want there to be no doubt."

The men left the room and shut the door.

Annabelle and Sarah looked at each other in awkward silence. Mrs. Rogers sat without showing any emotion and stared straight ahead.

Thank God they didn't make me go through this. A small shiver ran down Sarah's spine.

"Well," said Annabelle, "I suppose we should get on with it. Mrs. Rogers, would you be so kind as to remove your clothes? Fortunately, it is a warm evening."

Sarah pulled the blinds over the windows.

Mrs. Rogers pushed her chair back from the table, stood, and unfastened the myriad of buttons running down the front of her dress. She stepped out of it. A moment later, she threw her dress and undergarments upon the table and sat down.

"Your stockings and shoes as well," said Annabelle.

The older woman looked irritated but complied and set the items on the table.

"Isn't shoes on a table bad luck?" asked Sarah.

"For you, or for me?" Mrs. Rogers replied, speaking for the first time.

"A good question," said Annabelle. "Let's see what the evening brings."

Sarah picked up the shoes. She peered at the bottom of each and cringed both times she stuck her hand into their moist interiors to see if anything out of the ordinary lay within. Finding nothing, she set them on the floor.

"Okay," said Annabelle, "if you will please open your mouth."

Mrs. Rogers stuck her tongue at them with apparent insolence. Annabelle and Sarah checked in the woman's mouth, her hair, beneath her arms and breasts, and between her legs. Finally, they had her bend over and they stared at her rectum. While inspecting the latter, the older woman let go a prodigious amount of flatulence.

"You did that on purpose!" hissed Annabelle. "Whatever else you may be, you are certainly disgusting."

Mrs. Rogers sat down with a triumphant grin.

Annabelle swept the clothing off the table and into the woman's lap. "You may get dressed or not. Frankly, I don't give a damn."

Sarah and Annabelle withdrew to opposite corners of the room and fanned the air before them with their hands.

"The smell of flatulence mixed with incense is making me nauseated," confessed Anabelle. She walked over to the door and opened it about six inches. Mr. Rogers stood just outside and turned. His eyebrows were raised in expectation.

"Not quite yet, Mr. Rogers. We simply needed a little ventilation."

Sarah came across the room to join her.

They could hear the men outside the door.

"I think the demonstration tonight will speak for itself," Hodgson said. "Mrs. Rogers is a materializing medium of rare talent,"

"I hope you're right," said the professor. "Richard, I hold you in the highest regard, but I suspect you feel there is some rivalry between us. Nothing can be further from the truth. I hope this woman is everything you claim and so you may publish your findings as soon as possible. For my part, I cannot publish a thing about Miss Bradbury. It's a stipulation in agreeing to work with us. She'd been forced to be a carnival act for many years and now wants to work in relative anonymity. So, you see, we as an organization have everything to gain by your discovery."

"Harrumph," muttered Hodgson. "Are they ready for us?" he shouted. "There's not that much of her to check!"

Mr. Rogers knocked at the door and put his head toward the opening. Anabelle motioned for him to enter. He looked back at the others and said, "We're ready to begin."

The men returned to the room, but as they did so, Sarah overheard Professor James whisper to Edgar, "You have it handy?"

Edgar patted the breast of his jacket. "I do."

A grim smile crossed the professor's face.

Mr. Rogers shut the door. They all sat at the table. Edgar positioned himself on Mrs. Roger's immediate left. On her other side sat the professor. As they got settled, Mr. Rogers went around the room and blew out all but one lamp. He set the remaining one low, but before doing so, sprinkled more incense on its flame. The scent of sandalwood began to waft around the room.

Hodgson looked across the table at the professor. "She insists on the incense and says lowering the lights increases her sensitivity. Your search of her should have allayed any doubts. So, can we can indulge her?"

The professor agreed.

The participants joined hands around the table as directed. Mrs. Rogers closed her eyes.

After several anxious minutes, Mrs. Rogers began to moan. She panted between each utterance. These increased in intensity until she screamed. A fit of the shakes started. Edgar and the professor appeared to have difficulty maintaining a grip on her hand. With surprising suddenness, she became quiet.

Her eyes opened a fraction of an inch and closed again. Mrs. Roger's body began to convulse, and she began to gag. From her mouth emerged a white slimy mass. It worked its way down her chin, across the front of her dress, and onto the table, glistening in the faint lamplight.

"This is the ectoplasm I told you about!" said Hodgson. His voice betrayed his excitement. "She's quite remarkable in this regard!"

"I'll say!" said the professor. He sprang up and held both of Mrs. Rogers' hands flat on the table.

On her left, Edgar stood and produced a pair of sheers from the inner pocket of his jacket. Edgar reached down and cut off a large swatch of the ectoplasm. He grabbed the severed section, ran for the lamp, and turned the light up so high the flame began to smoke.

Edgar spread out the slimy mess in his hands and studied it in the light. "I will need to do some tests, but this appears to be cheesecloth."

"What?" roared Hodgson.

"Common drugstore cheesecloth," repeated Edgar.

Mr. Rogers now stood and hoisted his wooden chair above him. "Why you son of a bitch!" he yelled, running at Edgar with the chair held aloft. He brought the chair down, aiming for Edgar's head.

Edgar dodged the blow and instead, the chair came crashing down on the edge of the small table holding the lamp. The lamp toppled to the floor, shattering the glass. Flames leapt from the broken glass and kerosene. Ignoring the fire, the medium's husband ran at Edgar, who clipped the man under his jaw with such force. The little man reared up in a sudden stop and fell forward into Edgar's arms, unconscious.

Sarah and Annabelle stepped away from the flames, holding up the hems to their dresses. "Not again!" cried Sarah. She and Annabelle stood by the door and watched.

Hodgson and Meyers tried to stomp out the fire with no effect. The flames continued to spread.

"Step back!" yelled the professor. He shoved the large table in the direction of the fire and upended it so the tabletop crashed down and smothered the flames. The professor caught his breath and looked at his associates. "Well, an eventful evening in any case!"

Mrs. Rogers knocked Annabelle to the floor as she dashed from the room. Sarah ran after. "Hurry!" Sarah shouted, "She's escaping!"

Sarah chased the woman down the hall and out the open doorway onto the now-dark street. She glanced back and forth. The gas streetlights were on, and some light spilled from undraped windows up and down the street, providing islands of illumination. Sarah could see no sign of Mrs. Rogers. Annabelle came out and took Sarah's hand.

"Don't trouble yourself. Let her go," said Annabelle.

Sarah continued to look around for Mrs. Rogers. "But—"

Annabelle cut her off. "What would we do once we caught her? She has been found out. That is consequence enough."

Sarah lowered her head. She felt foolish at her impulsive pursuit.

Returning to the parlor, they could hear Hodgson's voice raised in anger.

"You planned this! Why did you persist in this humiliating charade?"

Sarah saw the professor shake his head in protest, though his protestations seemed insincere.

"I had suspicions," said the professor, "but I didn't know. I did not intend to humiliate you, only the Rogers."

"Well you've succeeded in doing both," fumed Hodgson, "creating several enemies tonight. I suspect you could care less about the Rogers—I now share that sentiment—but I promise you'll regret your underhanded behavior toward me."

Chapter Five

Over the next nine months, the Eidola Project investigated two dozen cases. Most proved hoaxes. One—despite their best efforts—remained a dangerous mystery. The most gratifying involved Sarah helping the ghost of Xavier Witworth, a former tax collector killed during the Whiskey Rebellion, move on to the next world. Despite this success, Hodgson gave no credence to their work and pursued formal censure and expulsion of the professor and the group from the American Society for Psychical Research. Thus far, supporters of the professor blocked such moves, but Hodgson had the tenacity of a bulldog, spurred on by his humiliation in the Rogers' debacle.

The professor felt their work would eventually be recognized, in spite of Hodgson's efforts, so he kept the group busy with correspondence, record-keeping, and following up on any and all reports of the supernatural.

In the course of things, Sarah appeared to be looking increasingly run-down. Annabelle attributed it to Sarah's penchant for working too hard and for taking every setback personally. This assessment changed the morning Sarah knocked at Annabelle's door, shortly after six.

The sight of Sarah startled Annabelle. The younger woman stood before Annabelle's doorway fully dressed, though her clothing looked as disheveled as her hair. Clearly, Sarah slept in her clothes. A dark circle orbited each bloodshot eye.

"Sarah? What's wrong?"

"May I come in?"

"Certainly." Annabelle held the door wide, still barefoot and in her white linen nightgown. "Are you ill?"

"No." Sarah came into the room and sat at the small table.

"Here, I'll fix us some tea." Sarah did not respond, so Annabelle busied herself putting water and tea leaves in the kettle, striking a lucifer on the grate, and turning on the gas. As the kettle heated, she threw on a light shawl, purely out of a sense of decorum—it being a warm summer morning. She fetched a few biscuits out of a tin and set them on a plate before Sarah, who looked at them wordlessly. When Annabelle set the mug of tea before her, she just looked at it as well.

"Have a biscuit," prompted Annabelle, "and tell me what's wrong. You've not looked well for days, but today is the worst."

"I've not been sleeping well. I'm plagued by a recurring dream—a nightmare, really." Sarah took a small sip of tea, took a deep breath, and began to speak.

"After drifting off to sleep, I find myself trying to stay afloat in a sea of blood. Panicking, I scream and flail my arms. My face is dripping with the stuff, and I spit every time some splashes into my mouth. Around me, frothy bubbles form as my arms beat at the bloody sea.

"The red surface stretches out in all directions until it merges with dark clouds at the horizon. Above me, bolts of lightning sear through the sky, followed by booming claps of thunder."

Annabelle set her mug of tea down and leaned over the table in rapt attention.

"Then, as they always do," Sarah continued, "dozens of bloody hands emerge from below and grab at me—in desperation, or to attack me, I don't know. Whatever the reason, I bat them away and continue screaming.

"A rowboat appears in the distance. The boat is propelled by some unseen force since its sole occupant simply stands and stares at me.

"He is dark and clean-shaven. Handsome. He holds a crystal ball before him.

"I'm never sure if he will reach me in time. The bloody hands from the depths have hold of my hair, my shoulders, my dress, and are pulling me down.

"At the last moment, the man on the boat throws aside the crystal ball, reaches down, and clasps my hand. He pulls me free of the others and into the boat.

"The man smiles and says the same thing every time. *Nigel Pickford, at your service*."

Annabelle shivered and pulled her wrap around her. She looked at Sarah, an attractive young woman whose looks were marred by the toll of these night terrors. "So…" she began tentatively, "what do you think it means?"

Sarah stood up. "Last night, for the first time, I could make out the name *Atlanta* painted on the bow of the boat. I need to go there as soon as possible. Today, if it can be arranged. This Nigel Pickford may save my life."

Chapter Six

Atlanta

When Madame Dobrescu, a fat medium, slumped forward on her chair, rivulets of sweat ran down the sides of her flabby face, dripped from her nose, and formed a puddle on the polished oak floor. No wonder, the crowded room was stifling.

Summers in Atlanta often became oppressively hot, and this evening's thundershower only increased the humidity. The draped windows and the backdrop of black curtains behind the medium made things worse—no air circulated.

Seated men and women filled the room, anxious to see what would happen next. They were overdressed for the heat, but at a society affair, one needed to maintain certain pretensions. Their shiny faces and drooping hairdos indicated the price they paid in addition to the admission.

In the front row, Annabelle Douglas and Sarah Bradbury fanned themselves with their programs. Within the folds of the makeshift fans, the text promised, *an extraordinary exhibition of supernatural power by Madame Dobrescu!*

Sarah only had limited ability to foresee events; nonetheless, she felt tonight would be a very different show. She also sensed she would find the man who haunted her sleep—someone who might save her life. That aspect alone convinced Professor James to pay for the trip and allow Annabelle and Edgar to accompany her. But Sarah could only provide his name, a vague description, and the sense he would be here tonight.

Sarah, Annabelle, and Edgar arrived early. A black servant ushered the two women to the front row, but he insisted Edgar stand in the rear, although empty chairs filled the room.

"So much for Southern hospitality," Sarah said.

Annabelle hushed her.

This sort of thing rankled Sarah, but she also knew he could have been banned from the place altogether.

In the ensuing half-hour, the room filled with patrons. Relegated to the rear, Edgar positioned himself near the double doors and queried each man who entered.

None answered to Nigel Pickford.

Well-dressed men and women now filled the dimly-lit room, watching. Those seated in the back craned their necks to see. Despite the sweltering heat, no one complained. Discomfort seemed a small inconvenience in order to communicate with the beyond.

Behind the medium stood a tall mahogany cupboard. Sarah leaned over to Annabelle and whispered, "That's where she keeps her best china for when the ghosts come to tea."

Annabelle motioned for her to be quiet, but smiled nonetheless.

Sarah stopped her flippancy and sat back with a start when the medium's rotund head came up to stare at the audience. The woman's eyes glowed green.

Several women in the audience gasped and even men made low utterances of surprise.

The medium's arms rose before her as electricity danced between the palms of her hands. She stood and raised her charged hands above her head, then threw her arms wide.

The room erupted in a flash of light with a deafening boom.

The medium collapsed back onto the chair as a green spectral girl formed in the mist floating above her head.

"Momma!" the girl wailed. "Help me, Momma. *It hurts!"*

A bejeweled woman in black, three chairs to Sarah's right, jumped to her feet. Tears streamed down her face. "It's her," she cried. "Oh, God, it's Mary!"

Standing, a bald man put a protective arm around the sobbing woman. The man looked up at the specter and then at the medium. His thick eyebrows knit together as he squeezed his eyes shut and fought back tears of his own. "We'll pay whatever you ask. Just give our daughter peace!"

A faint smile passed over the medium's lips.

Without warning, the entry doors behind the audience burst open like the gates of Hell. A demonic figure in dark rags stormed into the room, screaming.

Chapter Seven

Nigel Pickford crawled out from his lean-to shelter behind the tobacco warehouse, retrieved his near-empty bottle, and stumbled down Marietta Street. The rain from the thunderstorm stopped several minutes ago. Now the heat and humidity caused water vapor to rise off everything in thin ethereal clouds. It looked to him like the rapture, spirits rising from the earth, leaving Nigel behind.

The leaky shelter caused his long greasy black hair, beard, and filthy clothing to be sopping wet. The grime covering his skin made it hard to tell a white man of forty lay beneath. Moreover, his drunkenness made him seem older. But he was not drunk enough—he almost fell asleep in the lean-to. The only way to avoid the dreams was to pass out, to fall into an oblivion from which he could never be quite sure he would emerge. No matter. Nothing seemed worse than the dreams.

He needed more whiskey. He stumbled down the dusky street to where a thin man with a long taper lit the gas streetlights. Nigel gravitated toward the light, but as he approached, the lamplighter shook his head.

"Stay away!" he shouted and swung the taper at Nigel's head, "Or I'll give ya what for!"

Nigel avoided the blow and continued on his way. At the intersection with Peachtree Street, there milled a fair number of evening shoppers. A small boy pointed at him lumbering down the avenue.

“Look, Momma,” said the boy, as he pulled on the woman’s dress with his other hand, “a bear!”

The woman took one look at Nigel and hoisted the child into her arms. “No, honey,” she said as she scurried away. Her shopping list fluttered to the wet brick walkway, forgotten.

Nigel bent to retrieve it. He glanced at the list of sundries then called to the woman as he held the scrap of paper before him. The lady did not turn around. Instead, she and the child ducked into a store a half-block away.

Those left on the corner stared at him with familiar expressions of curiosity, pity, or disgust. Nigel put the list and his now empty bottle on the bricks and held his cupped hands before him. “A veteran of the war,” he said. “A lieutenant under Jubal Early, Gordon and Lee.” This yielded a few coins tossed at his feet.

A heavy man with a gold chain across the front of his checkered vest sneered, “Go back to Virginia. We don’t want ya!”

Nigel nodded as he gathered the coins. “The very reason why I’m soliciting. Help me with the train fare, sir?” But the man already turned away, as had the others.

Nigel continued down Peachtree. Additional shoppers he encountered backed away with revulsion. Some threw a few coins his way out of what he assumed to be pity or the hope this would satisfy him and keep him from approaching further. Nigel soon collected enough for a second bottle and smiled. He need not worry about dreams tonight.

A few minutes later, new purchase in hand, he

stumbled up Decatur Street and stopped now and then to sample the whiskey. The burning sensation felt like an antiseptic for his soul.

He found himself on a street crowded with carriages, some with their tops still up from the rain. A few coachmen dozed on the padded rear seats, others gathered in little groups, smoking and passing a flask or bottle of their own. Hearty laughter rose from one group, and Nigel turned to see if they were laughing at him. They weren't.

Large brick homes butted up against each other and bordered both sides of the street. Nigel stopped before one featuring a round white column on either side of a green door.

Nigel saw another crumpled piece of paper at his feet and retrieved it. The fact he could read and write surprised most other vagrants he met. When they saw him looking at one of his scavenged newspapers, they invariably asked him to read aloud and sometimes write letters. As a result, they gladly shared what they had—beans, alcohol, or even mulligan stew—sometimes known to contain an unfortunate dog or cat. But in spite of this welcome, since the war, Nigel spent most of his time alone.

He opened the wadded paper and held it up to catch the lamplight. The handbill advertised a séance at this location. He'd been drawn here, as to so many similar gatherings. *Perhaps this time*? He speculated for a moment then shook his head with disgust. He knew better—experience taught him otherwise.

Nigel climbed the damp stone steps to the front door. The brass knob felt cold in his hand. Unlocked. He entered a wood-paneled foyer with many doors and a narrow staircase going up along one wall to the second floor. The help—two mulatto maids and a very dark butler—apparently hadn't heard him come in. They seemed preoccupied, staring through a small opening in a set of double doors.

Nigel crept toward them until the butler turned his head and looked surprised. He reared up with self-importance. "Look, here," he said to Nigel, "You get the hell out before I throw you out!"

A flash of light came through the opening in the door followed by a thunderclap from the room within. Nigel could hear a young girl cry. "Momma! Help me, Momma. *It hurts!"*

The maids held hands over their mouths and quaked as they peered in, then turned to see the filthy stranger standing behind them. One gave a frightened yelp and ran off. The other's eyes went wide with real terror and backed into the door, closing it.

The butler grabbed Nigel's arm, but Nigel threw him off, and the man flew backward to slide across the polished wooden floor and bang his head on a baseboard.

Screaming like a madman, Nigel charged straight at the door and the maid who blocked it. At the last moment, the woman jumped aside. He smashed into the double doors and shattered the latch. The doors burst open and Nigel stormed into the séance.

Once inside, he stopped short, weaved back and forth and belched. Nigel took a long drink from his whiskey bottle and snapped to attention. He squinted, got his bearings, then resumed his charge.

He plowed through the crowded room, knocking some of Atlanta's wealthiest denizens from their chairs.

As he charged, he screamed one word, “Nooo!”

Nigel bumped into the fat medium as he passed, and she toppled over onto the floor.

He shoved the spectral girl aside. The girl screamed and began to swing in an arc across the front of the room, arms waving, with a shocked look on her green face.

At the cupboard, Nigel thrust his right arm through the black scrim-covered opening and yanked out a skinny young man who held a green-lensed lantern. The young man stumbled toward the audience and dropped the lamp. The glass shattered.

Nigel tore down the backdrop. This revealed two more of the medium’s assistants, both men burly. A man with huge biceps and a prominent jaw held a black rope to keep the not-so-spectral girl aloft. The other had a round sweaty face but looked just as strong. He pumped bellows above a small stove, heating glycerin to create the fog.

Turning back toward the shocked audience, Nigel raised his whiskey bottle in triumph. With his other hand, he gestured at the hapless girl still suspended in the air.

“There’s your ghost!” he said. “They’re all frauds! Charlatans! *Cheats!*”

A few moments later, Nigel staggered out the rear door of the séance house and knocked over a metal trash can. It clattered across the cobblestone walkway and into a flowerbed, strewing garbage along the way. Nigel lurched down the walk and out into a dark alley, whose cobblestones were covered in slippery muck. The alley ran along the back of the tightly-packed brick houses. There were no lamps, and what light existed came from the door Nigel left open when exiting the house and from a few windows on the alley without the curtains drawn. Everything remained wet and steamy. Nigel put a hand on a damp brick wall to steady himself.

"There he is!" the skinny assistant shouted from the doorway.

The two burly assistants joined him. The one with a round face grinned, revealing black and brown teeth and several gaps where teeth once resided. "Let's get 'im!" he shouted.

The skinny assistant broke out in front. As he neared him, Nigel whirled around and smashed his whiskey bottle over the young man's head. The kid's eyes rolled upward as if to see what hit him and then he crumpled into the mud.

Nigel brandished the broken bottle at the other two. He swung the jagged glass back and forth as the two attackers spread out to come at him from either side.

Chapter Eight

After the wild man's revelations, almost everyone stood up, many knocking over chairs which caused other people to trip and fall. Shouts of anger and disbelief filled the large room. Some folks made for the door while others pressed forward in anger toward the charlatan who deceived them. More chairs fell over. A white-haired man with a red face raised a cane above his head to menace the medium but then lost his footing and got swallowed by the surging crowd.

People turned up the lamps around the room, which ended the last vestiges of deceit. The green spectral girl, now looking pathetic in her makeup and gauzy gown, landed on the floor with a thump. The crowd shouted invectives—many demanded their money back.

"That was him!" Sarah yelled above the din.

"Are you sure?" Annabelle asked, incredulous.

"Yes! We must help. He's in danger!" Sarah pushed her way through the throng of people who crowded the front of the room to get a closer look at the props and devices used in the deception.

The fat medium removed her green glass eye-caps and surveyed the chaos around her. She raised her arms and shouted for everyone to be seated. No one listened. Out of desperation, she grabbed the bejeweled woman who thought the *ghost* to be her daughter. "Don't go!"

The bald husband shoved the medium aside and the

heavy woman fell back to the floor. Her two big assistants helped her stand. One of them started after the bald man, but the medium shook her head and told them to go after the tramp. “Now!” she demanded.

The burly men took off after Nigel. The skinny assistant joined them. Together they pushed through the crowd and ran after the vagrant.

****

Annabelle looked across the room and began to wave her arms until she caught Edgar’s eye. He gave a helpless shrug, trapped on the other side of the room by the swarming crowd. Annabelle motioned for him to go out the front door, but he looked at her with a quizzical expression. She yelled at the top of her lungs, to no effect. She waved her arms again as she tried to indicate he should go outside and then around to the rear of the building. Edgar indicated he understood and exited through the double doors.

Annabelle gathered her handbag and the one Sarah forgot beneath her seat. She ran after Sarah, who had charged off on the heels of the thugs working with the medium.

She caught up with Sarah in a large kitchen, standing by an open door. “They went this way!” Sarah shouted and ran out. Annabelle followed.

Outside, Annabelle saw the man Sarah believed to be Nigel Pickford whirl around and smash a bottle onto the skinny assistant’s head. The young man collapsed into the mud. Then the two burly thugs spread out to trap Nigel between them.

Annabelle held her gloved hand aloft. “Stop!” she shouted with authority. “Right this instant!”

The thugs glanced at her for a moment then looked

at each other and chuckled. They continued to press in on Nigel.

Rapid footfalls came down the alley signaling Edgar's approach. While he ran, Edgar removed his jacket and threw it to Sarah, who caught it and folded it over her left arm. Edgar rolled up his sleeves then tapped the shoulder of the round-faced thug with bad teeth. "You heard the lady."

The round-faced thug swung around and threw his left arm up to catch Edgar's face. At the same instant, he made a vicious uppercut with his right fist. Edgar dodged the blows, then stepped up and slammed a fist into the thug's nose. Blood ran from the man's nostrils like ale from a just-tapped keg.

The thug shook his head and rushed at Edgar, punching willy-nilly. Edgar held his bare fists up before him and crouched into a boxing stance. He blocked every punch, then delivered a series of devastating blows of his own. Annabelle recalled Edgar once telling her he had been on the Howard University boxing team. Nevertheless, she loosened the drawstrings on her handbag and clutched the heavy object within.

The lantern-jawed thug took a Bowie knife from a brown leather sheath on his belt. He lunged, thrusting the huge weapon at Nigel. Nigel swung the broken bottle, deflecting the blow.

Annabelle fired into the air then leveled her Smith & Wesson revolver at the thug with the knife. "I suggest you leave before you become a candidate for the next séance." Annabelle smiled without humor, prepared to follow-through on the threat.

The thug held up his free hand as he backed away several paces. He whirled around and fell face-first into the muck. The thug floundered on the slippery cobblestones, trying to find his Bowie knife, then abandoned the search. He struggled up and ran.

Annabelle swung her pistol around to the other thug. "You too."

The big man swiped his right sleeve over his eyes, wiping away some of the blood running from a cut on his forehead. Blood continued to stream from his crooked nose. He looked grateful for the chance to escape. The battered thug bent down and helped the skinny guy to his feet. The two hobbled away.

Edgar took out a handkerchief and mopped his brow. He retrieved his jacket from Sarah, and nodded his thanks.

Nigel stared at the three of them. "Who the hell are you?"

"My name is Annabelle Douglas," she said as she approached Nigel. "This is Sarah Bradbury and Dr. Edgar Gilpin." Annabelle deposited her pistol back into her purse and removed a business card. She offered it to Nigel who ignored it. "We are the Eidola Project," she continued, undaunted, "a group working with the Society for Psychical Research. We'd like you to consider joining—"

"Claptrap!" Nigel scoffed. He tossed the broken bottle aside and it shattered against a brick wall. "You're no better than those cretins I just vanquished."

Nigel shuffled past Edgar and Sarah, but Edgar grabbed Nigel's arm.

"Hold on there," said Edgar, "we just risked our lives—"

Nigel swung his arm free, grabbed Edgar's and twisted it behind the black man's back all in one quick motion. Pain shot across Edgar's face.

"And for that I am grateful." Nigel stuck his face up next to Edgar's, and the black man winced. "But if you ever lay a hand on me again, I'll break it clean off."

Nigel released his captive and turned away, but now Edgar tapped him on the shoulder from behind.

"Mr. Pickford?"

Nigel froze and growled, "How the hell does this darky know my name?" He spun around to face Edgar as he swung his fist in a roundhouse.

Edgar ducked, and then delivered a powerful blow to Nigel's chin.

Nigel stumbled back and hit his head against a brick wall. His legs buckled and he slid down the wall to collapse in the filthy alley, unconscious.

Annabelle turned to Sarah. "You said he would be difficult."

"He'll come around," said Sarah as she looked at the insensible derelict. "Sooner or later."

Annabelle sighed in resignation. "Well, let's get him cleaned up. I won't travel to Boston with him smelling like an outhouse."

Chapter Nine

Nantucket Island

The Mahogany farm did not get many visitors, so two in one evening seemed like something of a record. They'd expected the first, Reverend Malcolm Davis, the Baptist minister for their colored community on the island. The reverend, whose weathered dark skin reflected a youth spent aboard whaling vessels, would come by once or twice a month to harangue them good-naturedly about the need to get to church more often. Clarence Mahogany often wondered out loud if the reverend simply wanted a free meal.

His daughter, Maude, didn't hear these remarks—nor anything her father said since the age of two when the same fever that took her mother's life left her deaf. On the other hand, Maude could read lips. When she caught her father swearing or being rude, she would slap his shoulder with a dish towel, a book, or if nothing else was handy, her open hand. Her conditioning meant her father turned his back whenever he felt like swearing.

While unable to hear, Maude still learned her letters and read her Bible each day. However, her almost unintelligible speech could only be understood by her father, and not very well at that. As a result, Maude usually remained quiet. She also learned to cook well, the reason why her father suspected the reverend became a regular guest.

Reverend Davis put the last forkful of candied ham into his mouth and made a wide smile. He wiped his lips and set the blue cloth napkin down next to the empty plate. He turned to Maude who entered from the kitchen with an apple pie. "I know gluttony is a sin," said the reverend, "so I saved me some room for a piece of one of your excellent pies."

Maude smiled and set the pie before him. She cut the pie into quarters and started to dish one out, but the minister's hand stopped her.

The minister looked up at her. "So much *would* be a sin," he said. "An eighth would do me fine."

Maude cut the quarter in half. The minister retrieved his napkin and Maude set the pie piece on his plate.

A knock Maude could not hear came at the door.

The reverend looked toward the entry and then at Clarence. "A little late for visitors."

Clarence leveled his eyes at the minister and directed his comment to him as well. "I should say so." He got up and walked across the pinewood floor to the door. He opened it and at first, saw only darkness. "Hello?"

Out of the night came a timid woman's voice. "Mr. Mahogany?"

On the road, some distance away, a buggy drove by. A lantern hung off its side. The faint illumination outlined the form of a woman in the doorway wearing a large hat. There did not appear to be a buggy in the drive.

"Yes? What can I do for you?"

"Sorry to be calling on you at such a late hour. I wonder if I might impose upon you for a few moments."

"Surely. Come on in and join the reverend."

"No, no, I don't want to impose on you any more than I have already. I understand your daughter is a good cook. I am looking for one to put my kitchen to rights and prepare some meals for the next little while. I live in the old Hutchinson house out on Baxter Road. Do you know it?"

"I do. I've lived here twenty years, Miss—?"

"Lenore. Lenore Hutchinson."

"Twenty years and I can't say I've ever met you."

"I'm afraid I've become a bit of a recluse."

"I heard there used to be some disreputable parties out there."

"Oh, long ago, before I changed my ways and found our Lord, Jesus Christ. As I said, I am putting my place back in order and I could use your daughter's services. I would pay handsomely."

"There are rumors your place is haunted."

"Rumors, only. I am a gospel woman, Mr. Mahogany."

Clarence scratched the top of his balding head. "Well, I can't see sparing her in the evenings, when she is needed right here tending house for me, and rumors or not, I don't want her out and about in the dark. But we could sure use the cash." Clarence ran a hand over his face and looked back at the minister. "What do you think, Reverend?"

The minister put down his fork and dabbed his lips clean. He looked at Clarence standing before the darkened doorway. "Sounds like she was lost but now found in the glory of Jesus. Can't ask for a better reference." He grinned.

Clarence scratched his head again and turned back to the doorway. "If she came mid-morning and left mid-afternoon, would that work for you?"

"It would be adequate."

"You know she's deaf and dumb?"

"I do. But I also understand she can read as well as write and she has won several ribbons for her cooking at the Independence Day festivities in town."

Clarence ushered his daughter to the doorway and turned so she could read his lips. He recounted the offer and put it to her if she wanted the job. Maude nodded with vigor.

"Could she start tomorrow?" asked Lenore. "Guests will arrive soon, and I need to get things in order as soon as possible."

"Tell you what, Clarence," said the reverend, "I'll stop by whenever my circuit takes me that way. Tomorrow, in fact."

Clarence puffed out his cheeks as he let out a slow stream of air. At last, he said, "Well, all right. Tomorrow, then." He stuck out his hand and a woman's gloved hand emerged from the darkness to lightly shake his.

"Thank you," said Lenore, "and have a good evening."

"You as well," said Clarence, easing the door shut.

He walked with measured steps back to the table, then took another deep breath and sat down to a piece of his daughter's pie. "She's an odd duck."

"The Lord's tent is mighty big," said the reverend. "She seems shy, that's all. And as you said, you could use the money." The reverend looked down at his clean plate then up at Maude who just sat down. He grinned once more. "I do declare, there's still a little room left for more pie."

Chapter Ten

Atlanta

Edgar dragged the unconscious Nigel out to the street, but when Annabelle flagged down a cab, the driver took one look at Nigel and frowned. “Not on your life!” He announced and lifted the reins, prepared to go.

Edgar yanked off Nigel’s filthy coat and threw it on top of a magnolia bush. “There,” Annabelle announced to the driver. “The worst of it is off!”

The driver surveyed the potential customers a second time.

“We’re going to the Piedmont Hotel.” Annabelle waved a dollar at the driver, far more than the fare. “He’ll be on the floor. I guarantee your cab will not be damaged.”

The driver rolled his eyes, reached down for the money, and then waved them aboard.

They shoved the unconscious Nigel inside and laid him across the planking. Annabelle and Sarah kept their feet as far away as possible, but Edgar rested his shoes on Nigel, ostensibly to keep him from rolling.

At the hotel, they faced similar resistance, once the clerk woke up and became cognizant of the man on the floor in front of his desk. Edgar had hauled Nigel from the cab, one hand under each shoulder, and dragged him into the building. To protect the carpet, Sarah and Annabelle rolled up the rug in front of the reception desk so Edgar could set Nigel on the bare wood floor.

The desk clerk appeared to stand only about four-foot-ten-inches and combed his thin brown hair over the top of his otherwise bare head. Shiny spittle hung in the corner of his mouth from sleep, and Annabelle could not keep from staring at this when he spoke.

"We don't take in riffraff," the clerk told her. "I made an exception for your colored servant, but this is too much. For pity's sake, he stinks! Get him out!" He made little shooing motions with his hands.

Annabelle took out a lacey handkerchief and wiped the corner of the clerk's mouth. The man became nonplussed. "What are you doing?" he stammered.

"You were drooling on the guest registry when we came in. I'm sure the proprietor of the hotel would be happy to know he pays you to sleep."

"What? I never—"

"Moreover, this is not riffraff. Surely you've heard of Edgar Allan Poe? Yes, he has fallen on hard times, but we are rescuing him, just as I will rescue you by not reporting what I saw and causing you to lose your job. I see by the keys on the wall behind you that the room next to mine, number 401, is unoccupied. Now it is. You will also draw a bath and rouse the hotel barber."

"What? At this hour? He's probably drunk."

"Fine. They'll get along famously. We shall pay him for his troubles. Now go!"

The little man scurried about as ordered. He placed the key to 401 on the counter and went into the bathhouse, a room off the lobby. A few minutes later he emerged and went upstairs, presumably to get the barber.

"Were Poe still alive, I believe he'd be in his seventies," said Edgar with a smirk.

Annabelle smiled and gave an airy wave. "He's the first name with notoriety that came to mind."

When the barber descended the stairs, he carried a black leather bag, of the type favored by many physicians. He did smell of gin. His untucked white dress shirt struggled to cover his large belly and his suspenders hung limp at each side. Annabelle stated she wanted Nigel clean-shaven and with a respectable haircut. She volunteered Edgar's help and then gave the man two dollars.

The barber and Edgar carted Nigel into the bathroom and shut the door. Before long, the door opened and Edgar dropped Nigel's rags onto the floor. He withdrew back into the room and banged the door shut.

Annabelle removed her gloves, snatched a pen from the registry, and used the writing implement to gingerly pick up the fetid pile of clothing. She caught Sarah's eyes and grimaced with disgust. Annabelle set the rags on the desk in front of the clerk, who sat back, aghast. "Please incinerate these," she said.

The man picked up the clothes, held them at arm's length, and went out a rear door marked *Employees Only*.

"Well, you're getting him clean," said Sarah, "but what about new clothes? Edgar is taller. No shops are open at this hour."

"I've got an idea."

When the little clerk came scuttling back, Annabelle asked if there were any suitcases left by former patrons, perhaps those who skipped out on bills? She offered to buy anything Nigel's size.

The man returned, red-faced and puffing with exertion. He carried a small trunk, two suitcases, and a carpetbag. He set them on the floor. "As I recall," he said, wiping his face with a handkerchief, and then gesturing theatrically at the pile before him, "these were from people of a similar build.

"How often do people leave without paying?" Annabelle asked with surprise.

"The basement is half-full of this sort of thing." He stopped and eyed her. "Don't get any ideas," he warned, trying, but failing, to look intimidating.

Annabelle shook her head. "We'll settle our entire bill now, if it makes you feel any better."

Annabelle paid the clerk and then she and Sarah began to go through the luggage. They opened the trunk first and got a laugh when Sarah held up a pair of pants for an obviously obese man. The other luggage proved more fruitful, and they managed to assemble a suitcase full of clothes and shoes of various sizes, one of which they thought would fit. Annabelle took a nightshirt and knocked on the bathroom door.

Edgar opened it and took the garment. "The barber deserves a large tip," he said. "He helped me bathe the guy. My God, what filth!" Edgar shut the door.

****

A few minutes later the men emerged. The barber and Edgar held up either side of Nigel, who'd undergone a remarkable transformation.

"Well, I had my doubts, but it seems a man existed under all that grime," said Annabelle. "My compliments, gentlemen."

Sarah smiled. "He's actually handsome."

Nigel started to become aware. He staggered between the other two men as they brought him up the stairs and took him to his room on the fourth floor. But as they set him on the bed, Nigel came to and became agitated. "No, no!" he cried and fought to get off the bed. The barber threw his hands up in frustration and backed away.

"Hold him still," Annabelle told Edgar as she rummaged in her purse. She removed a small brown bottle and a handkerchief. Uncorking the bottle, she put drops of the liquid onto the cloth, then held the handkerchief over Nigel's nose and mouth. A few moments later, Nigel relaxed into what seemed to be a deep sleep.

Annabelle withdrew the cloth and looked at the others. "The professor gave me ether and the pistol, in case we should need them. Seems he was right on both counts."

Edgar turned to the barber and said, "Please excuse any appearance of impropriety."

"Quite understandable," said the barber.

Annabelle retrieved the suitcase and the shoes from the hall. She put them on the floor of Nigel's room. Then Sarah set an extra suit across the top of a dresser. As they all filed out, Annabelle removed the key from the inside lock, pulled the door shut and used the key on the outside to lock Nigel in.

Annabelle gave the barber a Morgan silver dollar as a tip. "Thank you for your trouble."

The man looked at the coin then at Annabelle and smiled. "No trouble at all, until he woke up. Good luck in the morning." The man ambled down the hall, flipping the coin up and catching it as he walked.

Edgar leaned back against the bright floral-papered wall of the hallway and exhaled with relief. “We should take turns here by the door in case he wakes up and starts causing a ruckus.”

“I agree,” said Annabelle. “I thought to suggest as much. I’ll take the first shift. Sarah, would you spell me in two hours?”

“I’ll take the first,” said Sarah. “My insistence got us into this.”

“All right. If I’m not here in two hours’ time, please wake me.” Annabelle entered her room and closed the door.

****

Edgar went into his room and returned with a plain wooden chair. He set it before Nigel’s door and gestured. “It’s not especially comfortable,” he told Sarah, “but may help keep you awake. You can call on me, instead, for the second shift.”

Edgar left and Sarah settled onto her chair.

As time passed, her mind began to wander. Later while abed, would she be subjected to the vision that brought her here? She’d find out in a couple of hours, as soon as her shift was over.

To keep her mind occupied, she decided to count the red roses on the wallpaper opposite her. She counted forty-two roses before sleep overtook her. Edgar happened to check on her a few minutes later and shooed her off to bed.

Sarah sank into an untroubled sleep.

The calm before the storm.

Chapter Eleven

Atlanta

"Well," said Annabelle, as they stood before Nigel Pickford's door the following morning, "shall we see what awaits us?"

Sarah and Edgar nodded.

The three announced themselves by knocking at the door several times, to no effect. *Perhaps I used too large a dose.* She knew ether could be fatal in large enough quantities, but the professor instructed her on how much to use. Nevertheless, as she turned the key in the lock, she ran several scenarios over in her mind—*if indeed this man were dead, she, Edgar, and Sarah would need to leave Atlanta with all due haste.*

Annabelle turned the knob and opened the door.

Nigel remained abed and Annabelle strode across the room and shook him.

"Mr. Pickford?"

No response.

"Oh, good God," she muttered. Annabelle bent down to check for breathing.

Nigel flung back the covers and put Annabelle in a chokehold, pulling her down onto the bed with him. Sarah and Edgar looked on from across the room in shock.

"I've been kidnapped and held captive," snarled

Nigel. "Plus, you've taken my belongings. I want some answers, damn you!"

Annabelle slapped at the arm across her throat, to indicate she could not breathe. Nigel loosened his hold and she gulped in air. Edgar edged closer to the bed.

After a moment, Annabelle croaked out "You have not been kidnapped."

"What do you call it?" Nigel shouted in her ear, tightening his grip.

Edgar sprang forward and grabbed the little finger of Nigel's left hand. He gave it one quick jerk. A popping sound occurred as the finger became dislocated.

Nigel let go of Annabelle and howled.

Annabelle clambered off the bed and turned to see Nigel, fully dressed, sitting up and holding his left hand in agony. The little finger stood at attention, but askew from the rest of the fingers.

"Help me!" begged Nigel.

"Will you listen to us? And not cause further commotion?" asked Annabelle.

"Anything," Nigel cried.

Annabelle reached down with both hands. She took hold of Nigel's left wrist in one hand and his little finger in the other. She yanked hard on the digit so it aligned with the others. Nigel screamed.

He began to calm down, still cradling his injured hand. After a while, he looked up at Annabelle with a hound dog expression. "It's better, but still hurts like a son of a gun. It seems I've fallen in with a pack of savages."

"You gave us no choice."

"What would you have done in my position?"

“Mr. Pickford, you have not been kidnapped. You were belligerent and uncooperative last night. We brought you here at our expense and have provided you with a room, a bath, and a fresh set of clothes, all of which it appears you have long been without. As soon as your behavior is reasonable, we will all go to breakfast.”

Silence occurred for a long while as Nigel considered the situation. He responded in a low voice, “Who’s payin’?”

“Our group is covering your expenses.”

“Why didn’t you say so? Let’s eat!”

“Let’s put your finger back to rights.” Annabelle turned to Sarah. “There’s some sewing scraps in the bag next to my bed. Would you please fetch a small length of linen and the scissors?”

When Sarah returned, Annabelle tied the little finger to the one next to it with two bits of cloth.

Nigel got off the bed and straightened his suit. He also had on a pair of shoes they had purchased for him.

Annabelle had to admit he looked good.

“These duds are a bit scratchy,” said Nigel, loosening his collar.

“You aren’t used to clothes free of vermin,” Annabelle said. “It may take some getting used to.”

****

In the hotel dining room, Nigel shoveled a huge forkful of eggs and grits into his mouth. He looked up at Annabelle and Sarah who ate with more refinement. He smiled and decided to speak with his mouth full.

“So, you go gallivanting around looking for spooks?”

Annabelle gave him a patronizing little smile. “We

mostly expose frauds, as you did last night—though we don't do so in a drunken stupor." She began what sounded like a practiced speech. "We are convinced something is out there and worthy of scientific investigation. So far we—" She stopped when Nigel shoved additional food into his mouth and ate with his mouth open.

Annabelle and Sarah both coughed into their napkins. "Mr. Pickford," Annabelle continued, "I'm glad you are enjoying your meal, but I ask you to please eat with your mouth closed."

Nigel swallowed the mouthful. "Sorry, ladies. Table niceties have fallen by the wayside these last few years."

"I imagine so," said Annabelle.

Nigel set down his fork, leaned on the table, and pointed at the two women. "You mentioned joining you on a trip to Boston. That's going to interfere with other plans of mine. Given the difficulty of rearranging my other commitments, I must ask for no less than fifty dollars for my time and trouble."

Sarah laughed at this and then coughed. She looked over at Annabelle.

Annabelle squinted at Nigel. "Agreed," she said at last, "once you have met with Professor James. You will not be able to extort a penny more from me, so let this be an end to it."

Nigel nodded and filled his mouth once more. Subsequently, they shared a somewhat amicable breakfast, although Annabelle reminded Nigel several times to use his fork and napkin.

After breakfast, they met Edgar in the lobby since he needed to eat in the kitchen with the colored help.

Annabelle asked the day clerk, a prim man of medium build, with a neat beard and mustache, to hail them a cab while the group went upstairs to pack.

The carriage dropped them off at Atlanta's Union Station, a hive of activity. Annabelle paid the cabbie and strode inside the crowded ornate building to find the ticket booth. The others followed with their belongings. Annabelle met them a short while later with their tickets to Boston.

Annabelle, Sarah, and Nigel would share a private room in a Pullman car with berths for sleeping. Edgar would travel in one of the colored coach cars. The Pullman car would go straight through to Boston, being transferred from one rail line to another. Edgar would have to wait in stations for each change of trains. "I'm sorry, Edgar," said Annabelle, "it's the best I could do. We can pursue different arrangements, once we get up north."

Edgar waved her off. "It's no different than what I've encountered before." He picked up his bags, took his ticket and moved to the waiting area for negroes.

****

"I need a drink," Nigel announced once seated in their compartment.

"I anticipated you having some difficulty without your liquor, so I bought a cough remedy this morning to help with any shakes. It smells of alcohol and should do nicely."

Annabelle rooted in her large handbag and removed a dark brown quart-sized bottle and a spoon she confessed to having taken from the hotel. She uncorked the bottle and poured a tablespoon of the liquor. She held the full spoon out before her. "For medicinal purposes only," she announced.

Nigel leaned forward and took the spoon in his mouth. He removed the utensil and handed it back to Annabelle. "Reminds me when I was a small boy and my mammy would feed me. You going to wipe me if I mess myself?"

"Really, Mr. Pickford. I ask you to speak with a little more refinement."

"I think I remember how, though I haven't given it much importance since the war. I honestly do need to use the facilities."

"Well, you'll have to wait."

Nigel stood. "I don't think so."

Annabelle looked up at him calmly from her seat. "Have you ever ridden on a train before?"

"Boxcars during the war."

"Well, the facilities you'd like to visit are simply rooms with a hole in the floor. Consequently, you are not allowed to use them in the station."

"I may need you to wash me after all if we take too long to depart."

Fortunately, for all concerned, the train soon pulled out of the station and began chugging its way north. Sarah accompanied Nigel down the hall to the men's restroom.

"I *am* able to do this all by myself."

"I have no doubt," said Sarah. "I'm making sure you do not stray from your mission."

"Why?"

"Self-interest. I believe our fates are intertwined."

Nigel stopped and appraised Sarah. "You're a little young for my tastes. Perhaps once we get to know each other."

"That's not what I meant."

"Hang on," he said as they reached the restroom.

Nigel opened the narrow restroom door and wedged his way inside. A few minutes later, he emerged with a grin. "Now I know why gandy dancers dance. I wouldn't want to step in it either."

"Is your crudity an attempt to control situations where you are uncomfortable?" asked Sarah.

Nigel looked at her wide-eyed. "How old *are* you?"

Back in their room, Annabelle tried to get Nigel to discuss his past.

"I've been trying to forget it for twenty years. I'd thank you not to raise the issue again." Nigel turned away and stared out the window at the scenery.

Much of the day passed in glum silence. The two women read, and Nigel stared outside or asked for more medicine. Annabelle doled this out no more than once an hour. Sarah produced a deck of cards and she and Nigel played several rounds of Hearts. When she tired of it, he sat on the floor and played solitaire. The two women watched him with some trepidation whenever the train pulled into a station or supply depot for water and coal, but Nigel did not bolt.

Eventually, they stopped for dinner and filed off to a nearby hotel catering to train passengers.

"Is your darky friend still with us?" Nigel asked as he sawed at a dry pork chop with his knife and fork. He gave up and grabbed the chop and began to gnaw at it.

"Edgar is facing the indignities associated with Negros traveling in the South," said Annabelle, after swallowing her mouthful of catfish. "He is in another part of the train and will join us later."

The three needed to rush through the pie and hurry back to the train before it departed.

****

At the station platform, Nigel saw a gray-haired fellow traveler sipping from a hip flask. Nigel felt compelled to knock the man aside and run off with it. Instead, he turned to the women and asked if they might buy him a newspaper. Annabelle obliged.

"So, you are literate, Mr. Pickford? Or will you just look at the pictures?" Annabelle's eyebrows arched with incredulity as she handed him the paper."

"You seem surprised I can read."

"You're one surprise after another, Mr. Pickford. One might say you're full of it."

Now Nigel raised an eyebrow and cocked his head. "Full of surprise, or something else?"

"The latter, I think." Annabelle stepped onto the train. Nigel smirked and followed her aboard. Sarah brought up the rear.

Nigel hid behind his newspaper for much of the evening until the cabin began to darken.

A colored porter with white hair around his cap, came into their room to light the lamp and to lower the sleeping berths. Annabelle informed Nigel he would sleep above, while she and Sarah shared the larger berth below.

They overcame the awkwardness due to the co-ed nature of their accommodations. The women took turns going to the restroom to change into their nightwear. Nigel chose to stay dressed. However, Annabelle insisted Nigel surrender his shoes for the night. Nigel shrugged at this, complied, and climbed up to his berth. He did not intend to fall asleep, but as soon as he lay back on the pillow sleep seized him.

****

"Why did you let us die, Lieutenant?" The question reverberated through Nigel's skull, as it did twenty years ago when his curse began—when he foresaw the slaughter of his men but could not prevent it.

Nigel awoke, covered in sweat.

Sometimes different visions plagued him, always calamities he couldn't stop from happening, like Cassandra in Greek mythology. At other times, what he saw happened in the past, evoked by a particular location, object, or touch—information he could not explain knowing. Sometimes visions came so clouded with symbolism he could not decipher them, until an event brought things into focus, after the fact. Most often, this precognitive vision from the war, when the curse began, returned to haunt him.

The frequency of these events, usually at the onset of sleep, and his inability to intervene, drove him to drink—which worked—albeit at the price of becoming a derelict. Fair enough, he thought, willing to pay the price.

Nigel stole down from the sleeping berth with every bit of stealth he could muster. In the moonlight streaming in through the windows, he studied Annabelle and Sarah who remained asleep. Beneath the ladies' berth, he found Annabelle's purse. Nigel rummaged inside and removed a money clip as well as the bottle of cough medicine.

He looked down at the wad of money in his hand and turned it over and over. He rifled through it. There appeared to be well over a hundred dollars. *I'm nobody's fool.*

Nigel stood, removed his jacket from the peg by the door, and put the bottle in one pocket and the money in the other. He retrieved his shoes from where they lay on the floor. With infinite care, he depressed the handle on the door and eased it open. He made his escape and closed it behind him with only the slightest of sounds. Nigel put on his shoes and strode toward the end of the car and freedom. He went out onto the divided platform between the two cars.

The night air rushed past him, and his hair and coat flapped in the breeze. Nigel crawled over the railing and leaned out so he could see past the side of the train car. The wind buffeted him as he judged the landscape for a jump. The moonlight revealed they were speeding along the bank of a river, but between the tracks and the water lay large boulders lining the shore for as far as he could see.

He waited. The rocky bank seemed to go on forever. He moved to the other side of the platform. A split rail fence ran along this side of the tracks. The longer he stared at the ground racing by the train, the more he doubted he could even survive a jump onto friendly terrain. *If I break my leg, my back, my neck, what then?* He could be lying there for days, injured, even dying. *Would I even be able to jump clear of the train?*

Nigel scrambled back over the railing, returned to his car and stole into his room. With regret, he knelt down and tucked the money clip back into Annabelle's purse. But before doing so, he extracted two dollars from the wad and tucked the bills into his pocket. He climbed back up to his berth.

Nigel stretched out across the bedding, propped

himself up on one elbow, and removed the bottle of cough medicine from his pocket. He uncorked it with his teeth, spat the plug across the blanket, and pulled a long drink. Nigel lifted the bottle in a little toast to no one in particular. "For medicinal purposes only," he said aloud.

In the morning the women discovered Nigel's theft of the bottle.

"You thieving sot!" Annabelle screamed at Nigel, who made a groggy smile at her.

"And good day to you, as well," Nigel said. He rolled over on the bed, facing away from her.

This only infuriated Annabelle further. In response, she yanked off the shoes he wore to bed.

He assumed she desired to make him more comfortable, so Nigel thanked her. Only later when he rose, still thick-headed from the medicine, did he discover Edgar held his shoes hostage in another car.

"You'll get them back when we arrive at Boston," Annabelle told him and reminded Nigel fifty dollars was at stake. She and Sarah took turns watching him and brought food back to the car so he didn't leave the compartment except when he needed to relieve himself. The line added a Pullman dining car to the train, which made fetching meals easier.

He reread the paper, and to keep from going crazy, Nigel asked them to share any reading material. Annabelle produced a small volume of Shakespearean tragedies from a bag beneath her seat and threw it at him. Nigel caught it neatly and grinned. And so they spent their day.

That night, they retired similarly to their perches, but this time Nigel stayed awake, waiting for the sounds of sleep from the other two. When it seemed propitious, he crawled back down. He looked beneath the women's berth; however, Annabelle's cloth purse was now secreted away.

No matter, Nigel thought as he stuck his hand into his jacket pocket and felt the two dollars he'd purloined the previous night. He withdrew his hand and gave the pocket a little pat. That should do it. *I'm willing to tag along with these lunatics, but I shall not do so sober.*

Once again, Nigel pried open the cabin door and slipped out. He wanted to see if the man with the hip flask, he'd spotted during their first dinner stop, still rode the train.

To his delight, after exploring two adjacent cars, Nigel discovered the gray-haired fellow inebriate in the third. He remained awake, sitting in the coach section reading a magazine. The man tilted his head back and drank from the flask, no doubt replenished since Nigel last saw him.

"Good evening to you, sir," said Nigel in a quiet voice, respectful of the sleeping passengers around them.

The man looked up from the *National Police Gazette* and raised his gray eyebrows in greeting. The man's clean-shaven face looked flush, his suit somewhat rumpled, and his tie hung loose around his neck. Bay rum cologne wafted off him.

Nigel continued. "I wonder if you, by chance, would know where I might procure a nip as well. A nightcap, so to speak."

The man removed his feet from the seat opposite him and motioned for Nigel to sit. Nigel obliged him and the man offered his flask. "I happen to have a bit of the stuff with me here." Like Nigel, he spoke with a Virginian accent. "And an obliging porter has helped to keep me supplied through three states. Raymond Davis, at your service."

Nigel accepted the flask and shook Mr. Davis's hand. After introducing himself, he took a swig and winced. Whiskey and not well-aged—Nigel's usual vintage. He took a second drink and returned the flask. "Mr. Davis, you are a gentleman—" Nigel indicated the magazine and grinned "—and a scholar."

They both laughed.

Mr. Davis would be traveling on to Portland, Maine, and so made the perfect traveling companion. When they finished the flask, they found the obliging Negro porter and parlayed Nigel's two dollars into two bottles of cheap whiskey.

****

Edgar sat, uncomfortable and unable to sleep, in a car toward the rear of the train. The wooden bench hurt his backside and the iron armrests every foot and a half made it impossible to stretch out and sleep. The air felt hot and stuffy, but most of the windows in the car were painted shut, as they had been in the last one. Edgar took out his penknife and freed many of the windows so that they would open. Other passengers thanked him, and he waved off their appreciation. "Nothing any of you couldn't have done."

It's a long way to Boston, thought Edgar as he yawned and retrieved his copy of *Nature* magazine. Well, I ended up with a position at Harvard after all, he mused, but not the one I imagined…

Chapter Twelve

On the Train from Atlanta

"Good morning, Mr. Pickford," Annabelle called from the lower berth as she sat up. She lifted the dark blue gingham robe from where it lay on top of the bedclothes and put it on. "Mr. Pickford?" Annabelle tied the sash around her waist, climbed out and looked up. The berth above her was empty.

Sarah entered the compartment, fully dressed. "I found him three cars up, passed out. It seems he and another passenger share the same affinity for cheap alcohol."

A rap came at the door and a muffled voice from outside announced they would be arriving in Boston within the hour.

"Well, at least he may be more malleable in this state," Sarah observed, "but difficult to carry. Perhaps we'll be able to wake him."

"I need to get my clothes on before we consider our next move." Annabelle snatched her raiment from a hook on the wall and dressed. "I'd just as soon leave him."

"You have good cause, but I am confident he will prove useful. My visions have never led me astray." Sarah smiled at Annabelle, who simply frowned.

Dressed and their luggage packed, Annabelle and

Sarah made their way back to the coach seats and reclaimed Nigel. They managed to rouse him enough so he could stumble down the aisle, through the next two cars, and into their own. Annabelle shoved him into the restroom.

"Relieve yourself, sir," shouted Annabelle, "and I hope you fall down the hole!"

After several minutes she pounded on the door but got no answer. Fortunately, Nigel forgot to throw the bolt. They opened the door and saw him squat down in the corner with his trousers around his knees. They almost gave up but finally got him extricated from the small room.

Sarah and Annabelle brought him back to their cabin and changed his shirt. As the train pulled into the Boston and Providence Railway Station, Sarah flagged down a porter who carried their bags out to the platform. The two women wrestled Nigel, in his stocking feet, out to the platform as well. There Nigel began to sing loudly and out of tune. Fortunately for everyone within earshot, he soon sat down on their pile of belongings and went to sleep.

Edgar, carrying his suitcase and Nigel's shoes, joined Annabelle and Sarah. "I see Mr. Pickford has comported himself well," he said. "At least as well as could be expected."

Chapter Thirteen

Nantucket Island

The Black Baptist minister, Reverend Davis, rose shortly after six AM. He threw off the quilt and climbed out of bed, then reached back and pulled the bedding over his wife's backside. Marriage to Carmilla, his former housekeeper, was a mixed blessing. One or two nights a week, he felt spent and utterly happy. Still, from the moment she said her vows, breakfasts became a thing of the past. Well, what did he expect? Carmilla had never been much for mornings, and not much of a cook at any hour.

Reverend Davis went into the kitchen and lit the small pile of paper and kindling he'd put into the stove. It soon caught so he added larger pieces of wood and shut the hatch. Next, he'd grabbed the coffee pot, pulled off the lid and set the insert on the counter. He held the pot beneath the pump until, after several up and down motions with the handle, water ran from the faucet. He set the pot on top of the stove, ground some beans, and put them into the insert, then set the contraption into the pot and replaced the lid.

The reverend got dressed and brushed his teeth with a god-awful mixture of tobacco ash, salt, and charcoal. Carmilla read about this in a magazine and insisted they try it. He rinsed his mouth with water and wanted coffee to clear the nasty taste from his mouth.

He rejoiced in discovering the coffee already brewed, so he poured himself some. As he lifted the cup to drink, he noticed Carmilla regarding him with her frowzy morning hair and a beautiful smile on her brown face. The minister smiled in return and handed her his cup. "Brewed this especially for you."

"It's a sin to lie."

"I'm hoping my prayers and contrition will make up for a whole lot of sins."

"Don't go putting expectations on the Lord."

The minister shook his head and poured himself more coffee, this time in a tin cup. "You know I wouldn't do that, but I *can* hope and pray."

"You can at that, and very well, I hear. You home for supper? I hope and pray."

"I expect so."

"The age of miracles hasn't passed."

"No indeed." The reverend put on his suit jacket.

"Hold up, Minister." Carmilla came up to him, pulled him down by his lapels, and kissed him. "Now you can go."

Smiling, Reverend Davis went out into the foggy morning. He made his way around the house to the shed where Horace, his bay gelding, waited. He set a blanket upon the horse's back and then set the saddle in place. As he reached under the horse for the straps to buckle the saddle, he saw the lower half of a woman—an inexpensive blue skirt and scuffed black shoes. "Carmilla?" he called.

"No, Reverend. It's Katty Baldwin."

The reverend squeezed out along the side of the horse and wiped his hands clean on a rag. He took the pregnant woman's offered hand and made a little bow. "Why, Mrs. Baldwin. This is a surprise. A pleasure, but a surprise nonetheless."

A light-skinned Negro, Katty's brown eyes were downcast and her voice little more than a whisper. "I saw you come out."

"You been waiting? How long?

"I couldn't sleep. Folks spotted Louis's ship yesterday evening. It'll put into port as soon as the fog lifts, and I'm powerful afraid." Katty Balwin began to sob.

The reverend touched her shoulder. "Come on in the house. We got coffee, and you can collect yourself." He led the woman through the rear door and into the kitchen. Carmilla must have heard them come in and emerged from the other room wearing a robe. They helped Katty onto a chair and Carmilla poured the last of the coffee. The crying woman took the cup in two shaking hands, so Carmilla put her hands over the distraught woman's and helped lift the cup to Katty's lips. The younger woman stopped her sobbing, blew on the coffee, and took a tentative sip.

Carmilla looked at Reverend Davis, but he shook his head in dismay.

"Why don't you tell us what has you in such a state, Katty?" said Carmilla.

"I *am* in a state," she said, her voice shaking, "That's the trouble. The last time I got in such a state, Louis returned home and accused me of whoring. He hit my belly so hard the baby, a little girl—his little girl, was born dead. I've never been with another man, but Louis don't pay that any mind when he's been gone and comes back to find me with child. I don't wanna lose this baby. I can't face him again! Lord, I should have left Nantucket, but I have no place to go!"

Carmilla stood up and leveled a hard gaze at the reverend. "You know about this?"

Katty reached out and grabbed Carmilla's forearm. "No, no. I ain't told no one before."

Carmilla looked back at the reverend. "What are you going to do about this?"

The reverend raised his hands in a gesture of helplessness. "Apart from talking to Louis, I'm not sure what I can do."

"I know where Louis keeps his gun," admitted Katty. "I won't let him kill another innocent."

Carmilla turned to the reverend. "I'll tell you what we're going to do. I'm going to get dressed and then we're going to accompany Katty to the police station. When Louis's ship gets in, he can be arrested."

"Carmilla," the reverend tried to reason with his wife, "There's no proof of a crime, so the police will not get involved."

"We're damn well gonna try." Carmilla looked at Katty. "Pardon my French."

Five minutes later, the three of them walked down the foggy street to the station house.

They reached the darkened building a few minutes before seven o'clock. Carmilla pounded on the locked door to no effect.

"Well, now what?" asked the reverend.

"We wait," announced Carmilla.

"I am powerful sorry for all this trouble," said Katty.

"No trouble at all," Carmilla said. She gave the reverend a hard look daring him to contradict her.

"Don't trouble yourself on our account," the reverend mumbled in a half-hearted voice. "We want to be sure you and the baby are safe."

"That's right," said Carmilla with conviction.

After waiting for an hour on the stone steps, the conviction started to wear a little thin. The reverend suggested they return home for more coffee.

"I think we should stay close," Carmilla told him. "Her husband's boat hasn't docked yet, but it could happen any time. Let's have breakfast at the Snug."

The reverend sighed in resignation and ushered the ladies before him.

"Don't mind his sighs," said Carmilla in a loud whisper so the reverend could hear. "He pinches pennies so tight they scream in protest. We can well afford this."

In a blue house across the street from the station, The Snug Café featured breakfast and lunch fare prepared by the owner, a colored woman from the West Indies, Babette Didion. Both whites and colored folk frequented the place.

The reverend and the two women made for an open table in the corner by the kitchen. The waitress, Mamma White, a very large black woman and Babette's partner in all things, approached them with a wide smile.

"Why Reverend Davis and Carmilla, plus Kitty Baldwin!"

"It's Katty."

The waitress looked her over. "Yes, I guess you're right." She turned back to the reverend. "We don't see you much in here, Reverend. Carmilla keeping the leash too tight?"

The reverend made a smile, bigger than the one worn by the waitress. “And I haven’t seen you and Babette none too often at Sunday service. Perhaps we can all resolve to do better.”

The waitress guffawed. “That we can. So what might I get you, folks?”

Katty seemed reluctant to order anything, but Carmilla prodded her until she ordered the same as her—eggs, bacon, potatoes, and toast. The reverend ordered a coffee and a roll.

“Now how you gonna keep your strength up with a breakfast like that?” the waitress asked.

“I’ll manage.”

Mamma White looked at him and at the two women. “Yes, I guess you’re right. I don’t think you can get any more on your plate.” She laughed at her own joke and went off to the kitchen.

As anticipated, the women left half their food, so the reverend ate plenty.

The police station opened during their breakfast, but the fog remained. Sergeant Sean O’Connell, a husky man with a handlebar mustache and slicked-back brown hair looked up from some paperwork as the reverend and the two women entered.

“Good mornin’ to you, Reverend,” said the sergeant with a thick Boston accent.

“We’ve been waiting for hours to speak to someone, but the place was locked up tight.”

“When no one’s in a cell, we don’t usually stay here. The station officially opens at nine. Now, what can I do for you?”

Carmilla stepped forward and conveyed the story. The sergeant listened sympathetically and noted things down in a small black notebook he took from his breast pocket. When she finished, the officer bade Katty to step forward.

"This all true?"

"Yes, sir," said Katty. "He beats me regular too, but it's the baby I gotta protect. It's his, it's just he don't ever see it that way."

The sergeant set down his pencil. "Your husband on a whaler?"

"The Firm Resolve."

"Well, I'm goin' to firmly resolve to meet Louis when his ship comes in. Perhaps between the reverend and I, we can put the fear of both God and the law into him. I'm afraid, at this point, that's all I can do."

Katty lowered her gaze. "I appreciate it, but I don't think it's gonna do much good. Especially when he takes to drink, there's no stopping him."

The officer made a patronizing smile at the pregnant woman. "If he touches so much as a hair on yours or the baby's head, in a manner of speakin'"—the policeman stood for emphasis—"I'll take his off at the neck."

The reverend, Carmilla, and Katty gave their thanks to the officer and went back out onto the street.

"I want to thank you both for what you done," said Katty. She turned to go, but Carmilla grabbed her hand and stopped her.

"Where do you think you're going?"

"Home. You heard the officer."

"No, child, you're coming with us. You'll stay until we're assured you're safe, or we'll get you someplace far from here, if you're ready to leave him. In the meantime, the reverend will sleep on the floor."

"Now hold on a minute!" the reverend protested.

Carmilla turned to confront him head-on. "We will welcome this poor soul into our home. It's the Christian thing to do."

She used the "C" word. The reverend knew from experience that further protest went nowhere. She fired the big gun. "You are right, as usual," he said in resignation.

"Perhaps we should take Katty to her place to gather some belongings while the coast is clear."

"Why not?" sighed the reverend, indicating his assent. The three walked across town to Louis and Katty Baldwin's home, a small gray Cape Cod cottage with a host of flowers in the front garden. "Them's my other babies," said Katty, indicating the flowers. "Them are the ones he don't trouble."

Carmilla and the reverend waited at the doorway as Katty put her necessities into a carpet bag and readied herself. The place looked simple but clean. Two chairs bordered the fireplace and another chair sat by a window with a basket of items to mend on the floor next to it. A small vase of wilting chrysanthemums sat on the dining table. The only book in sight was a large family Bible on a small table next to the fireplace. *Did they use pages from it to start their fires?* The reverend shook his head to clear it of the uncharitable thought.

Katty approached them with a nervous smile. She held up her bag. "I gots what I need," she announced. The reverend reached over and took the surprisingly heavy bag from Katty. They filed out of the house and Katty locked the door. She put the key under the mat. "He doesn't always have one handy when he gets in," she said.

They walked back to the minister's house, next to the Baptist church, Katty and Carmilla nattering all the way about a variety of topics. The reverend followed in sullen silence while he carried Katty's bag.

Once there, Carmilla buzzed around their little place, helping Katty get situated, and the reverend said goodbye.

"There's a couple with a sick infant out in Shawkemo, and some other people who are expecting me, so it's time I left. Looks like the two of you will keep each other company."

Carmilla came over and kissed him on the cheek. "Don't worry about us. Katty has offered to help darn your socks, so you'll at least have warm feet while you're sleeping on the floor."

"We each care for souls in our own way," he said with a smile.

Out back, Horace waited patiently in the shed, still with the saddle half on. "Sorry, my friend. Both our patience have been tried."

The reverend secured the saddle and put on the rest of the tack. He led the bay out of the shed and mounted the horse. *You know, if I cut things short this morning, I might still be able to make the Browns' house for a midday meal*. He would check on Clarence Mahogany's daughter, Maude, afterward.

But first, he needed to get to Shawkemo. The Meadowlarks wanted their new baby dedicated into the church. Usually a part of Sunday service, their child might not last till then.

He arrived at the Meadowlark's ramshackle hut and thought it looked about to fall in on itself. Somehow it managed to remain intact despite the hurricane-force winds that regularly buffeted the island. The reverend tied his horse to the broken railing on a dilapidated porch and went to the door. He needed to knock three times before it opened.

Inside of the doorway stood a skinny black man, already stoop-shouldered, despite his youth. “Sorry, Reverend, couldn’t get to the door right away. Ida, our baby, got the whooping cough. Polly’s so worried, she can’t stop crying. Please come in.”

The one-room shack was dark, dingy, and full of wailing. Reverend Davis purposely left the door open as he entered to let out some of the contagion and gloom. Across the bare wood floor lay a straw mattress. Polly wept face-down on the bed. Next to the mattress sat a homemade cradle, fashioned from a crate for canned salmon. Burned into the side of the cradle were the words *Winchell’s Seafood.* The sick baby, who alternated between wails and wracking coughing fits, lay within.

The reverend came forward, crouched, and put a hand on Polly’s shoulder. “I’m so sorry,” he shouted above the din. “Perhaps our act today, dedicating her to the Lord, will aid in her recovery. In any case, as an innocent child of the church, she is already part of God’s flock and she will be welcome in God’s heavenly home.”

Polly stopped to peer up at him over her left shoulder, then buried her head in the mattress and resumed crying. Her eyes were so red, she appeared sick too. Sick at heart, he realized.

The reverend straightened and regarded the infant girl for the first time. The child scrunched her eyes as she cried. Green mucus poured from her wide nose and bubbled up from the mouth during coughing fits. Crusty trails of the stuff hung on both cheeks.

“Please wipe her face, Mr. Meadowlark, and lift her into your arms.”

The man did so, and the baby seemed to breathe a little easier.

The reverend placed his hand on the baby’s warm moist forehead and for a moment the infant quit its wailing. The reverend spoke the ordinance aloud, and in doing so told the Meadowlarks to lead exemplary lives and teach the child the ways of the Lord. Polly sat up to watch the dedication and her crying quieted to little whimpers into a wet hanky.

Sensing the need to do something more, the reverend bent down and kissed the top of the baby’s head. He looked at the father.

“I’m no doctor, but as I understand it, keeping the child on your shoulder, or with its head raised in your arms may help. Steam might also be good. If she can’t suckle, have Polly squeeze milk from herself and put drops into the child’s mouth whenever she’s not coughing. Beyond that, it’s in God’s hands.”

Chapter Fourteen

Nantucket Island

By mid-morning, the fog still lay thick over the island. Maude didn't realize she had arrived until the Hutchinson place rose out of the mist with imposing suddenness. Large and rambling, with a porch running along the full front of the house, it once enjoyed the reputation of being the finest home on the island.

The yellow and white exterior needed considerable attention. The chipped and blistered paint, absent in many places, reveal the weathered wood beneath. It made Maude think of the pox. One shutter on the upper floor hung askew. It didn't look haunted to her, just sad.

Maude pulled the wagon up before the front and climbed off. She fetched a full water bucket from the rear of the wagon, removed the lid and watered the horse, letting her drink deeply. Maude replaced the bucket and went onto the porch.

She knocked on the door and it swung open, revealing a white and black marble foyer.

"Hello?" she called. Her father told her before it didn't sound much like the word, and she couldn't hear any answer, but this signaled her arrival. Maude worried her deafness would ultimately prove too frustrating for her employer. Still, she told herself, Miss Hutchinson knew about it before she came by our house last night to offer me the job. *Nothin' I can do but try my best.*

Maude took a step inside the spacious marble foyer and looked around. Several rooms led off in different directions and a hallway ran to the rear of the house. Also from the foyer rose a wide staircase to the second floor. Maude opened a doorway to the right of where she came in and saw an unoccupied library.

"Hello?" she called again.

Maude crept back and opened another door. This led into a dining room with a huge wooden table she reckoned could easily seat two dozen. She walked through the room and pushed open a swinging door at the rear. She found the kitchen.

The large room contained a white enameled oven big enough to crawl in, and the stovetop looked at least six feet across. She noticed the full coal bin next to the oven and grinned. She wouldn't need to haul any for a while. While clean, the room did not look used. Enamel and copper cookware hung above an island workstation. They gleamed as though new. The double sink had a cast-iron pump and long counters on either side. Maude opened the icebox. Empty.

There were three other doors leading out of the kitchen. One led to the back of the house, another to the hall she'd seen from the foyer. The final one opened into a large pantry with a staircase at the far end. The stairs descended to a basement no doubt used for cool storage. A box of lucifers and a lamp sat on the otherwise empty shelves. Must be for forays below, she realized.

Maude shut the pantry door and opened the one to the hall. She shouted again, as loudly as she could, but no one appeared. In frustration, she stamped her foot so hard it hurt. There didn't seem to be anything for her to do but wait, and she hated to be idle. She recalled the library. At least she wouldn't be bored. Maude noticed a piece of paper on the floor near the island and bent to retrieve it. A note, which must've blown off when she entered the kitchen. Something caught the corner of her eye and she straightened with a start.

A shadow of a person fell across the curtains on the back door. *Her employer?*

Maude opened the door and saw a heavy-set white man in overalls. He had blond hair and a walrus mustache. She could tell he was speaking to her, but his mustache concealed his lips, making them difficult to read. He appeared to be saying something about never being here before.

Maude glanced at the note.

Good morning! I apologize, several errands today prevent me from being here to meet you. I have ordered a number of supplies (food and sundries) to be delivered this morning. Please have the delivery man bring these into the kitchen. Your task today is to put the kitchen to rights. Place things where you feel they belong. The kitchen is now your domain!

Sincerely,

Miss Lenore Hutchinson

Maude handed the man the note and indicated she could not hear. The man looked at the note, nodded, and turned away. Maude followed him down the steps to the rear drive and saw a wagon loaded with goods. The man unfastened a rope from one side, threw it over the load, and pulled back the tarp.

The delivery man pulled the top off a packing crate

and tipped it on its side. He removed fistfuls of loose straw, which he threw to the ground. The man put a burlap bag over one shoulder and used a pair of tongs to grab a block of ice from the crate. He hoisted it up onto his shoulder and headed for the back door.

The man said something Maude couldn't comprehend.

Intuiting his needs, Maude ran before the man and held open the kitchen door. She then opened the icebox.

This time Maude managed to discern what the man said. "Well, you ain't stupid, even if you are dumb."

The delivery man put the block on the floor and wiped it clean with the burlap. After muscling the ice into the compartment in the icebox, he swiped the burlap around on the floor, gathering up most of the water and pieces of straw.

After numerous trips, the delivery man filled the kitchen with wooden boxes containing eggs, bacon, ham, salami, three chickens—already plucked and cleaned—cheese, a half-dozen jugs of apple cider, produce, canned milk, and other goods. He also hauled in sacks of flour, coffee, rice, sugar, beans, and cornmeal. Maude had never seen so much food, except in a store.

Before she launched into her work, she brought the horse around back, unhitched her and set up a tether to allow her to roam the ill-kept yard and crop the grass. She spent the next five hours unpacking, sorting, cleaning, and putting things away. Not knowing what meal to prepare, she hard-boiled and peeled some eggs. She also carved up the ham and put damp pieces of cheesecloth over each to keep them moist before putting them into the icebox.

Maude finished by her mid-afternoon departure time. She scrawled a note—in her best penmanship—to Miss Hutchinson saying she would be back again in the morning. She asked for more information on the guests, so she might plan some meals.

When her horse saw Maude emerge from the house, the mare swished her tail back and forth and raised and lowered her head, as though indicating approval. Maude hitched her to the wagon and gave her the rest of the water.

They headed home through the glowing brightness of the lifting fog.

Chapter Fifteen

Nantucket Island

The reverend thought the Browns' farm looked like the Promised Land, compared to the Meadowlarks' hovel. The fog thinned enough for the reverend to see the well-tended fields and the handsome farm animals as he approached the house. Crushed oyster shells covered the drive and the path to the front door, a door distinguished by a large oval window with beveled glass. Despite the bucolic splendor, he knew his tardiness would not sit right with Chester Brown, who kept his watch wound tight.

The reverend tied the horse to the hitching post. He pulled two sugar cubes from his coat pocket and picked off the lint. No sense Horace should suffer, he thought. The animal seemed appreciative. The reverend climbed the stone steps and gave the door several raps. A moment later, Patrice Brown, a full-figured black woman with a warm smile and eyes he could get lost in, opened the door.

"I see the sun has come out already!" said the reverend, smiling back at her. "A very good day to you, Mrs. Brown. I hope I'm not too late."

Patrice Brown stepped back and held the door wide. "Welcome! The table is set and will soon be laid out with all your favorites. We were waiting on you."

The reverend walked down the familiar hall to the kitchen, where Mr. Brown sat at the table glowering as he held a cup of coffee.

"I'm sorry for my tardiness," said the reverend. "Needed to bring some comfort to the Meadowlark family out in Shawkemo. Their little girl is powerful sick, and I believe the Good Lord may be calling her home in a day or two. I hope you'll forgive me."

"There's nothing to forgive," said Patrice using a towel to take a covered dish from the warming oven and setting it on the table. She lifted the lid to reveal the pieces of fried chicken and looked at her husband to second her courtesy. It didn't come.

"You an expert on doctoring, as well as everything else?" asked Mr. Brown.

"Chester!" Patrice said in shock. The sunshine drained from Patrice's demeanor. "What on earth has gotten into you?"

"Nothin' and that's the problem." Her husband banged the cup down on the table and helped himself to a drumstick and a thigh. "I'm sure the reverend's mission of mercy provided great comfort to all except my stomach. Oh, and there's the fact I need to get back to work. I've been here half the day, waiting around for his holiness, and I'm not going to wait a minute more. I'm sure you understand, reverend, and will forgive *me*."

"Of course. Again, my apologies."

Mr. Brown's parting words were made incomprehensible by him gnawing on the drumstick as he left the room.

Patrice looked close to tears. "I—I can't understand—" she stammered.

"No matter at all," said the reverend, putting a hand on her shoulder.

Patrice turned and hugged him, crying for some time onto his shoulder. "I wanted everything perfect for you," she sobbed.

"Again, it is I who need your forgiveness for being so late." While the reverend enjoyed the fresh smell of Patrice's hair and the warmth of her embrace, he also eyed the chicken. "Let's sit down and not let all your efforts go to waste." The reverend held her shoulders and stepped back so that she could see his most disarming smile.

The reverend continued to grin through most of the meal due to its deliciousness. After they ate, the two chatted about spiritual matters and together they prayed for a good harvest. In the course of things, Patrice's knee pushed up hard against his. With some regret, he scooted the chair back to maintain a sense of propriety.

When the two parted company, the reverend steered his horse in the direction of the Hutchinson house. He would be late arriving there as well. As he rode, he considered the attraction he felt for Patrice.

Stop it. Carmilla's a good woman. He remained glad he made an honest woman of her, yet he couldn't help a wistful consideration of Patrice and other women on his circuit. No one told him before becoming a man of the cloth, being a minister acted as a powerful aphrodisiac. *Is it because I listen and spend time with them?*

The fog had fully lifted during his time with Patrice. The reverend lifted his face toward the sun and smiled. As he approached the old Hutchinson place, he checked his watch. 4:36 If he missed Maude, he resolved to stop by the Mahogany farm on his way home to make his apology. Perhaps, as a result, he would benefit from another free meal and the opportunity to put off returning to his own crowded home and to Carmilla's cooking. *There's always a silver lining.*

He rode around to the rear of the house, where he assumed the help would come and go. No horse or wagon waited there. He started to turn the horse away then noticed the rear door stood wide open. *She still here?*

Curious, he dismounted and attempted to tie the horse's reins to the post for the small roof above the entry, but the horse shied away. The reverend pulled at the reins, "Come on, Horace," he said, but the gelding planted its hooves and refused to move. "Maybe they should have cut off something more," he muttered. Deciding on the path of least resistance, he crossed the drive, away from the house, and tied the horse to a bush.

The reverend came up to the doorway and removed his hat. "Hello?" he called into the kitchen. "Maude?"

No answer. He called again, much louder than before. He stopped shouting and grinned.

Of course, if Maude were the only one here, she wouldn't hear him. He looked around and listened. No sign of anyone.

"No harm in checking," he told himself out loud. "In for a penny, in for a pound."

The huge kitchen appeared to be well-stocked and orderly. He sensed Maude's handiwork. The reverend moved through the room to the open door to the pantry. In the rear were stairs leading down to where faint light shone in the cellar.

"Maude?" he called and shook his head again, feeling foolish.

He descended the steep stairs and held onto a rail on one side for safety. The lamp shone from back behind the stairs, so he needed to descend fully to see if she were there. At the bottom of the steps, he noticed the basement's packed-earth floor. The dim light also revealed a wall twenty feet ahead with a door set into it.

The reverend turned and saw the lamp sitting on a bench halfway across the large basement. He squinted in the weak light and judged the dingy room to run the length of the house in this direction. Shadows cloaked much of the room. The reverend began moving toward the light. He glanced around to see if he could catch a glimpse of Maude.

Something tripped him and he went down hard, smacking the side of his face onto the dirt floor. He kicked at whatever grabbed him, and a rod swung around and hit his chest. The reverend snatched at it and realized he had hold of a rake. He gave a little laugh to calm himself and threw it aside. His eyes, adjusting to the faint light, could now discern tools of various kinds—shovels, hoes, scythes, buckets, and a wheelbarrow nearby.

He got up, brushed himself off a bit, and retrieved his hat. He started forward again. The lamp sat on a wooden bench in front of shelves stocked with dusty mason jars. The reverend assumed the unidentifiable brown, green or red contents were once fruits and vegetables.

Had she simply forgotten about the lamp and left it burning? The reverend peered into the shadows all around for any sign of the girl.

The hairs on the back of his neck suddenly rose.

The light went out.

Talons grabbed his hair from behind and jerked his head back. Tears sprang to his eyes.

"Hey!" he managed to shout before something—not sure what—ripped into his throat. The reverend's body jerked with pain and he inhaled blood from the wound. Then came spasmodic coughing.

The reverend felt warm wetness down his front from a fountain of blood and from the urine pooling in his crotch before it ran down both legs. He wondered why his assailant held him in such a cruel embrace before consciousness slipped away.

Chapter Sixteen

Cambridge, Massachusetts

Professor James took his eyes off the test subject for a moment to survey his messy laboratory while he and his assistants waited. He did keep the floor clear, his one concession to his mother's frequent adage about cleanliness being next to godliness. Were that so, the shelves and glass-fronted cabinets around the room were the devil's own playground, stuffed to overflowing with papers, books, and the debris from prior experiments. Similar materials lay on top of the shelves and cabinets, stacked to the ceiling. There were various optical illusion devices, distorted paintings, dolls—some without heads—and small bits of machinery. While inexplicable to the casual observer these were once crucial objects in experiments, used and now set aside—probably for good. *The devil be damned*, he liked the clutter. He considered everything as touchstones to past lab work and what they continued doing in the exciting new field of psychology.

Today the professor wore a white lab coat over his usual charcoal-colored suit and carried a board clip, with papers attached, and his favorite fountain pen. He and three graduate students, also dressed in suits and ties, were conducting an arcane experiment on a similarly well-dressed man suspended in a metal cage.

The experiment purported to be about perception, particularly hearing. The subject, bound to a chair and blindfolded, also wore padded stoppers—screwed inward from the cage's frame—plugging his ears. They sought to deprive him of sensory input.

Various noise-making devices—a metronome, drums, a xylophone, bells and buzzers of numerous type—lay on the table before the professor. None of these were sounded. They were part of a ruse. Instead, Professor James and his protégés watched the test subject and remained absolutely silent. After a long while, the man in the cage, whose forearms were free, tentatively raised his right hand. James checked the time and recorded it on the clipboard. He looked at the others.

"As you can see," said the professor, in a low voice, with evident fascination, "when deprived of stimuli, the brain begins to hallucinate. All five subjects have exhibited the same phenomenon; they *think* they hear something."

Unannounced, Sarah threw open the laboratory door and held it wide. James turned with a start as Annabelle and Edgar entered, propping up either side of Nigel Pickford. The drunk sang *My Wild Irish Rose* at the top of his lungs.

Bemused, the professor put the cap on his pen and tapped it on the pages of his board clip as he approached the intruders.

"Well, what have we here?" he asked.

Annabelle's face flushed with embarrassment. "Sorry, Professor. He got hold of some whiskey on the train."

"Why bring him here in this condition? It would be useless to speak to him now."

Nigel broke free. He stumbled across the room and smashed into the suspended cage. The contraption swung away.

"Whoa!" shouted the bound and blindfolded test subject, who sensed movement.

"Beg pardon," Nigel apologized to the man in the cage.

The cage swung back and knocked Nigel off his feet. "Hey!" he yelled, "I said sorry."

The grad students looked flummoxed.

Annabelle and Edgar grabbed Nigel and pulled him away. Nigel resumed singing.

Edgar looked up at the professor. "If you want him sober, keep him under lock and key. He's incorrigible."

"I prefer to think no one is irredeemable. Nevertheless…" The professor motioned for them to bring Nigel across the room and opened a small closet, filled mostly with boxes of books. "We do need to help him achieve a more rational state."

Annabelle and Edgar shoved Nigel into the closet. Professor James slammed the door and locked it.

Though muffled, Nigel's singing continued.

The professor turned to his assistants, who still wore looks of complete shock. "That's it for today, gentlemen. Let's reconvene at nine AM tomorrow."

The students, now given direction, snapped to. They released the subject—who appeared relieved—and departed.

The professor smiled at the others. "As you know, my wife has the uncanny ability to sense when I will bring surprise guests for supper and invariably has enough food for all. In the interest of science, let's see if this precognitive ability stands up to another test."

The professor cocked his head toward the closet. "He seems happy enough in there."

Professor James ushered Annabelle, Sarah, and Edgar out the door and pulled it shut behind him.

****

Nigel's singing continued for perhaps a minute more, then stopped.

The closet door rattled.

"You folks can let me out now."

Silence.

The door rattled again.

"Hey! I gotta pee!"

****

At 95 Irving Street in Cambridge, the members of the Eidola Project sat down to a fine supper of turtle soup, roasted chicken, beans, and fresh greens. Alice seemed gracious but wary in their company.

As they ate, Annabelle recounted the events in Atlanta. The professor chuckled at their exploits and patted Annabelle's hand. "If you pulled out that pistol as a student at the Harvard Annex, you might not have needed to work for your good grades!" Everyone laughed but Alice.

Harry, now four years old, burst in from the kitchen. "Boo!" he shouted and laughed. Harry's two younger brothers and the nanny feeding them could be seen in the kitchen as the door swung the other way. "Boo!" he repeated. "I want the ghost hunters to chase me!"

The professor coughed around his mouthful of food and smiled.

Alice stood up from the table and shooed her son away. "Harry James, if you do not give your father some space, a ghost *is* what you will become when I'm through with you." She pushed him through the door and into the arms of the nanny. Alice turned back to her guests and forced a smile.

"Thank you, Alice," said Annabelle, "for accommodating all of us unexpectedly."

"I always prepare more than needed, as William picks up guests like a dog does fleas."

Annabelle sat up with a start.

"Alice!" said Professor James with surprise.

Annabelle, Edgar, and Sarah looked at each other uncomfortably.

Alice took out a handkerchief from a pocket and held it over her mouth. She turned and walked briskly from the room and into the parlor. Professor James followed.

"That was uncalled for," he told her.

Tearful, Alice shook her head and walked into his study. The professor trailed her and shut the door behind them.

Professor James ran a hand through his hair and over his beard. "What is it? This isn't like you."

Alice turned. She ran into her husband's arms and blubbered, "All I do is tend your home and bear you children. I can't compete with that woman."

"What woman?"

"Annabelle. She's clearly in love with you."

"Nonsense. I assure you, you've always had and will continue to have my heart."

A knock came at the study door.

"Yes, what is it?" the professor asked with some

irritation.

"It's Esther, sir," said their maid. "A telegram just arrived."

The husband and wife parted. Alice used her handkerchief to dry her eyes. Professor James opened the door and stepped into the parlor. The maid handed him the telegram. Near the front door stood a boy in brown knickers and a gray shirt and cap. The boy tipped his cap at the professor.

"Will there be a reply, sir?" the boy asked.

"If it's what I'm expecting, then yes," said the professor. He tore open the envelope. "Have a seat, young man, and I'll be right with you."

The professor read the message and returned to the dining room. It didn't look as though anyone moved an inch in his absence. "You may all relax. The warm weather is bothering Alice, nothing more. Are you all worn out from your recent sojourn south, or do you have the stamina to begin a new investigation right away?"

Chapter Seventeen

Nantucket Island

The sun descended below the horizon before the *Firm Resolve* slid into port, met by a few shore hands and some family members of the crew.

In the twilight, the crew could see their wooden whaler had the distinction of being the only whaler in the bay. Before the popularity of kerosene, the port would have been clogged with whalers. A market still existed for the cargo they unloaded in New Bedford—spermaceti for perfume and high-quality oil, baleen for corsets, and barrels of rendered blubber that continued to be desired by some. All the men had money in their pockets. Still, the *Firm Resolve* numbered among a dying breed, due to both petroleum and the increasing difficulty of finding whales.

The steam-driven tug released them, and shore crew and deckhands tied off the ship.

Back after eight months at sea, Captain Chandler stood on the forecastle and assembled all the crew on the main deck below him, as he always did when they put into port. "Those with no homes, or whose wives throw you out, may use the ship as a rooming house for a dollar a night, but there's to be no fornicating aboard my ship."

"Does that include sea lions?" asked one of his best

harpoon men.

"If you can coax one into your hammock, I may make an exception." The captain grinned. "Now off with you!"

Louis and the rest of the crew fled to meet the women and children at the end of the wharf. They clambered down the gangplank and along the dock on legs made rubbery from their long voyage. Shouts of good cheer arose, cries of delight, and people embracing all around him. Louis waded into the sea of people. He looked for Katty in the fading light.

Nowhere to be seen.

What the hell?

Humiliated, Louis broke free of the crowd and ran across town to his and Katty's home on Bayview Street. He discovered a dark house, locked up tight. Louis pounded on the door but got no answer. He pounded again before he kicked it open. The wood around the latch shattered and the door swung into the darkness within.

Louis stepped through the doorway and fumbled around for the tin lamp and box of lucifers on the small table to the left. He lit the lamp and held it aloft.

Deserted. *Could she be out visiting*? No. She would've known, like the others, of their arrival.

The flowers on the dining table proved she'd been here recently. But now, no Katty and no note.

Where could she be? Had she left him? When the cat's away…

Louis swung his free arm across the tabletop and sent the jar of flowers sailing across the room to smash on the wall. Water, glass shards, and chrysanthemums flew in every direction. To make sure, he stepped into the bedroom and confirmed no one was there. He turned back and set the lamp down on the dining table. Louis scratched his chin and considered his next move. Suddenly, without much thought, he grabbed the lamp and threw it against the wall. Its glass chimney shattered, and the tin base, still aflame, bounced off the wall and rolled on the floor to where several wet chrysanthemums extinguished the light.

Darkness enveloped him, but moonlight shone through the doorway to guide his way. However, as he exited, Louis stumbled into the rocking chair and he pitched it aside with such force the chair flew across the room. It hit something which then fell. *Probably the family Bible.* He didn't care.

Outside, he halted on the flagstones and looked around. *Where was the bitch?* The moon illuminated the flowers Katty tended in front of the house. He took a few moments to stomp them into oblivion.

An hour later, Louis nursed his fourth glass of rum at Davy Jones' Locker, a decrepit dockside pub. Some crewmates in the place at first tried to cheer him, but after being told to fuck off enough times, they left him to brood at the bar.

Babette Didion and Mamma White from the Snug entered the pub shortly before ten, arm in arm, laughing at some intimate joke. They came up to the bar next to Louis and ordered gin and a bowl of sugar cubes. When the drinks arrived, they put a cube into each other's mouth. Before drinking, Mamma White lifted her glass to Louis as a way of hello and smiled, the sugar cube held between her teeth.

After a long drink, Mamma White set her glass down and faced him. "So, Mr. Baldwin, why are you not home pleasuring your wife? Can it be you don't find women in a motherly way attractive?"

"She's with child?"

Babette leaned over the bar to see Louis around Mamma White. "Oh yes, man. That or she's carrying a watermelon under her dress!"

The two ladies laughed.

Momma White added, "When we saw her this morning with Reverend Davis and Carmilla, your Katty looked big enough to burst. I kidded the reverend about having two women in tow."

Louis's voice became steel-hard. "Is that so?" He tossed back the last of the rum and slammed the glass down onto the counter. He pushed off from the bar and headed for the door.

"Hey!" yelled the bartender. "You haven't paid!"

Louis did not turn around nor slow his stride. A very dark, bald-headed bouncer, with huge biceps and a thick chest, suddenly appeared before him. He carried a sap.

"Settle up, or else," the bouncer snarled.

Louis kicked out with sudden savagery and his heavy boot connected with the bouncer's crotch. The bouncer collapsed to the floor and held his privates. He curled into a fetal position and emitted a strangled groan.

Louis staggered out onto the street. Bands of fog seemed to reach up from the bay to stop his progress, but they were no more effective than the bouncer. Louis set his course for the Pleasant Street Baptist Church.

The fucking bitch! He cursed as he stormed down the street. *And with the preacher!* He dealt with her being untrue after his last voyage with a well-placed blow. He'd do a whole lot more this time—to all three of them.

After several blocks, he reached his destination, but the church, a gray square building, had its doors locked and no light in its windows. However, the small white-washed parsonage next door had its windows lit up, acting as a beacon for his wrath.

****

Carmilla looked at the clock again—ten-seventeen. Only four minutes later than the last time she checked. Where could Malcolm be? He'd never been this late without having sent some word. Katty lay in the small bedroom, snoring, exhausted by the day's events, but Carmilla was on edge. She decided to warm some milk.

As she stirred the milk on the stove, the door to their home crashed open behind her. She jumped and screamed, knocking over the pot. A hissing sound arose as the milk spread across the cast-iron stove and burned. She involuntarily put a hand to her mouth and swung around to see the madman in the doorway.

The stink of burning milk filled the room.

Carmilla forced her hand down, stood erect, and tried to put some power into her voice. "Louis Baldwin, what in God's name are you doing?"

"You know damn well! Where's my wife?" The man looked filthy and sweaty. His thick brows knit together in anger.

She took a step toward him. "We got her a safe place to stay while she decides what to do next. Turn your tail around and get out of my doorway. The police already know of your violence toward women." She attempted to push him out. "Get on out of here before you dig your hole any deeper!"

Louis backhanded Carmilla across the face. She flew against the dining table and scattered the place setting for the minister's uneaten meal. Carmilla fell to the floor, dragging the checkered tablecloth and everything on it down with her.

****

"Stop, Louis!"

Louis looked up to see Katty in the bedroom doorway holding a pistol before her. Katty's hands shook. She tried to stop the shakes, but they would not cooperate.

Louis edged toward her.

"Is it the minister's?" he said as he pointed at her swollen belly. "What were the three of you doing while I was away?"

"It's yours—I swear. I'm not going to let you hurt it, or me, or anybody else. Stop or believe me I'll shoot." The gun shook more as she said this and Louis smiled.

He dove forward, reaching for the pistol.

The gun fired with a deafening blast. Its kick caused Katty to fall backward to the floor. The weapon flew behind her and slid beneath the bed.

Katty tried to scream, but nothing came out. The fall knocked the wind from her. She fought to regain her breath and clawed her way across the wood floor to retrieve the pistol. She grabbed it and swung around on her knees. She held the gun out before her with both hands, the shaking gone.

A few feet in front of her, in the bedroom doorway, Louis also knelt.

"Get out!" she screamed.

Louis didn't move. He appeared to cry as a red

drop ran from his mangled eye and down his cheek. More followed, and soon a torrent. Louis swayed and toppled over.

Dead.

Chapter Eighteen

Cambridge, Massachusetts

When the professor returned to his psychology lab, long shadows filled the room. He unlocked the closet door and saw Nigel sitting on a small upturned crate. Further back in the closet a large wet stain marred a pile of books.

"Good God, man!" exclaimed the professor, "You urinated all over my books!"

"I've been held captive for hours. This a sample of Yankee hospitality?"

Professor James shook his head with incredulity.

"I suppose it couldn't be helped." He motioned for Nigel to step out. "Come, we haven't a moment to lose."

They were soon inside a carriage, being jostled about by the vehicle's progress on cobblestones. Despite the shaking, the professor was able to pour a cup of coffee from a wicker-wrapped flask. He offered the tin cup to Nigel, who shook his head.

"What the Sam Hell is going on?"

"Go ahead and drink," prompted the professor. "It's god-awful—my wife's one weakness—but it'll have to do."

Nigel took the cup just as the carriage went over a bump, and he spilled a good deal of its hot contents onto his lap.

"Jesus!" Nigel swore. He reflexively stood up and bumped his head on the carriage roof, spilling the remaining coffee on himself. The cup dropped and clattered away on the carriage floor.

"I warned you it was bad," said James and set the flask aside.

Nigel sat down and ineffectually wiped at his suit with a handkerchief.

The professor regarded Nigel with a penetrating stare, causing Nigel to squirm.

"So, Mr. Pickford," the professor began, "let me tell you about our little enterprise."

****

When the carriage pulled up before the train station, Annabelle, Sarah, and Edgar were paying porters to take numerous pieces of luggage and two large wooden crates onto the train. Nigel stepped out of the carriage and held the door open for Professor James. The professor shook his head, no.

"I must return to Harvard. The Eidola Project is a passionate sideline, but my other work pays the bills. All the more important since the Society for Psychical Research has cut our funds—a little spat between the director and me. I expect it shall soon be smoothed over." The professor pulled the carriage door closed. He stuck his head out the window and smiled at Nigel. "Thank you for agreeing to give us a try."

Nigel looked at the others with a smug expression and back at the professor.

"Hell, if you fruitcakes want to keep buying me whiskey and new clothes, I'm prepared to give you a whole week."

Annabelle waved her hand back and forth to intercede. "No alcohol," she insisted.

Nigel turned to William James in protest, but the professor shrugged.

"I agree," he said. "To change one's life, do it immediately. Do it flamboyantly. No exceptions."

Annabelle and Nigel glared at each other in a test of wills.

Finally, Nigel broke off and glanced down at his clothes. The coffee stains weren't visible. He gave the lapels of his new suit a strong tug.

"Well, all right…"

The professor looked elated. "Fine! Fine! I leave you in capable hands."

Nigel turned back to Annabelle and grinned lecherously. "If Annie's capable, I'm willin'."

Professor James pointed to the station's large ornate clock. "Hurry, now, the train is about to depart. I'll join you in a few days."

****

Nigel followed Annabelle as she entered the train car. Their room contained two banks of leather upholstered seats facing each other and three windows on the far side. Annabelle sat down and Nigel plopped down next to her, but when Sarah and Edgar entered, he bounded back up. Nigel stepped in front of Edgar.

"Go sit with the other coloreds," he said.

Annabelle stood and stepped between them, facing Nigel. Her cheeks were flushed with anger, and he thought she looked rather fetching.

"Mr. Pickford, this boorish behavior must stop!" Annabelle spoke with righteous indignation. "Edgar is both brilliant and a valuable member of the team. If you are to accompany us, you must set your prejudice aside."

Sarah came up and took Edgar's arm, steering him from the room without a word.

"Of all the god-damned nerve," swore Nigel after Edgar's departure. He retook his seat.

"Massachusetts integrated its trains years ago. It is you whose behavior is intolerable."

Annabelle moved to the opposite seat and sat down with a huff. She folded her arms across her chest and shook her head in disgust. "*Really!*"

Nigel folded his arms and leaned back. "*Really!*" he echoed, mocking her.

Annabelle's face flushed with even more rage. "If Sarah weren't so adamant we need you, I would shoot you right now."

Nigel slid further down in his seat, leaned into the corner and shut his eyes. "Really?" he asked with nonchalance. He intended to close his eyes only for a few moments, to feign indifference, but the instant he did so, he fell asleep.

Chapter Nineteen

October 19th, 1864 - March 25th, 1865

The Army of Northern Virginia promoted Nigel to lieutenant a few days before his twentieth birthday, a rare, but not unheard of occurrence for one his age. It happened after a Union cannonball took the head off Lieutenant Thaddeus Faringsworth. One moment, their unit commander sat astride his horse, barking orders and waving his sword, and in the next, he lacked a head. A brief spout of blood ran from his neck and the lieutenant, sword still raised high, tumbled into the tall weeds surrounding his men. The lieutenant's horse continued to stand there as though nothing happened.

"Get down!" Nigel yelled. He slapped the horse on the rump and sent it running. Nigel joined the rest of the men on the ground. Several more cannonballs whizzed overhead and missed them entirely.

Corporal Dowd, whose proudest achievement in life seemed to be his waist-long beard, pushed the weeds aside so he could see the young sergeant. Nigel nodded his hello. "We'd best skedaddle," the corporal offered his unsolicited advice.

"We stay put." Nigel raised his voice. "Did y'all hear that? We stay put! The Yanks are coming over the rise any minute. We need to give 'em a welcome."

Just as he said, a short while later, a wide column

of Blue Coats came up over the slope and let out whoops of delight. It appeared they took the hill with no resistance. Some slapped each other good-naturedly and others removed their caps to wipe their brows.

"I guess they heard we were coming!" one Union soldier shouted.

"They went home to hide their womenfolk!" added another.

"Their gals are attracted to us like flies to shit," added a third.

"Shut your damned mouths!" yelled an officer, the only one who looked uneasy as they crested the hill.

They continued to advance on the neglected field, whose high weeds held their quarry.

"Now!" shouted Nigel. A fusillade of lead—round balls and pointed Minié bullets—flew through the air and cut the Union column to shreds. Gut-shot men fell backward and fumbled with their shirts to check their abdomen for the bad news. Others screamed as the metal smashed into bones and soft tissue. The remainder of the column turned and ran back down the hill.

A cheer went up in the weeds among the Confederates, but Nigel would not let them celebrate, not while they fought a rearguard action.

Nigel stood up. "Now we skedaddle! Get your asses outta here!" he yelled.

The men picked up their guns, grinning as they ran.

When they got back to the Second Corps and everyone heard what happened, Nigel was promoted by Lieutenant General Jubal A. Early. The general wanted to highlight one bit of good news in what had otherwise been a rout in the Battle of Belle Grove.

Over the next few months, they faced a number of engagements, hit and run—mostly run, until there was no place left to go. More and more talk circulated about the possibility of losing. Early was replaced by Major General John B. Gordon. When the Union surrounded Petersburg, Virginia, Gordon and Lee formulated a plan to break the siege.

As a consequence, Nigel and his men waited in the darkness on the eve of the Battle of Fort Stedman.

Lieutenant Nigel Pickford sat upon his horse with his men arrayed around him, much as Lieutenant Faringsworth, months before. The irony was not lost on Nigel. His mind often flashed on the grisly tableau of a real headless horseman. This time, however, Nigel and his men were on the edge of the woods.

His band of anxious soldiers looked ragged. Many didn't have shoes. At least it wasn't winter anymore.

In his short time as their leader, the men became fiercely loyal to him. He successfully steered them through these final days of the war with limited casualties. Only two of his men were shot since he made lieutenant. While one losing an arm and the other a leg were not easy things, these men could still look forward to a life ahead of them. Corporal Dowd, on the other hand, died of dysentery—what they called "screamers" because of the terrible cramps—in December. Nigel missed the man and the pride he took in his long greasy beard.

Last week, while making his evening rounds, Nigel overheard a group of his men talking about him around a campfire. "He's got some sort of gift," said Saunders, a rifleman attached to his unit. "He *knows* things, I tell ya. It's spooky, but with him on our side, we got some hope of getting through this damned thing alive."

Nigel walked out of the darkness and startled the men. Surprised, Saunders dropped the flask of whiskey he'd stolen off a dead Union officer earlier in the day. The flask landed in the fire, flared up and exploded. None of them were injured, nevertheless, it made for quite an entrance.

"Who the hell put that fool notion into your heads?" Nigel asked.

"The proof is in the pudding, Lieutenant," Saunders grinned. "We're still here."

Now, moments before the battle, Nigel's unit waited in the frosty pre-dawn light. The gunfire of sharpshooters began in the distance. A farmhouse, also some distance away, began to burn, and its light faintly illuminated Nigel and his men. The main thrust of the battle centered on Fort Stedman, in the center of an arc of forts and parapets stretching for miles. Nigel's men were to move against a fort on the flank, Fort Haskell.

Nigel raised his arm to signal the attack but stopped short. In a panic, he glanced back and forth at his men—all of whom appeared horribly disfigured.

How can this be? We haven't engaged the enemy. An instant earlier they looked fine.

Seventeen-year-old Tim Hayton whimpered as he tried to hold in guts spilling from his abdomen. He looked up at Nigel in anguish. "Why'd you let us die, Lieutenant?"

Corporal Archibald Smith, another battlefield promotion after Dowd died, stepped forward out of the shadows. His brain glistened and throbbed in the flickering light, due to half his skull being gone. "It's a trap, sir," said Smith.

"Lieutenant Pickford!" General Evans spat fire as he rode through Nigel's men, who suddenly appeared normal. Following the general were two aides-de-camp. "Why the devil do you not advance as ordered? We are waiting to follow!"

Still stunned by his vision, Nigel echoed Corporal Smith, "It's a trap, sir," he mumbled.

"Speak up."

"It's a trap."

"I don't care if the gates of Hell await you in that valley. You were ordered to advance, and you will bloody well do so. Gordon has opened a hole in the Union line. We need to support him on his flank. Move out!"

"I can't do that, Sir."

The general drew his revolver and leveled it at Nigel's skull. "You will proceed as ordered, or I'll find some other bastard who will."

An outcry arose among Nigel's men. "We ain't afraid, Sir!" Corporal Smith told the general, "And neither is our lieutenant. He just gave us the signal to advance before you arrived." Everyone shouted in affirmation.

"Very well." The general lowered his pistol. "Proceed, Lieutenant."

The corporal grabbed the reins to Nigel's horse and led him forward. The rest of the men followed.

The men descended through the underbrush and came out on the road leading to a cornfield and the forts in the distance. They began to work their way through the withered stalks, some still standing since the fall, others fallen and covered in a coating of frost. They breathed air redolent with damp earth, molding vegetation, and cordite drifting their way from the battle some ways off.

"Thank you, Corporal," said Nigel, "I don't know what came over me."

Smith shook his head and grinned. "We know you ain't a coward, Lieutenant. You only want to look out for us. So far, so good."

Indeed, proceeding through the field, they encountered no resistance by Union troops. All the action happened far to their left—rifle fire, cannon blasts, and the shouts and screams of men at war. Nigel's unit began to cross a recently plowed field. The frost acted as a thin crust to the muddy earth below, and their shoes or bare feet sank into the muck as they walked.

They were now forty yards from Fort Haskell's earthworks.

"Steady, men," he heard General Evans say to the column behind him, "'nearly there."

"Have the Yanks run off?" whispered Saunders, who stood on Nigel's left.

If I were to hit us, it would be now.

As if they heard Nigel's thoughts, a fusillade of shots came from the earthworks ahead. Cannonballs and canisters tore through the men. At one moment, Saunders stood next to Nigel, whispering to him. The next instant Saunders disappeared, except for his shoes, which remained stuck in the mud, still filled with Saunders's feet.

A bullet struck Nigel's horse in the haunches and it reared up and screamed. Nigel fell backward. He struggled to stand as his head spun from the fall.

Union troops cascaded from the fort with bayonets

thrust before them. Nigel, still dizzy, managed to knock a bayonet aside with his sword, but the Union private who wielded it brought the butt of the gun up and clipped Nigel hard across the side of the head. Before he could follow-up with a downward thrust of the blade, a bullet caught the private in the chest and he flew backward, spraying blood onto Nigel.

Semi-conscious, Nigel could not account for the number of soldiers from both sides who stepped or tripped on him. His eyes flickered open to see a Union major charge at Tim Hayton. Tim fired, missed, and held up his rifle to block the officer's sword. The major feigned a downward blow, then switched sideways to slice open the young soldier's stomach like a sack of wheat.

Tim's intestines spilled out and fell around his legs. He looked down in shock at his innards—long red and gray ropes of intestines looked like sausage. He dropped to his knees as though in prayer, expired, and collapsed into the mud. Tim's comrades fared no better.

Nigel regained consciousness sometime later. He opened his eyes to see a young red-headed Union private with a face full of freckles stealing his watch. Nigel grabbed the offending hand and its owner screamed and broke free—though he still held Nigel's timepiece.

"Stop!" Nigel shouted at the thief with what little force he could muster.

The sun shone in a bright blue sky, and despite the recent battle, birds sang as per their usual morning ritual.

Nigel tried to sit up but fell back into the bloody mud and passed out.

The next day when Nigel awoke, he found himself in a hospital tent. He wore a bandage wrapped around his forehead.

His eyes fluttered open and he stared at the nurse as she wiped his face with a sponge. Her pockmarked face broke into a buck-tooth smile, but at first, Nigel thought her an angel.

"Morning, Reb. Seems you're a lucky man. War's over for you."

To his left, two Union men bore a Confederate soldier in on a stretcher and set their load down on a pair of crates—a makeshift operating table. The surgeon approached. He held a nub of a cigar clenched in his teeth and wore an apron covered in blood. Nigel noticed the piles of severed arms and legs on the floor.

"What the hell am I to do with him?" yelled the surgeon. "His head's half gone!"

One of the stretcher-bearers stopped at the door to the tent. "He was talkin' a minute ago as though nothin' were wrong. Said his name was Smith."

The doctor took his cigar from his mouth and blew smoke upwards. With his other hand, he shook Smith's shoulder. "That right? You Corporal Smith?"

Smith didn't respond. Instead, his head flopped over to reveal his brain through the open skull. His lifeless eyes stared straight at Nigel.

Chapter Twenty

July 30th, 1885 - Present Day

The train pulled into the Nantucket Ferry Station with a squeal of brakes, jostling the cabin back and forth as it slowed to a stop.

Nigel jerked awake, freeing himself from the vision plaguing him for twenty years. He sat up, disoriented, and covered in sweat. Annabelle, Sarah, and Edgar stared at him from the opposite bench seat.

"You were dreaming of the war again," announced Sarah.

Stunned by her comment, Nigel's jaw dropped. She looked at him with such intensity he needed to turn away. *How could she know?*

Sarah stood. "Come, Edgar. Let's see to the luggage."

She and Edgar departed without another word.

Nigel loosened his tie and put a palm over each eye for several moments. He lowered his hands and looked at Annabelle. "I need a drink."

Annabelle shook her head. "No, you don't. Your dipsomania is a result of not knowing how to handle your visions. Didn't the professor discuss this with you?"

Nigel looked out the window at the bustling station. "He said this group would help me come to terms. He called it a gift. I call it a curse."

Annabelle stood in the cabin doorway and motioned to him with her gloved hand. "Come. We need to transfer to the ferry."

"What am I getting myself into?"

"You hid in a bottle for almost twenty years. Where did that get you?"

They departed the train and entered the station. Once tickets to Nantucket were procured, Nigel went to the restroom. He splashed water on his face and straightened up. The figure in the mirror opposite him looked unfamiliar. He avoided mirrors for a long time and caught only occasional glimpses of the filthy beast he became.

Who am I now? Cleaned up, he didn't look half bad, but a haunted look could be seen in his eyes.

Annabelle met him outside the restroom and the two went out along the dock to the wooden ferry. It seemed to be a huge creature swallowing wagons, carriages, and people whole. Well ahead of them were Sarah and Edgar, following a pair of roustabouts who hauled a flatbed hand truck with their luggage and crates onto the ferry.

No sooner were they seated than the ferry departed. Annabelle and Nigel again sat on opposite bench seats, this time alongside a large porthole. Through the circular window, the moon reflected on the choppy water as they sped along. The steam engine below caused a low hum and caused the passenger deck to vibrate.

Sarah and Edgar perambulated the interior. They each gave a little bow to Annabelle as they passed. After which, they moved down the aisle and out the rear door onto the outer deck.

Annabelle rummaged in her purse and counted out a number of bills. She handed them to Nigel. "As promised."

"Thank you." He took the money, folded it, and put it into his coat pocket. Nigel stretched and leaned back in his seat. "The professor explained your organization to me, but what I don't grasp is you. What's your reason for being part of this?"

Instead of answering, she threw the question back at him. "Why do *you* do it?"

"Expose mediums?"

Annabelle nodded.

"I want to find one that isn't a fraud."

"Well, you found her."

Nigel sat up, startled. He scowled. "You?"

Annabelle blushed. "Goodness no. Though I sometimes wish— It's Sarah."

"Sarah?" He sounded dubious.

"Sarah's parents sold her to a carnival as a child. She escaped last year and presented herself to the professor during one of his classes. She has talents the rest of us don't possess. In fact, we undertook the trip to Atlanta when she told us about you."

"Told you what?"

"That you're a gifted but tortured soul."

Nigel dismissed her comment with a snort, but his mind reeled with the possibility of Sarah's authenticity. She seemed to know what haunted his sleep.

The boat made a sudden sharp jerk, and the sound from the ship's engines changed in character. Momentum pulled Nigel forward in his seat as the ship slowed to a stop.

Annabelle looked worried. “What is it?” she asked. “Did we hit something?”

“Don’t know. Never been on one of these things.”

Sarah dashed in from the outer deck. Breathless. Troubled. “Someone’s drowned,” she announced.

Nigel, Annabelle, and Sarah joined Edgar and the other passengers who crowded the outer deck and promenade.

The naked body of a man floated face-down in the sound.

From the lower deck, several crew members with mean-looking gaffing hooks leaned out. Another crew member held a lantern at the end of a long pole above the corpse. One hook snagged the body and caused it to turn over. The lamplight revealed the grisly condition of the man’s throat, torn open to the spine.

Various sounds of revulsion arose from the crowd. There were numerous comments about sharks.

Nigel took Annabelle by the arm and tried to lead her away. “A lady should not subject herself to such indecencies.”

Annabelle twisted free and turned back to look.

Two other crew members sank hooks into the bloated corpse. As they drew the body toward the boat and began to haul it up along the barnacle-crusted side of the ship, the head detached and splashed back into the water. A woman in the crowd screamed. The head, mouth agape in apparent protest, sank below the surface.

The crowd erupted into shocked comments and opinions.

“My God!” Nigel added to the chorus of voices.

Annabelle turned to Sarah. “Any thoughts?”

Sarah shook her head.

"Edgar?" Annabelle said as she turned to the physicist.

"Sharks?" he echoed the speculation heard from others.

Annabelle turned back to Nigel, who, in a fugue state, stared down the promenade.

A vision of the same headless corpse just hauled from the water, now stood on the walkway, naked. The whitish-gray body swayed slightly and dripped seawater, forming a pool on the deck. Torn tendons, veins, and arteries issued from its neck and resembled gray spaghetti. Fresh tears and stab wounds from the recovery efforts further rent the man's flesh but caused no bleeding. The corpse raised an arm and pointed straight at Nigel.

"Nigel?" Annabelle touched Nigel's shoulder, and the vision disappeared.

Back inside, Nigel spent the remainder of the trip ruminating on the vision. What did it mean? A threat? A warning? Ever since the war, whenever he foresaw things, he'd been unable to stop their occurrence. This and the frequent reprise of the vision he'd had before the Battle of Fort Stedman were what drove him to drink.

He felt the compulsion to anesthetize himself with alcohol more than ever. But now, as the focus of one of his visions, might drink be his undoing? Should he keep his mind clear?

He imagined the disembodied head at the bottom of the sea moving its lips, trying to answer his questions.

Chapter Twenty-One

Nantucket Island

With a blast of its horn, the boat lowered its deck ramp through wisps of fog onto the Nantucket Ferry Landing. Passengers streamed forward and ferrymen directed them to the side to allow horse-drawn wagons and carriages to disembark.

As the passengers neared the terminal building, several people came out to greet them. The headless corpse became an instant topic of conversation. A boy's voice carried above the rest. "—and the man's head came clean off!"

The last to exit the boat, Annabelle, Sarah, Nigel, and Edgar led a pair of brawny ferry workers who pulled a large flatbed cart loaded with the group's belongings. They stopped at the terminal building, which now stood deserted.

Edgar removed two silver dollars from his vest pocket and handed one to each of the ferry workers. "Thank you for your pains, gentlemen."

The men looked at the coins with surprise.

"Who knew pickin' cotton paid so well?" quipped one with an Irish brogue. The two workers laughed and headed back to the ferry.

Nigel saw Edgar's hands ball into fists and noticed him fight to control himself. Sarah came up and touched the black man's shoulder, but Edgar shook it free.

Nigel turned to Annabelle. "Seems some of your Yankee brethren are boorish too."

A slender mousy woman appeared around the side of the terminal and approached them through the thickening fog. She walked with quick steps and turned her head furtively one way then the other. She held her handbag clutched to her bosom like a shield. The woman wore a long coat, a wide-brimmed hat, and a pair of dark glasses masked her eyes. She spoke in a tentative voice. "Are you the folks I was given to believe would be arriving from Boston? Associates of Professor James?"

A sudden gust of wind buffeted the group and knocked the timid woman's hat from her head. The hat tumbled across the dock. Nigel sprinted after and snagged it.

"Perhaps we should speak inside," suggested Annabelle.

The group moved into the empty waiting room and composed themselves, smoothing hair and clothing. The room's light revealed the mousy woman's abnormally pale skin and pure white hair, drawn back in a severe bun.

Nigel entered the room and returned the rescued hat with a bow. "Nigel Pickford, at your service."

"Lenore Hutchinson."

The lady presented her hand, and the touch lasted for several moments longer than Nigel expected. He looked at the woman's face. Below her dark glasses, a smile flickered across the woman's full lips before she disengaged her hand from his.

"Much obliged, Mr. Pickford. You are the perfect Southern gentleman."

Lenore glanced at each member of the group with a nervous smile. "Please forgive my tardiness. I have been hiring a wagon and arranging rooms for us at the Nantucket Inn."

Annabelle stepped forward and shook Lenore's hand. She introduced herself and presented Sarah and Edgar. "I speak for the entire group in saying we would like to proceed to your house directly. The professor said your home could accommodate us all."

"To be quite honest, I was looking forward to a stay in town—a welcome reprieve from what I've been dealing with at home."

Annabelle shook her head. "This is not a holiday. The prospect of an authentic haunting is tremendously exciting. We'd like to get started."

Lenore looked downcast. "Very well," she said.

The group hauled the cart with their belongings around the building to a wagon, whose driver waited in front of the terminal. Lenore renegotiated with the driver who, at the promise of a hefty fee, agreed to drive them across the island to her home. Once they loaded everything, they climbed aboard. Nigel chose to sit on the buckboard next to the driver, and Lenore came up and sat next to him. The others were forced to contend with the backend of the wagon.

They made their way through the tidy city of Nantucket. Despite the lateness of the hour, lamps still shone in many homes.

Lenore seemed to overcome her timidity and spoke to Nigel over the sound of the wagon and clopping hooves. "Most of these homes were once owned by

Quaker whalers or their crew—many of whom were former slaves. Whaling is a dangerous occupation but it provided a good livelihood for those who didn't perish in the process. My father, though not a Quaker, owned a number of whalers at one time. He wanted a house away from town, perhaps because we were Presbyterian and didn't fit in."

"What does your father think of our coming?"

"Father died some time ago. Ironically, many of the Quakers are gone, too. Not that they died—well, some no doubt—only the whaling industry is not what it was. And I am left with a large isolated house.

"Alone?"

"Yes, aside from a part-time cook, and for the unwelcome guests I hope your group will evict."

Nigel scoffed. "You truly believe your home is haunted?"

"I believe my circumstance will speak for itself."

The two lapsed into silence for the remainder of the trip. The wagon proceeded through the outskirts of the city, past rolling pastureland and widely scattered homes making up much of the island. The fog became thicker and soon hid almost everything. At length, Lenore indicated their arrival. The darkness and fog made it difficult for the group to make out the place.

"I'll go in and light some lamps," Lenore said. She thrust some money at the driver and disappeared into the dark structure.

The rest of them, except the driver, unloaded the wagon. The driver sat silent, staring straight ahead into the fog.

"Perhaps one shouldn't be paid until the job is completed," scolded Annabelle.

The driver ignored her. Once Edgar, Nigel, and the ladies unloaded everything, the driver said, "Good luck to ya. Ya'll need it." He spat and gave the reins a shake. The wagon disappeared into the darkness and mist in mere seconds.

The ladies carried the smaller pieces of luggage inside while Edgar and Nigel carried a large wooden crate into the house and set it in the marble foyer. The larger crate was left outside, but Edgar and Nigel moved it under the eaves of the porch, in case of rain.

Edgar followed him in and shut the door. "A device I expect will prove useful."

Lenore cleared her throat. "The cook is gone till morning. I'll see what I can manage in the kitchen." She took one of the kerosene lamps from a table, went off down a long hallway, turned, and disappeared from sight.

Nigel noticed the black and white marble on the floor formed a huge compass rose. Vases, lamps, and small items of statuary sat on accent tables around the room. Across from the group, a large staircase ascended to the next floor. An unlit chandelier hung from the ceiling. Nigel gave a small whistle. "It appears our hostess does not lack for means."

"We'll see none of it," said Edgar. "We don't charge for our services."

Nigel looked incredulous. "What kind of fools are you?"

"The kind eschewing the lies and thievery of so many purported mediums," interjected Annabelle. "The professor insists we take no money. In the past, the Society for Psychical Research paid us a stipend and covered our expenses, but lately, the professor has been doing so out of his own pocket."

"We have exposed a lot of frauds who would sooner pay to have us killed," Sarah said.

"Great. Can't wait to join." Nigel responded, his voice thick with sarcasm.

Lenore opened a mahogany door on one side of the foyer and ushered them into a dark-paneled rectangular dining room. "I've located some food and drink. I hope they will suffice."

A short while later, the remnants of a light meal were scattered about on one end of the long table where they sat. In front of everyone but Nigel stood a crystal glass of red wine. Before Nigel sat an untouched glass of water.

When Edgar sat back to wipe his mouth with a napkin, Nigel shot out a hand and grabbed Edgar's glass. He downed the contents in one gulp. Edgar slammed a fist down on the table, but Sarah put her hand over his and shook her head. Seeing he could get away with it, Nigel reached for the bottle in front of Annabelle, but she snatched it away. She and Nigel glowered at each other for a moment, until he dismissed the situation with a grunt.

Nigel turned to Lenore. "This may seem intemperate, but why do you wear dark spectacles at this hour?"

Lenore put a tentative hand to her face. She paused, took a deep breath, and removed her smoked glasses to reveal eyes bright red with albinism. She replaced the spectacles and stood.

"I hope you will forgive my awkward attempt at vanity."

Lenore began to move away, but Nigel took hold

of her arm and stood.

"Forgive me," he said. "Please sit."

Lenore regarded him for several moments through her dark glasses. She acquiesced and retook her chair. Nigel also sat.

An awkward silence hung over the table before Annabelle changed the topic.

"Sarah feels the gust of wind on the dock could have been a sign, as though something were trying to drive us away. Mr. Pickford, did you sense anything?"

"No."

"Huh." Annabelle shook her head. "Why am I not surprised?"

Nigel felt blood rush to his cheeks.

Annabelle continued. "I propose we conduct a séance before we turn in. Perhaps we can make contact right away."

Edgar turned to Lenore. "Have you a pry-bar or a hammer?"

"For a séance?" she asked with surprise.

"The crate in your entryway contains a camera and other equipment we need to capture any sightings."

"I'll see what I can find. Then you'll need to excuse me. A séance goes against my faith. I will allow it in this home if you feel it is necessary, but you cannot expect me to participate."

Nigel followed Edgar out to the foyer and watched as the black man moved the baggage away from the crate. Lenore arrived with an iron crowbar and handed it to Edgar.

"Thank you," he said. "This will do nicely."

Edgar went to work on the pine box whose nailed boards separated with what sounded like agonizing moans. Many of the boards splintered into long wooden shards, despite his evident attempt to maintain the boards' integrity for the return trip. "I'll need to find replacements for the broken wood," he stated as he worked, but Nigel said nothing.

Inside the crate lay packing straw, and Edgar removed great fistfuls of the stuff and dropped it onto the marble floor. Ultimately he exposed a camera, tripod, and boxes of other materials.

He carried the equipment into the dining room, as Nigel looked on. The others cleared the table of everything but a solitary lamp. As promised, Lenore left the room.

Edgar set up the tripod and attached the camera, a black lacquered box about a foot square with a glass lens on one side. There existed a glass viewfinder on the side opposite the lens which Edgar used to position the camera, then draped it with black fabric.

"It's the new Eastman Interchangeable View," he said with evident pride. "It uses the new flexible film George Eastman has developed." He attached the roll holder for the film and advanced the celluloid. Then he snaked a long hose with a black rubber bulb on the end across the tabletop to where he would be seated. Edgar returned to the camera and poured flash powder into the long narrow pan above the lacquered box. As he retook his seat, he smiled again and said, "I've made a few modifications, allowing me to both ignite the flash powder and open the shutter from a distance. I hope to catch the first legitimate photo of a spirit."

Sarah moved to the head of the table and the group sat down. Annabelle dimmed the kerosene lamp. Shadows moved in and obscured the room.

Annabelle, Sarah, and Edgar put their palms down on the tabletop. Nigel took the cue and did the same. He looked around expectantly and waited.

After some time, Sarah's breaths became long and deep. Her breathing turned ragged, as she seemed to fight for air. She suddenly gasped and lurched back in her chair with her eyes wide. Then her eyes closed as the color drained from her face. She began to gag.

From her mouth issued a pulsing mass of translucent red slime. As the ectoplasm poured from her mouth, it rose up along one side of Sarah's face and began to float above the table.

Edgar snatched the camera bulb and squeezed. At the flash of the powder, the slime immediately darted back down Sarah's gullet and disappeared.

"No more photographs!" Annabelle hissed.

Edgar looked at her in disbelief. "But—"

Annabelle shot him an icy stare, visible through the gloom. After a moment, Edgar gave in and set the camera bulb aside.

Sarah's trance continued, and her ragged breathing resumed. She began to moan and sob.

"Who are you?" asked Annabelle. "With whom do I speak?"

Sarah's moans ceased, but pain could be heard in the chorus of voices that came from her mouth—male, female, children, and adults—speaking as one. "We are many," they said.

"Why do you haunt this house?" asked Annabelle.

Sarah moaned again in pain, took a raspy breath, and stood. Her eyelids opened to reveal glassy orbs. Many voices shouted. "Leave! Get out!"

Annabelle stood to challenge them. "We will not

leave until we understand why you are here and help you to—"

Sarah turned away and began to walk from the room. Edgar and Nigel looked at Annabelle for guidance, and she motioned to follow. The three trailed Sarah through the dining room, the foyer, and out the front door into the misty darkness.

A strong breeze came up again and whipped bands of fog around them in the weak light from the open door. Nigel could hear the sound of pounding surf from somewhere off in the distance.

They followed Sarah across the drive, over an ill-kept lawn, and around to the rear of the house. Faint illumination shone from the kitchen windows, but it sufficed for Nigel to see Sarah stop, stretch out an arm and point.

He shook his head in frustration. "There's nothing to see in this darkness."

Annabelle turned to Sarah. "What do you want to show us?"

Sarah emphatically pointed but did not speak.

Annabelle looked off in the direction Sarah pointed. Only fog and inky darkness lay ahead. "You want us to go in that direction?"

"That must be it," said Edgar.

Annabelle took Edgar's arm and edged forward. Nigel joined them, their steps awkward on the bent tufts of grass forming lumpy mounds beneath their feet. That and the mist caused everything to become slick. The sound of crashing surf grew louder.

"Stop!" shouted Lenore, who suddenly appeared before them.

"What? Why?" asked Annabelle.

Lenore lifted a shutter on the blackout lantern she carried. A few feet beyond where they stood the ground dropped away in a precipice.

"My God," said Edgar, "she nearly sent us off a cliff."

"What are you doing here?" asked Nigel.

"I needed some air and wanted to get away from your sacrilege. I thought you folks were scientists."

"Why would Sarah have sent us to our deaths?" Annabelle asked.

"I don't know, I'm sure," said Lenore. "Perhaps the Devil had a hand in it."

"Let's ask her," said Nigel.

They turned and in the lantern light saw Sarah collapsed onto the ground, unconscious.

Chapter Twenty-Two

Nigel insisted he, rather than Edgar, carry Sarah to her bedroom. Now the two men waited in silence in the upstairs hall. Annabelle and Lenore saw to Sarah's needs behind the closed door. Ten minutes passed. Then twenty. Finally, Annabelle and Lenore emerged from the room.

"Is she all right?" Edgar asked.

Annabelle smiled with reassurance. "Yes." She turned to Nigel. "Thank you for carrying her upstairs. She seems to be sleeping peacefully."

Nigel smirked. "I shouldn't wonder. Nearly killing us would tire anyone out."

Annabelle rolled her eyes and turned away.

Lenore smiled nervously. "Perhaps we should all get some rest."

Edgar yawned. "I'm for that. I'm done in."

Annabelle crossed to her room and opened the door. She turned back. "An auspicious start, in any case. It appears the home is truly haunted."

Lenore's dark glasses turned from one of them to the other. She smoothed back her hair and ran her hands down the front of her dress to smooth the wrinkles. Nigel cocked his head and stared at her, trying to get the measure of the woman. *Is this modesty? Preening?*

"I hope none of you are troubled further this evening," Lenore said. "Thank you again for being here." She gave another nervous smile and turned toward her room.

Nigel pushed himself off where he had been leaning against the wall. "Wouldn't miss this for the world," he muttered.

****

A short while later, now in her white cotton gown and gingham robe, Annabelle finished unpacking. She removed her tortoiseshell hairbrush and comb from her carpetbag, set them on a bureau, then unpinned her hair and let it fall to her shoulders.

Annabelle took up the brush and ran it through her tresses, as she regarded herself in the oval mirror above the bureau. Had the professor ever noticed her luxuriant brunette hair?

I'm twenty-eight—an old maid, she thought, suddenly despondent. She remembered reading that in Japan, she would be called a Christmas cake because no one wanted Christmas things after the twenty-fifth. She could be married with children by now, like most of the girls she grew up with. She then dismissed these thoughts. *I have my own road to follow.* Where it led, she didn't know, but she did not aspire to domesticity.

In the meantime, her road led to this strange Nantucket house, and the prospect of unlocking its secrets excited her.

Annabelle stopped fussing with her hair and set the brush down next to the comb. She gave herself a little smile and turned away from the reflection. She returned to her bag and removed a final item—the folding golden-colored frame contained the picture of her father on one side and her mother on the other. The same one that prompted Sarah's visions. Her parents gave her this gift when she left for college. Annabelle crossed the room, opened the picture frame, and set it on the bedside table next to the lamp.

No sooner did she place it down than Annabelle retrieved it. She sat on the bedside and regarded the portraits. Her gaze focused on her deceased mother, and she slowly stroked the image with her right thumb as tears formed in the corners of her eyes.

"Annabelle?"

Her mother's voice. She could never forget.

"Annabelle?"

Annabelle put the picture frame on the bed and blinked her eyes clear. An odd tingling ran through both arms as goosebumps rose beneath the robe and nightshirt. She stood and shot her gaze around the room. Her shaky voice answered. "M-Mother?"

"Get out!"

Annabelle's door flew open and smashed against the bedroom wall.

No one stood in the doorway.

Chapter Twenty-Three

Nigel stood next to a large bookshelf in the library when he saw Annabelle enter the room. In addition to the shelves of leather-clad volumes, the room featured a red velvet settee and several similarly upholstered English Regency styled club chairs—the kind of high back affairs where elderly and middle-aged men dozed in English gentlemen clubs. The chairs sat on either side of an unlit fireplace. In one corner stood a huge globe, about three feet in diameter, on a walnut-colored stand. Around the room, small circular tables with marble tops held ornate lamps. Nigel lit a lamp with an amber-colored globe, and it bathed the room in a sickly yellow light.

Annabelle, dressed in her gingham robe, padded into the room in bare feet. Her dark hair hung free and her face looked flushed. Seeing him, her eyebrows knit together. *Had she been crying?*

"Can't sleep?" he asked.

Annabelle shook her head. "No."

"Nor I. But with me it's a matter of choice."

Nigel picked a book off the shelf and blew a cloud of dust from its top end. "Despite appearances, seems our hostess is not much of a reader."

"And you?"

"Used to be. Was quite the bookworm before the war. Was a lot of things."

"What happened? Sarah has been uncharacteristically vague."

"Moby Dick," Nigel read aloud and looked up at Annabelle. "A man haunted by a whale. Seems appropriate." He tucked the book under his arm and moved to go.

Annabelle reached out and touched his shoulder.

Nigel stopped. He glanced at her hand and then into her eyes. He grinned. "This a capable hand you're offering me, Annie? Does it come with the rest?"

Annabelle snatched her hand away. "I was going to tell you about what just happened, but I think not. Frankly, I can't understand what Sarah sees in you."

"I know why I'm here. It beats sleeping under a bridge. Why are *you* here? You lookin' for your mamma? I could hear you calling for her when I was on the stairs."

Annabelle's face reddened. "I thought I heard—" She stopped mid-sentence. "Y-you couldn't understand," she stammered. "We are scientists. Some of the best minds of our time support our work—clergymen, scientists, politicians, painters, writers…even Samuel Clemens."

"I don't think any of them will find their momma here. Every so-called spiritualist I have met has been a fraud."

"How do you explain tonight's séance?"

"I can't. Not yet anyway. Perhaps I'll take my time and enjoy clean sheets for a while. You know, I could use a little help taking the chill off them sheets."

Annabelle recoiled. "You disgust me."

"That makes two of us."

Upstairs, Nigel tossed the book onto the bed. He

took off his jacket and vest and threw them carelessly over the back of a Morris chair. *Why did I insult her? You only succeeded in pushing her further away.*

But it's what you wanted, isn't it?

Nigel liked Annabelle, in spite of the friction between them. Because of her, the entire group, and the vision on the ship, he'd decided to try to pass the night without going in search of alcohol—a battle he needed to fight alone—or with only Herman Melville for company.

Sober, he thought he might confide in Sarah tomorrow. If a bona fide medium, perhaps she could help him find a way to break his curse. He'd never confided in anyone before. Never trusted anyone to understand…

An hour later, despite his resolve, Nigel slept fitfully on top of his bed, his face covered in sweat. *Moby Dick* lay on the edge of the mattress, where it fell after sliding from his fingers when he succumbed to sleep.

Now he lay in the throes of another vision, one that came on him recently and occurred almost as often as the one showing his men slaughtered in the war. This new vision showed him rescuing Sarah from drowning in a blood-red sea and from a hoard of hands that tried to pull her under.

He hoisted Sarah aboard, smiled, and introduced himself.

But as soon as she sat in his small vessel, the planks on the bottom of the boat began to separate and the bloody sea seeped in.

Nigel splashed the blood from the boat as best he could, but Sarah just sat there with a stunned look on her face.

"Bail, damn you!" he shouted.

The bloody hands started grabbing the edge of the boat on all sides. Nigel stomped on them and pried others free, but more kept coming, weighing the boat down and causing the blood to seep in from the bottom even faster. He looked at Sarah and screamed, "I can't swim!"

Nigel jolted awake, his hair plastered to his forehead with sweat and his shirt soaked. He sat up and glanced around in a panic. The book fell from the bed and hit the floor. After a few moments, he realized where he was. Nigel lay back, looked up at the red paisley-patterned ceiling, and tried to calm himself.

He emulated the pattern of breathing he'd seem Sarah use earlier. A slow deep breath through his nose, holding it, then exhaling from his mouth. As he did so, he looked up at the design above and tried to think of nothing else. After several minutes of this, he felt better.

Then, as he stared above him, the paisley pattern on the ceiling transmogrified into a mass of intertwined naked bodies, male and female. The figures began to writhe. Faint moans and grunts of pleasure grew louder. Above the sounds of rutting came a woman's ear-piercing scream of terror.

Nigel grimaced but continued to stare upward, transfixed. Something dark dripped from the ceiling onto his forehead. Nigel wiped it away as another drop hit his cheek. Another. He stared at the fingers of his right hand and saw blood.

Nigel cried out in surprise and pushed off the bed. He struggled toward the door and swiped at his face and shirt as more drops fell.

Someone or something pounded at the door. Louder. Louder still.

Should he find another exit? The window? He decided to risk the door, ran to it, and fumbled with the key in the lock. He finally managed to turn it and threw the door wide. He staggered out and ran into Annabelle and Edgar.

At the sight of him covered in blood, Annabelle screamed.

Lenore emerged from her room at the end of the hall, tying the waist cord to a white robe as she ran. No glasses obscured her blood-red eyes and her long white hair hung free.

"You're hurt!" Lenore cried as she ran to him.

Stunned, Nigel regarded his blood-spattered clothes and slowly shook his head. "No."

He turned around to look back into his room. The bedclothes were in disarray, but no blood lay on the bed or elsewhere in the room.

"We heard you screaming," said Annabelle.

"Ectoplasmic manifestation," said Edgar as he stared at him in fascination. "We need a sample." Edgar tried to wipe Nigel's face with a handkerchief, but Nigel grabbed Edgar's arm.

"Keep your god-damned hands off me!"

Chapter Twenty-Four

A knock came at the Mahogany's front door while Clarence and Maude ate breakfast. Clarence got up to answer and discovered a stocky policeman with a handlebar mustache on their doorstep. Clarence recognized him as one of the officers the town recently hired from Boston.

"Top of the mornin'," said the policeman in a thick Boston accent. "Sergeant Sean O'Connell. Have you seen the Reverend Davis hereabouts?"

Clarence shook his head. "The reverend is more apt to put in an appearance around supper time."

The policeman looked past Clarence and gave a little nod to Maude, who stared at him from where she sat at the table. The sergeant returned his gaze to Clarence. "I'm visitin' people on Reverend Davis's regular circuit. It seems he has disappeared. His horse showed up yesterday evenin' near Tom Nevers' pond at the Unitarian picnic—in distress and still saddled, but with no sign of the reverend. The man has not turned up this mornin'."

"He enjoyed dinner here night before last," said Clarence, "and yesterday he was supposed to check-in on my daughter. She has a new job as a cook at the Hutchinson place."

The officer removed a small notebook and pencil from his breast pocket. He consulted his notes. "I know he stopped at Chester and Patrice Brown's farm for a late lunch. There seems to be some bad blood between the husband and the reverend, which makes him a suspect. Did the reverend show up at the Hutchinson house?"

Clarence waved his daughter over and faced her to explain the policeman's inquiry. He asked if the reverend checked on her, as promised. Maude shook her head no.

The policeman furrowed his brow as he eyed the girl. He looked at her father. "She's not much for makin' long speeches, in a manner of speakin'. She hidin' somethin'?"

Clarence shook his head in disbelief. "My daughter's deafness hasn't affected her eyesight. She can spot a fool at one hundred yards."

The officer started at this, but instead of taking umbrage said, "Well, I suppose I should poke around the Hutchinson house next. I'm new hereabouts. Can you direct me? The fog makes it doubly difficult."

"My daughter will be leaving for the place shortly. If you wait, you can follow her."

"That would be fine. I'll wait out here with my horse—wouldn't want it to take off for Tom Never's pond."

****

When they arrived at the Hutchinson place, Maude drove around to the rear, but the police officer steered his horse toward the front.

The sergeant dismounted and approached the house, but his horse balked. All four hooves planted themselves on the drive and it refused to be led nearer. O'Connell yanked on the reigns and swore. It became a test of wills, neither willing to give up. In the end, O'Connell lost and, tied the horse to a bush across the road from the house.

Sergeant O'Connell strode over the dirt and gravel drive, marched across the porch and gave the door a sharp series of knocks. A few moments later a pretty dark-haired woman opened the door.

"Are you the lady of the house?" he asked. He removed his helmet and smoothed back his oiled hair, both out of courtesy and to make a favorable impression on the woman.

"No, Sergeant, I'm a house guest."

"M-may I help you, Officer?" called a pale woman in smoked glasses, who appeared dressed to go out, with a long coat and hat. The woman descended the steps to the foyer. "Thank you, Miss Douglas." The dark-haired woman stepped back, and the pale woman came to the doorway. She offered her gloved hand, and he shook it. "Miss Lenore Hutchinson," she said.

Officer O'Connell introduced himself. "I'm here looking for a colored preacher by the name of Davis. I understand he planned to stop by yesterday."

"If so, I-I didn't see him," said Lenore, her timidity conveying sincerity. "Moreover, I don't know this reverend, and I'm not sure why he would be here, except perhaps to see Maude, my cook—a deaf colored girl I have recently employed. I spent most of yesterday out, arranging for the arrival of my house guests. Perhaps you should ask Maude. I believe she is here."

"No need. I came with her. Well, if that's all you can offer, I'll take my leave." Sergeant O'Connell replaced the helmet on his head and tipped the brim a little as a goodbye to the ladies.

"Sorry I can't be of more help, Officer," Lenore said as she eased the door shut.

****

Lenore turned to Annabelle after shutting the door. "With Maude here, I expect she'll have breakfast prepared shortly. Are the others waiting to eat?"

Annabelle shook her head. "No, I am the first one up. In fact, I didn't sleep much last night."

Lenore gave her a thin smile. "Perhaps once the house is rid of spirits we shall all rest in peace."

****

Nigel pushed away from the table, leaned back in his chair and belched. He saw Edgar snigger, but Annabelle didn't look amused.

"Good God," she muttered and shifted around in her chair so she no longer faced him.

"Not the best repast," said Nigel, "but filling."

Maude came out of the kitchen and began to clear away breakfast—now-cold scrambled eggs, fried ham, muffins, gooseberry jam, coffee, and apple cider. Nigel grabbed her sleeve to stop her. "Please leave it. Not everyone has eaten!" he shouted.

Annabelle turned her head to him and said, "I suspect the deaf, like foreigners, don't understand you no matter how loud you yell."

Embarrassed, Nigel let go of the woman's sleeve. Maude gave them an anxious smile and continued to clear the table.

"It seems our hostess is a radical," said Nigel. "Few folks would hire a crippled colored girl."

"Her generosity is akin to white people sending donations to Africa. It's a salve to one's conscience," Edgar opined before he took a bite of his muffin and jam. As he did so, the red preserves squeezed out and ran down both corners of his mouth. Edgar quickly wiped himself clean with a white napkin, leaving red splotches on the fabric.

"They're no concern of mine," grumbled Nigel.

Edgar glowered and wiped his mouth a second time.

Sarah entered the room and broke the tension, as she so often did. She took a seat. Little remained on the table for her, cups for coffee, a pitcher of apple cider, and a couple of glasses.

Sarah poured some juice as Maude returned with the place setting she just cleared. Sarah touched the servant's hand and shook her head. Maude shrugged and took the plate and silverware away.

"You seem to speak her language," observed Nigel, his voice a little testy. "As we witnessed last night, you can speak in many tongues—even all at once." He decided in the light of day Sarah possessed no more legitimacy than a plug nickel.

Sarah drank her cider and smiled pleasantly at him. "I don't recall much of last night, except our trip here. Did we do a séance? It sometimes provokes amnesia."

Nigel frowned. "Séance or dangerous play-acting. You nearly sent us off a cliff."

Sarah's smile faded, and she shook her head. "It's not possible. One's true self can always intercede. I assure you, I never would have done that."

Nigel's expression turned ugly. "I assure you that you did. The others can attest to it. Perhaps deep down, you're a killer."

"Perhaps you misinterpreted what I, or the spirits, tried to convey," said Sarah.

"It seemed pretty clear."

"That's enough!" said Annabelle. "This house appears to be setting us against ourselves. Perhaps a malevolent force *is* at work."

"Hogwash." Nigel stood up and threw his soiled napkin down on the table. He turned and left the room.

****

In the late afternoon, Lenore met Nigel in the library and he accepted her offer to tour the grounds. There wasn't much to see outside due to the fog and low clouds, which hung like an oppressive shroud over the Hutchinson estate. The visibility extended only about forty feet. Dark indistinguishable shapes stood in the distance until they approached close enough to make them out—a gnarled tree, twisted by a century of wind storms, berry bushes, and poison ivy.

Lenore still wore her protective clothing—the long coat, hat, and gloves—in spite of the lack of sunshine.

"Is it always so foggy here?" Nigel asked.

"I believe it's starting to lift. The stars should be beautiful tonight." Lenore stopped and turned to Nigel. "About last night. I'm so sorry. Now, at least, you can see what I'm up against."

"I wonder if Sarah faked the séance, nearly sending us to our doom."

Lenore drew back, affronted. "Are you saying I am deluded, believing my house to be haunted?"

"No, I—"

"And what about your nightmare and the blood on you last night? You looked as though you'd seen a ghost."

"I don't have a ready explanation. Is it possible someone has rigged your house, in an attempt to drive you mad or drive us away?"

"Don't be ridiculous." Lenore took his arm and gave it a squeeze. "Are you sure you're all right? It sounds like you're grasping at straws. I thought your group studied the supernatural. You seem to have a disdain for it."

"I am not really part of this troop. I was asked to join—God, or at least Sarah, knows why."

"So, you're not afraid of ghosts?"

"Not in the least. Not sure they even exist. In twenty years, I've seen nothing to prove they're more than parlor tricks."

"I think you are trying to convince yourself more than anyone."

Nigel put his free hand over the gloved hand resting on his other arm. They commenced walking.

After a few moments of silence, Lenore continued. "I do find it hard to believe your Miss Bradbury has no memory of nearly sending you all off the cliff. It's lucky I came along."

"Do you often go about in the dark?"

"With my affliction, it's the only time I can move about freely."

"It must be difficult."

"One must play the cards one is dealt."

Nigel stopped and did a double-take. He stared at Lenore with surprise.

"What's wrong?" asked Lenore.

"Professor James used those very words to convince me to join this endeavor."

"That's because they're true. Perhaps you should take those words to heart. Are you glad you came?"

"I'm grateful it gave us the opportunity to meet."

Lenore's pale face became a vivid red as she blushed. Nigel patted her gloved hand on his arm once again, and they strolled on.

When the two came to a small family cemetery, Lenore reached down and pulled some weeds away from a weathered tombstone, a joint marker for Samuel E. and Deborah T. Hutchinson.

"Mother died giving birth to me. Father from influenza when I was twenty-three."

"And there?" Nigel indicated a mound of turned earth lacking a tombstone.

"My beloved dog, Willie. I've yet to receive the headstone. Once he died, the haunting became much more intense." Lenore's voice cracked and a tear worked its way past her glasses and ran down her cheek.

Instinctively, Nigel reached out and hugged her. Lenore hugged him back and put her head on his chest. This knocked Lenore's hat back, so it hung from her neck by a wide ribbon.

After a few moments, she looked up with a fragile smile and said, "I guess what I need is a new protector."

Nigel and Lenore entered the house sometime later, arm in arm.

Annabelle, standing in the foyer, saw them come in. She averted her eyes. In response, Nigel and Lenore looked at each other and smiled. Lenore went up the staircase to her room.

Nigel hung back near the door and whistled a little tune to affect nonchalance. Annabelle crossed the foyer to confront him. She needed to step around the open crate, crowbar, packing straw, and all the splintered and broken wood laying on the marble floor.

"What have you been up to?" Annabelle nearly spat the words, though she kept her voice low.

"What business is it of yours?"

"We are here to investigate and help end this haunting. She is a client. Don't make this anything more. Honestly, I don't like her. She's peculiar."

"She can't help being albino. She's all alone and under tremendous stress. Perhaps you're jealous?"

Annabelle snorted derisively, turned away, and motioned for Nigel to follow. "We need you for another séance."

"So we can be led off a cliff like lemmings? No thanks."

"Sarah convinced us to pick you out of the gutter and dress you up like the dandy you've become. She sees something in you, frankly, I don't. Perhaps you can honor her faith in you, if nothing else."

Nigel grimaced, started to shake his head but raised his hands in surrender. "'Lay on, Macduff,' or is it Lady Macbeth?"

****

As before, the group clustered around the end of the long dining room table. With all the shades drawn, the room looked gloomy. A kerosene lamp, turned low, sat between them. They placed their palms on the table. As they did so, Nigel rolled his eyes. Annabelle shot him an icy stare. "Mr. Pickford, without your cooperation, you are worthless to us."

"I believe your whole enterprise is worthless. These things are always a product of smoke and mirrors. Someone may have rigged this house with devices to suggest a haunting, someone who wishes Miss Hutchinson ill—"

"Hush!" said Annabelle as she stared at Sarah.

Sarah became agitated, her breathing fast and shallow. Her cheeks flushed, face sweaty. She bent forward, craning her neck, and her eyes went wide. Her mouth worked as though trying to say something. She lurched back in her chair with so much force, it nearly toppled over.

Then her eyes closed, and she relaxed. A moment later, she opened her eyes and licked her lips lasciviously.

"With whom am I speaking?" asked Annabelle.

Sarah looked at Annabelle, smiled and raised her arms in a long languorous stretch. "You should know, you hired me." She rose from her chair and sauntered behind Edgar, who remained seated, as did the others. Sarah ran her hands over Edgar's short-cropped nappy hair and smiled at the rest of them. "I didn't realize you were serving dark meat at this party."

"Who are you?" Annabelle persisted.

Sarah leaned over and rubbed Edgar's chest. She worked her hands lower. In a husky voice, she whispered in Edgar's ear, "You can call me Ruby."

Edgar grabbed her hands to stop her before she reached his crotch. "Enough!" he said.

Sarah laughed. "I'm surprised to hear that coming from you." She smiled, and her voice changed. "I save you. I save you," she moaned in a perfect imitation of Eusapia. Abruptly, Sarah straightened and began to look around in alarm. "Wait! Where am I? What's happening? Oh, my God! No! *No!*" She screamed and thrashed about. In doing so she struck the back of Edgar's head.

"Ouch!" Edgar yelled and followed it with a curse.

Sarah screamed and fell to the floor. Her body shook with spasms and foam bubbled from her mouth in an apparent epileptic fit.

"Stick something in her mouth!" directed Annabelle.

"No!" Edgar shouted. "It can do more harm than good. Let her be."

"To hell with that." Nigel pulled out a clean handkerchief and twisted it into a cord. He put it between her teeth. Sarah clamped down on the twisted material and continued to jerk in spasms. A stream of urine ran from beneath her and across the wooden floor.

After what seemed an eternity the seizure stopped.

Nigel scooped up Sarah, unmindful of her soiled clothes. Edgar ran ahead and opened her bedroom door. Annabelle spread a towel on top of the comforter and Nigel lay Sarah on the bed. Sarah became conscious and started thrashing about and babbling incoherently. Nigel and Edgar tried their best to calm her, without success. Annabelle left for a few minutes and returned with a washcloth, a towel, soap and a basin of water. She also carried the small brown bottle of ether.

Annabelle uncorked the bottle and placed some drops onto a washcloth. She held the cloth over Sarah's nose and mouth. A short while later, Sarah went limp and she became unconscious.

The men exited to allow Annabelle to wash Sarah and change her clothes. They found Lenore pacing in the hallway.

"What happened?" Lenore asked, her brow creased with worry.

They filled her in, and after a while, Annabelle emerged from the room and shut the door.

"How is she?" Lenore asked, wringing her hands.

"The ether I administered will give her a headache," Annabelle confessed, "otherwise, I think she'll be fine by morning."

"I wonder if having you all here is really for the best. I know some Catholics. Perhaps they could help me get a priest..." Lenore's voice trailed off as she looked at Annabelle.

Nigel saw Annabelle's face become a livid red.

"What you're suggesting is a breach of contract," Annabelle said in a quiet but icy voice. "Despite considerable expense and distress, we've come to your aid. At your behest, the group agreed to help you end the haunting as quickly as possible, instead of studying it fully. If Edgar is correct, your home should be free of spirits by this time tomorrow."

Annabelle strode toward her room and opened the door. She turned back to face Lenore. "How about some gratitude!" she said before entering her room and slamming the door behind her.

****

Only Nigel and Edgar came down for dinner, a meal featuring a very rare roast beef that filled its platter with sanguinary juices. The two sat opposite each other and ate in silence. The cook somehow knew there were issues with alcohol. Instead of placing the wine on the table, she left an unopened bottle and a set of glasses on the sideboard. Edgar uncorked the bottle and poured himself a glass. He raised the goblet in a silent toast to Nigel and drank it all in one go. After which, he recorked the bottle and took it into the kitchen. He returned to the table without the wine and continued his meal.

Nigel broke off a piece of bread and sopped up the last of the bloody juices on his plate. He popped it into his mouth and leaned back in his chair. "So how do you propose to do it?"

Edgar wiped his lips and looked up at Nigel. "Do what?"

"Rid the house of ghosts."

"With a dynamo—a machine for generating electricity."

"Nonsense!"

"What do you know?"

"I know there's a wealthy young lady living here all alone and you and your people have cooked up some scheme to bilk her. I know you profess to work for free, but I don't believe it. What? Did you get some confederate to come here earlier to make eerie noises and frighten Miss Hutchinson so she'd hire you? I admit it's a far more sophisticated scheme than I've ever encountered, but you're frauds nonetheless. I plan to tell Miss Hutchinson to be rid of you in the morning."

"Your ignorance knows no bounds."

"That's rich when you and the spinsters travel around and take advantage of folks like Miss Hutchinson."

"So, you think today was a charade?"

"I've seen better."

"Why did you rush to help her when she collapsed? You seemed to take Sarah's wretched condition at face value."

"I have a natural inclination to rush to the aid of women in distress, but upon reflection, I doubt the performance. You're a well-educated lot, bully for you.

You're using your machine, your polish, and your fifty-dollar words to steal from the lady of the house, and I won't have it. You can dress a pig in man's clothing, but it's still a pig."

"*Why do you hate me?*"

"I don't hate you in particular. I hate all darkies."

"Why? What in God's name have we done?"

"I saw men torn to shreds in the war, both sides. The root cause was your people. Had you accepted your lot and not appealed to bleeding hearts in the North, there would have been no Lincoln, no need for secession, and no god-damned war. Yeah, I lay it all upon your people."

"You blame the victim."

"You were once valuable property. After your freedom, you became nothin'."

Edgar stood up from the table and threw down his napkin, just as Nigel did in the morning. "Let me tell you something, Mr. Peckerwood. Yes, I was born a slave, like my daddy before me. God gave my daddy a son who could get ahead, and when I won a scholarship to Howard, he told me to never look back. A year later, there was nothing to look back on. A band of white-robed vigilantes murdered my family—burned our house with them inside. They accused my daddy of being an agitator because he led an effort to buy new books for the Negro school. You're cut from the same bolt of cloth as those white-clad monsters!"

Nigel stood up from the table to challenge him, but Edgar headed out the door.

****

Sarah's room looked similar to Nigel's, except pink, red, and blue floral patterns covered the upper half of the walls, above the wainscoting, and a full-length mirror stood in one corner.

Before Annabelle left, she dressed Sarah in a nightshirt and put her beneath the covers. But as she slept, Sarah pushed the comforter off and now rested on her side, with only a sheet and a thin blanket to cover her.

She stirred when the bedside lamp brightened. Sarah opened her eyes and turned toward the light.

A young girl of about nine stood by the lamp. She stared at Sarah. The girl had a pretty face, blonde hair, and wore a fancy pink and white dress, as though headed to a party. Her appearance, however, was marred by her torn and bloody throat. Flaps of skin revealed muscle tissue and pieces of veins and arteries dangling beneath her chin.

A ghost? Sarah's head still felt clouded with ether, but she told herself to flee. In attempting to do so, she became tangled in the sheet and blanket and fought to escape. She yanked at the bedclothes with one hand and raised the back of the other to her face in horror.

At last, she freed herself and edged off the side of the bed opposite the hideous apparition. Sarah turned to run, but the ghost materialized before her, cutting off her escape.

"Miss?" the girl cried. "My name is Betsy. My throat hurts."

Sarah considered crawling back across the bed, but the girl pleaded with her.

"Miss? *Please help me!*"

Sarah stopped. Though panicked, she tried to employ logic. It seemed an honest appeal for help. *The girl isn't menacing me...* Sarah stared at the apparition for some time. As she did so, her expression softened. Eventually, and without much thought, she opened her arms, and the girl ran the few steps to embrace her. The solidness to the girl surprised her. Now, they both began crying.

"There, there," said Sarah as she stroked the back of the young girl's head. "It's going to be all right."

Chapter Twenty-Five

The nightmare of the previous night visited him again, and Nigel bolted from his room in terror and covered in sweat. His rumpled clothes betrayed him having slept in them.

He looked each way down the hall, illuminated by a small oil lamp on a table near Lenore's door. He saw no one.

Nigel strode back and forth before his doorway, glanced back in at his disheveled bed, and stopped. He shook his head and turned from his room. His experiment with sobriety over, he fetched the oil lamp and used the little flame to help guide his way downstairs to the main floor. The debris from the crate still lay strewn across the foyer. *Strange, one would think she'd have a housekeeper.*

He made his way around the mess and entered the dining room. The kerosene lamp still sat on the table, so he traded the oil lamp for it, using the small lamp to light the larger. He carried the kerosene lamp into the kitchen, spotless except for the dirty dishes from dinner sitting in the sink. Well, the cook is certainly neat, he thought. *Now, where did Edgar stash that bottle?*

He could not find it.

The icebox contained nothing of interest, but the door to the pantry stood open, and Nigel stepped in. The stairway at the back descended into the darkness below and called to him. He realized, if there was one bottle, there might be more in the cellar. Slowly, he navigated the steep stairs, carrying the lamp into the bowels of the house.

The packed dirt betrayed a path across the room to a scraped half-circle pattern where a door met the floor when opened. Nigel crossed the room and entered the next room. He held the lamp high. "Eureka!" he said aloud.

Racks upon racks of dusty wine bottles filled the room.

He chose one at random and attempted to blow off the carpet of dust. When this didn't work, he wiped it with a hand. The dust came away, as did the label, which landed between a pair of bottles and slid down, out of reach. Nigel didn't care. He glanced around for a corkscrew. Without one at hand, he peeled off the lead cap and shoved the cork inside. He raised the bottle to his lips and drank. The wine tasted good. In fact, very good and went down fast.

A short while later, Nigel staggered across the basement, juggling his second bottle of wine and the kerosene lamp. The ascent to the kitchen turned out to be difficult—the stairs seemed to move. He pressed himself against the handrail and used it as a guide. When he reached the foyer, he took a long drink from the bottle before attempting the staircase to the second floor.

With a herculean effort, he reached the second-floor summit. Nigel took a congratulatory swig, wobbled, and nearly fell backward. He caught himself, turned, and saluted the stairs with bottle in hand.

As he weaved along the carpeted hallway, he

glanced down the hall at Lenore's room and dropped the open bottle to the floor. Blood seeped into the hall from under her door.

No! Nigel thought as he stumbled toward Lenore's room.

"Lenore?" he called as he entered through the unlocked door. Deserted. The blood at his feet disappeared.

Lenore's bed looked untouched.

Heavy floor to ceiling curtains were pushed back from a bank of large windows and a pair of French doors stood open to the night. Nigel ran out onto a balcony. Lenore's forecast about the fog proved correct and a gibbous moon shown in the starry sky. Nigel lowered his gaze and could see the beach and roiling surf below the bluff. He could also see the white of Lenore's bathrobe and unbound hair blowing in the wind as she approached the waves.

"Lenore!" he shouted, but his voice was lost in the wind and pounding surf.

Frantic, he descended the stairs to the yard below. Nigel worked his way along the edge of the cliff, the lamp held high. At last he found a route, though a steep one, and he slid half the way on his backside, catching bushes along the way with his free hand to slow his descent. He made it to the base of the cliff and clambered over driftwood to the open beach beyond.

Nigel ran as best as he could in the soft sand, shouting all the while. "Lenore! Lenore!" Finding Lenore's robe, he came to an abrupt stop. He retrieved it from where it lay in the sand. Nigel ran to the edge of the surf and held up the lamp. He called her name until his voice became hoarse.

What possessed her to do such a thing? Was she in a trance? Could a spirit exert such control? Was she somehow driven to suicide? He didn't know.

Nigel shivered. The cold night air and the shock of Lenore's disappearance sobered him considerably. Perhaps she'll return, he told himself. He moved up the beach and built a fire of driftwood, using some of the kerosene as an accelerant. He soon created a raging blaze.

The wind blew spectral shapes of smoke and embers into the night air. Nigel sat on a log as he held Lenore's robe and stared into the fire and at the shapes spawned above it.

Time passed. An hour? Two? He wasn't sure but became increasingly aware of the likelihood of Lenore's death. Nigel brought the robe to his face and filled his lungs with Lenore's scent—lavender. He fell to his knees and started to cry.

"Mr. Pickford, I would thank you to return my robe at once. *Do not turn around!* I'm not decent."

Shock and then relief washed over Nigel like successive tidal waves. After a few stunned moments, he grinned. He lifted the robe with one hand and in the corner of one eye, spotted Lenore's right arm as it extended out of the darkness to grab it.

"Weren't you cold?"

"Not until I emerged from my swim and discovered someone absconded with my robe!" She touched his shoulder and her voice became tender. "You were worried about me."

Nigel stood and turned to face her. In the firelight, he could see Lenore's bare shapely legs and arms extending from the robe. *Might she be naked beneath?*

She wore no glasses and strands of her white hair flew around her head in the breeze. “What about sharks?” he asked.

Lenore shook her head no and smiled.

Nigel took Lenore’s arms and pulled her to him. “You should be worried.”

They kissed with intense passion. Nigel felt Lenore’s tongue snake into his mouth. A shiver of pleasure ran through his body, and his crotch swelled. He held Lenore still tighter.

Bravado aside, Nigel had not been with a woman in many years. He’d been a drunk, living in filth, longer than he could remember, with only brief periods of sobriety. Despite what he consumed tonight, he now felt free of it—filled with a new type of intoxication, her.

Locked in an embrace, the two sank to the sand.

Chapter Twenty-Six

After their lovemaking on the beach, Lenore showed Nigel an easier trail up the cliff. She led him back to her room where they brushed the sand from each other's hair and clothing. As she wiped the last of the sand from a spot near his eye, Lenore let her hand remain on his cheek and smiled. She guided his lips to hers and kissed him lightly. Nigel responded with renewed passion, and they began another round of lovemaking. Eventually, Nigel fell asleep on her bed. Lenore smiled and turned to stare up at the ceiling.

Her mind drifted back in time to when her father, whose room this used to be, informed her she needed to live with her invalid aunt. It changed everything…

****

Lenore's father finished his breakfast as he sat at the dining room table reading a book. A former whaling captain, he stood six-foot-one and remained strong, despite his fifty-five years and his growing midsection. He had a distinguished salt and pepper beard, the same color as his hair.

Lenore cleared the table of breakfast items. It fell on her to prepare the meals on the weekends when their cook went home to her own family. Lenore returned from the kitchen and picked up the small pitcher of cream. She leaned across the table to see the title of her father's book, *The Life and Morals of Jesus of Nazareth* by Thomas Jefferson.

"Have you found religion, Father?"

Her father looked up from the book. "Never lost it. I believe in common sense. It appears Jesus did too, according to Mr. Jefferson. Speaking of good sense, it seems I should fend for myself on weekends or get the cook to prepare food in advance."

"I don't mind being a domestic for a few days each week."

"I'm afraid you are needed seven days a week with your Aunt Eustace—to play Florence Nightingale."

Lenore reeled around to face him, then collapsed onto a chair in shock. "I-I don't understand," she stammered.

Her father closed his book. "You're needed to nurse my sister during her final days."

"Why not keep the hired nurse?"

"Your aunt is short on funds."

Lenore's normally pale cheeks became flushed with anger. She slapped her right palm down on the table. "But you are not!"

"There is no sense squandering good money on some stranger when a loving niece can fit the bill. Besides, you have no responsibilities, aside from me, and I can fend for myself."

"Do I have no voice in this?"

Her father stood up with his book, turned, and began to walk away. "There is no sense in belaboring this. You're twenty-three and are in danger of becoming an old maid. You rarely venture from the house. Nursing your aunt will provide your days with meaning and purpose, to say nothing of it being a gift to a woman who has loved you."

Lenore stood and kept pace with her father on the other side of the table. "If I'm a spinster, it is because you and mother made me so!" Lenore tore off her dark glasses and pulled her white hair free of its pins. "What man would want a woman such as me!" she cried.

Her father put down his book and came around to the other side of the table. He hugged his daughter. "Shhh," he said trying to soothe her. Eventually, Lenore regained her composure. "Any man worth his salt," he said with quiet conviction, "would be lucky to have you. You're isolated in this home. At least when you can get away, you'll be in town." He bent down, kissed the top of her head, and walked from the room, leaving *The Life and Morals of Jesus of Nazareth* behind.

Later that day, her father took her into Nantucket. Lenore sat glumly next to him in the carriage. She wore her typical long coat, gloves, dark glasses, and a large hat she anchored to her hair with several long pins. In addition to the pins, Lenore needed to hold her hat down onto her head for much of the trip, as it kept trying to fly off in the strong breeze. She wished to do the same.

When they reached her aunt's home, her father jumped from the carriage and tied the horse's reins to a green hitching post, the same color as the house. He came around the carriage, helped Lenore down, and retrieved her bags. Aunt Eustace's home looked utterly normal, a bluish-gray saltbox affair on Easton Street with similar structures surrounding it. The road ended one hundred yards west at Brant's Point Park.

Lenore and her father stepped onto the porch and crossed to the front door. Lenore's father set down the bags and knocked. After what seemed an eternity, the door opened. A matron with a round face surrounded by a white cap, and wearing a stained white apron over a simple gray dress, stood in the doorway.

"Good afternoon, Mrs. Blumhouse. I hope you are well." Her father's cordiality sounded forced.

"As well as could be expected under the circumstances." Mrs. Blumhouse's frown made clear her unhappiness about losing her position.

"I understand," said Lenore's father. He picked up the bags and pushed his way past the gatekeeper. Lenore followed him in. The nurse simply grunted.

The strong scent of bleach filled the inside, but it did not cover the smell of sickness. Lenore took out her lavender-scented handkerchief and used it to cover her nose and mouth. It didn't help.

She'd been avoiding accompanying her father here for months, grateful to miss the deterioration of her aunt. Her father acquiesced in this, but for some reason, changed his tune. Was it the book? In any case, she felt as though she were being sentenced to prison.

Bric-a-brac and uncomfortable furniture cluttered the parlor. An elephant-foot table stood in one corner, and in another a stuffed chimpanzee. The animal snarled and looked ready to spring onto whoever strayed too near. There were lit oil and kerosene lights around the room and a fire ablaze in the hearth, despite the heat of the day.

Mrs. Blumhouse shut the door, turned, and regarded Lenore. "Are you up to the task?" she asked.

Her father dropped the bags onto the polished wooden floor behind her, causing Lenore to jump. He came up from behind and braced her, squeezing her arms and lifting her up onto her toes.

"Of course she is."

He set her down, stepped to her side, and gave her a sideways hug.

"Now," her father continued, "if you will kindly orient Lenore to the daily tasks of caring for my sister, I will draw up a check for the balance of your wages, plus a severance allowance I hope will take the sting out of being let go."

Mrs. Blumhouse smiled with tight thin lips. "Very well." She looked again at Lenore. "Young lady, please follow me."

The older woman crossed the room to a door and opened it. The stench from within nearly bowled Lenore over. She gagged.

Mrs. Blumhouse smiled her thin smile again.

Across the dimly-lit room, what remained of Lenore's aunt lay propped up on the bed. The shades were drawn, Lenore figured, to prevent the world from seeing the deteriorating woman within.

Erupting from the top of her aunt's head of thick gray hair were two large tumors, one the size of an orange and the other like an egg. Both were red and scabrous with a few strands of wispy hair on each.

"Your aunt is unable to speak or move any longer, so you'll need to check on her regularly."

Mrs. Blumhouse raised one side of the blankets and peered beneath. "Just as I thought." She dropped the covers and looked at Lenore. "She's wet. Good, I need to show you how to change her bedding."

The older woman crossed the room to a loveseat stacked with linen and other items. She returned with a white nightgown, a white flat sheet and a three-foot by six-foot piece of rubberized canvas.

"It is important to prepare everything beforehand, because when you remove the pillows, Eustace will no longer be able to breathe. You must work quickly, so in a matter of moments, you are able to prop her up again. Understood?"

Mute, Lenore fully realized the demands and responsibilities being forced upon her. She just stood there.

Near the foot of the bed, Mrs. Blumhouse prepared the clean linen.

"Watch very carefully."

First, Mrs. Blumhouse pulled back the covers and removed her aunt's soiled nightgown, cut up the back for easy removal. She dropped the nightgown to the floor.

Lenore's aunt lay naked for a moment, the first time Lenore ever saw a naked person—other than her own reflection in the bedroom mirror. She noticed her aunt's emaciated body and her flat withered breasts. *Will that be me one day? Will I have tumors too?*

The caregiver placed the new nightgown, also slit up the back, onto the old woman, but kept it bunched up over the breasts. Next, Mrs. Blumhouse lifted the soiled rubber canvas protecting the mattress from the wet sheet, tucked-in the clean linen, and rolled up the soiled material. Mrs. Blumhouse moved to the other side of the bed and held up the ailing woman, whose eyes popped open at the embrace. Despite Eustace's illness, Lenore could tell she knew what would soon be coming. The caregiver pulled out the pillows from behind Eustace and stacked them on the side of the bed. She carefully laid Eustace on the mattress.

As Lenore's aunt lay back, she let out a loud pitiful

moan, but the sound choked-off as Eustace lay supine. The woman's eyes bulged, and her face became beet-red as she fought for breath.

Mrs. Blumhouse rolled Eustace onto the clean bedclothes and removed the soiled linen, tossing them to the floor. She quickly stepped to the head of the bed and helped the ill woman sit.

When she rose, Eustace could finally breathe. Her eyes looked filmy with tears.

Mrs. Blumhouse packed the back of the old woman with the pillows so Eustace would remain propped up. When finished with those, the nurse smoothed out the nightgown and brought the top sheet and blankets back up to cover the woman. Finally, she set Eustace's arms on top of the bedspread and patted the old woman's hand.

"You rest a bit, Eustace, then we'll wash you and give you something to eat."

Mrs. Blumhouse bent down and gathered up the wet bedding and nightgown. She thrust them at Lenore. "These will need to be cleaned and hung out to dry. You'll need to keep on top of this, as you will change her several times a day. If she has a bowel movement, wash her off first and put the towel between her and the waste before changing the bedding." She leveled her gaze at Lenore. "You sure you're up to this?"

Lenore stood frozen in place. Mrs. Blumhouse took the soiled linen back. "Get a hold of yourself, or you'll be no help at all."

Once her father and Mrs. Blumhouse left the house, and before caring for her aunt, Lenore took her belongings into the room Mrs. Blumhouse had occupied. Lenore stayed in this room many times before, whenever she came for extended visits, back when her aunt had her health.

Her uncle, a whaling captain, like Lenore's father, died at sea with his whole crew. Prior to her marriage, Eustace taught primary school, and once a widow, she returned to the profession. She taught the younger grades on the island for another nineteen years, until the headaches started. She slowly lost her ability to walk and other bodily functions. Two boil-like eruptions grew from her head, and the losses continued until she could do little more than breathe, swallow, and move her eyes.

Lenore fed her invalid aunt a dinner of bread pieces dipped in warm milk. The meal took the better part of an hour, as her aunt would rarely open her mouth. Lenore discovered that if she flicked her fingers up and down on her aunt's lips the old woman's mouth would open. But sometimes the food just sat in her aunt's mouth until milk ran from her lips in little white rivulets.

At last they finished, but of course when Lenore checked, she discovered wet bedclothes.

Lenore went to the loveseat and retrieved the items Mrs. Blumhouse showed her. She prepared the rolled-up rubber pad with the sheet inside and set up the bed as directed. Lenore changed her aunt's gown and held her in place as she pulled out the pillows. She laid her aunt back. The choked-off moan occurred as before.

As quick as she could, Lenore changed the bedding. She glanced at her aunt. The woman's eyes bulged wide with panic, her face turning blue. Lenore stepped up to the side of the bed and began to help her aunt sit, but in the process, she knocked the pillows off the bed and they tumbled out of reach. Her aunt's eyes bulged further. Lenore sat on the bed and pushed the old woman up into a sitting position. She heard her aunt's desperate gasp of air.

Lenore wrapped her arms around the old woman to keep her from tottering off one side or the other. She tried to keep her own head back, away from the tumors. The two stayed in this position for what seemed like years. Lenore wept freely. "I'm sorry, Auntie. Please forgive me," she wailed.

After a while, Lenore knew she must try again. She let her aunt lie back, and she flinched as the old woman's moan choked-off. It could not be helped. Lenore let go of her and scrambled to retrieve the pillows. She piled them on the bed and helped her aunt to sit again. Lenore at last packed the pillows behind the old woman's back.

After she put the bed in order, Lenore reached out and caressed her aunt's cheek. The old woman didn't respond at first, but in time, the wild glances became less panicked. After an anxious wait, Aunt Eustace closed her eyes, and her breaths became slow and regular.

Lenore left the soiled bedding on the floor and ran through the parlor and out the front door. Crying with self-pity, Lenore gulped for air, much as her aunt did a few minutes earlier. The fresh air, pungent with the scent of the sea, revived her, and she began to calm. As she stood in the middle of the street, she realized she'd forgotten her protective coat, gloves, and hat. Fortunately, it was close to sunset and the danger of getting burned had passed. She could not face going back in her aunt's house just yet.

Lenore moved past the well-manicured yards of her aunt's neighbors. Through the unshaded windows, she could see evening lamps being lit. She kept walking and entered Brant's Point Park.

The park contained a series of trails through sandy soil and tall grass. Overlooking the entrance to the bay, she saw a new park bench, installed since her last visit.

Lenore sat down. In the light of the setting sun, she watched the waves breaking on the rocks just outside the bay and the fishing boats making their way to the calm waters of the harbor. Life went on as usual, despite her calamity. It made her feel small.

As the sun sank below the horizon, the sky filled with florid shades of pink and red. A dark-haired man approached the bench.

"Might I join you to appreciate the last rays of the sun?" The man spoke with a cultured British accent. His clothes were dark and well-cut. He carried a silver-tipped walking stick and wore a long coat but no hat.

Lenore, self-conscious as always about her looks, turned away, but before doing so she noticed the man looked as pale as she. "You-you're welcome to sit," she stammered, "but I'm about to leave."

"Thanks, but please don't rush off on my account." The man regarded the stunning sunset. "Red sky at night—"

"Sailors delight," finished Lenore in a mousy voice.

The man laughed and proclaimed, "We are both aficionados of natural beauty and poetry!"

Lenore laughed, in spite of herself. A few minutes earlier she wondered if she'd ever be able to laugh again.

"Been cooped up in a ship the past few weeks, on my way from Trinidad to Nova Scotia. When we put in here, I needed to get off and stretch my wings."

"I understand. I've been cooped up practically my whole life. Sometimes, I just want to fly away."

"See! Again, we are kindred spirits. Oh, please forgive me," he stuck out his hand, "Roland Varney. Very pleased to make your acquaintance."

"Lenore Hutchinson," she responded and shook his hand. At the touch, Lenore shivered.

"You're cold. Apt to happen once the sun sets. Allow me..." Roland scooted a little closer, removed his coat, and put it over her shoulders.

She shivered even more...

****

Lenore broke free of her reverie, turned onto her side, and began to tickle Nigel's nose. He swiped her hand away and opened his eyes.

"Hello," said Lenore in a low voice, "after your scandalous behavior, don't you think you should head back to your room?"

"I don't care what they think." Nigel scooted closer and nuzzled his head next to hers.

"Well, I do. They say they can end the haunting. I want them to finish what they've started, not run away in a fit of puritanical horror."

"All right," he whined. Nigel turned over and sat on the edge of the bed. "You think they can do what they promise?" He stood and pulled up his pants.

"We shall see."

Nigel buttoned his shirt as he walked across the room. "I think this may be an elaborate confidence game." He swung around to look at her. "Have they asked for any funds?"

She smiled. "You're worried about me again." Lenore ran to him, her face beaming. "I do have a new protector…a gallant knight!"

"Hardly," said Nigel, "It's just that I—"

Lenore hushed him by putting a finger to his lips. "There's always tonight," she said coyly.

Nigel swept her up into his arms and carried her back to the bed. "There's always right now!" he said with a grin.

Lenore laughed. "You're insatiable!"

****

Nigel emerged from Lenore's room an hour later and eased the door shut behind him. He carried his shoes, with the socks stuffed inside, and tiptoed down the hallway. He noticed the spilled bottle of wine and the red stain on the carpet.

Nigel retrieved the half-full bottle and stole back into his room. A little insurance, he told himself, just in case.

Chapter Twenty-Seven

Nigel spooned a silver ladle of strawberry compote over a plate of pancakes. The red sauce ran over his food and nearly off his plate. He wiped the excess from the edge of the white china with his index finger and licked it clean.

"Self-cannibalism, Mr. Pickford?" Annabelle inquired upon entering the room to see Nigel with much of his index finger in his mouth.

Nigel extracted his finger. "Yes, well, you are what you eat," he said with a grin. He drank some coffee. Nigel felt sleepy but happier than he could remember.

"You sleep well?" Annabelle asked as she sat down.

"Never better."

"Seems haunted houses agree with you."

"This one, haunted or not, certainly does."

Sarah came into the room, sat at the table, and poured herself some coffee. She cradled the cup in her hands and stared at it, mute. While Nigel seemed to be on an upward trajectory, Sarah appeared headed in the opposite direction. She looked wan and troubled, her hair uncombed, and dark circles orbited her eyes.

"Good morning, Sarah," said Annabelle. "May I serve you some pancakes?"

Sarah remained mute.

"Sarah?"

Sarah looked up as though hearing Annabelle for the first time. “Yes?”

“What may I serve you?”

“Nothing, thanks,” said Sarah. She took a sip of the coffee, set down the cup, and wiped her lips on her sleeve.

“Sarah!” Shocked, Annabelle grabbed the soiled arm. “What’s wrong? This isn’t like you. You missed dinner last night.”

“And ate nothing for breakfast yesterday, far as I could tell,” added Nigel around a mouthful of pancakes.

“I’m worried about you,” said Annabelle. “Perhaps these séances have made you ill.”

“No. It’s nothing like that.”

“Then what?” pressed Annabelle.

“I’m not sure how we should proceed.”

“Edgar says his device will be operational later today, perhaps before the professor arrives this evening.”

“The professor? I was beginning to think he was afraid of ghosts,” Nigel quipped before putting another forkful of pancakes into his mouth.

“I assure you, he is anything but,” said Annabelle. “He hopes to see Edgar’s device in action, but it will depend on which ferry he catches. Our hostess is adamant—she wants us finished today.”

“But I’m not sure the spirits mean us harm,” said Sarah.

Nigel choked on a mouthful of pancake. Coughing it up, some landed in the center of his plate. He coughed several times further and looked at Sarah, red-faced. “No harm? What do you call the stunt on the cliff? Or was that your idea?”

Sarah appeared frustrated and about to cry. “Perhaps if I talked to Miss Hutchinson—”

Annabelle shook her head. “It’s no use. She put a note under my door sometime last night apologizing for her lack of faith in us, yet reiterating her plan to bring in a priest if we do not resolve things today.”

“But we don’t know what Edgar’s device will do to them!” Sarah cried, slapping her hand on the table. Her coffee sloshed out of her cup and filled the saucer beneath. Sarah shoved her chair from the table and stood. “Where’s Edgar. I want to speak to him.”

Annabelle calmly poured herself more coffee. “He’s already outside assembling his device.”

Sarah made for the door. Annabelle turned to Nigel. “Please go after her.”

Nigel pushed his plate aside. “Fine,” he muttered, “I’ve lost my appetite.”

He caught up to Sarah before she reached the front door and opened it with mock gallantry. Sarah marched out onto the porch and did not bother to acknowledge his gesture. Nigel followed her out.

On the gravel drive, Edgar stood in the sunshine next to another opened crate. As before, large pieces of splintered wood and piles of packing straw lay strewn about. This time the crate contained a cast-iron machine, parts of a bicycle, and a spool of copper wire.

Sarah regarded the contents with a frown.

“So, this is the gizmo you spoke of?” queried Nigel.

“Dynamo,” said Edgar, as he picked pieces of straw from the machine.

“Huh?”

“Dynamo, not gizmo.”

"This whatchamacallit is supposed to kill ghosts?' Nigel asked with disdain.

"No, no."

"Then what good is it?"

Exasperated, Edgar stood up and brushed straw from his clothes. "They're already dead, so it won't kill them, just neutralize them." Edgar took out his handkerchief and used it to bat away flecks of straw from the machine. "All life is energy. Even spirits possess it—in fact, that's all they are. I am going to surround this house with a powerful charge, like a giant electromagnet. The spirits won't be able to resist. Then I'm going to ground them like a lightning rod dissipates a charge into the earth."

"So you're sending 'em straight to Hell?"

"What does Hell have to do with it?" Edgar's voice sounded brittle.

"Don't get all uppity."

Edgar walked off in disgust.

Nigel turned to Sarah. "What did I say?" he asked.

"He helped save your life in Atlanta," she said, distractedly, still staring at the equipment.

"So, I need to show him respect? That'll be a cold day in Hell."

Nigel forgot his reason for being there, turned around, and started to walk back into the house. Before he entered, he heard a loud metallic clang and then another. He looked back to see Sarah slamming the crowbar against Edgar's machine again and again.

Nigel ran up and grabbed her from behind in a bear hug.

****

"Let me go!" screamed Sarah. She kicked her legs

and struggled to get free.

Edgar raced back and snatched the crowbar from Sarah. "What in God's name were you doing?"

"You can't use this thing! They're not bad. We must help them to move on without destroying them!"

Nigel grinned. "Did some handsome gentleman ghost come to call?"

Sarah stomped down hard on Nigel's foot.

"Ow!" he yelled and released her.

Sarah stepped away and turned to confront Nigel. "You're impossible!" She turned to Edgar, who shook his head in dismay.

"What's gotten into you?" Edgar asked. "We can free this place of its curse. Where spirits go after we're done, I don't know, and I don't care."

"You're just as impossible!" shouted Sarah. "Somehow I expected more from you!"

Sarah ran back into the house and began to look around every which way. "Betsy!" she called out just before her feet tangled in the debris in the foyer. Sarah fell and slid across the marble floor. She picked herself up, unhurt. "Betsy!" she called again and hoisted her skirts so she could run up the staircase.

****

Annabelle came into the foyer as Nigel and Edgar entered through the front door. "Where's Sarah? I heard her shouting."

Edgar looked dismayed. "She went berserk and tried to wreck the dynamo. Fortunately, she didn't know what to strike."

Nigel made an unconcerned gesture and grinned. "I think she's taken a shine to a ghostly gentleman."

They could hear Sarah's shouts from the second

floor.

Annabelle shook her head. "She's calling a girl's name, but you're right about her becoming too involved. Come, we must hurry!"

****

Sarah ascended the stairs and ran down the hall. She flung open the doors to all the rooms along the way and continued to call for Betsy, her voice becoming hoarse.

She burst into her own room.

Betsy stood next to the bed, appearing like the night before, in the party dress with the horrendous wound in her neck.

"Betsy, you're in danger! Let me show you to the others—convince them not to destroy you—"

The little girl shook her head. "I'm not in danger. You are."

Sarah stopped moving and scrutinized the apparition with new anxiety. Betsy smiled in reassurance, stepped up to Sarah, and took her hand. "Let me help you."

Betsy led Sarah across the room to the full-length mirror. She halted for a moment, looked up to smile again at Sarah, and then pulled her into the mirror where they both disappeared.

****

Annabelle raced up the staircase, followed by the two men.

They ran from room to room, and when they came to Sarah's, Annabelle ran inside and called her name. No sign of her. Annabelle looked under the bed and began to move around the room, but when she approached the mirror, she put her hand to her mouth and reflexively took a step back. “Oh, my God! *No*!”

Nigel and Edgar sprang to her side as Annabelle reached out to touch the solid surface of the mirror.

On the other side of the glass, through a swirling red fog, Sarah appeared to be desperately screaming for help though no sound emerged. She pounded on the mirror, unable to escape. The rest of the group stared at her, dumbfounded, and Sarah’s panic escalated.

Suddenly, Sarah stopped beating on the glass and froze. She cocked her head, turned, and looked behind her, then drifted off into the mist.

“No!” shouted Annabelle, going to the mirror. “Sarah, don’t go!”

Nigel stepped up and wedged himself between Annabelle and the glass. “Annie, step away. We don’t want to lose you too.”

“Stop!”

“No,” Nigel said, shaking his head, “I’m serious! Step away.”

“Don’t move,” Annabelle commanded with as much authority as she could muster. She took a deep breath and tried to regain her composure. “Look at your right elbow.”

Nigel did so and saw part of his arm disappeared into the mirror. He jerked it free. Blood-red slime covered his elbow, but it otherwise felt fine.

Edgar came up and touched the now-solid surface of the mirror. “Remarkable.”

“Well, Mr. Pickford,” said Annabelle, “it appears you may be of some use after all.”

Nigel stared in shock at the impossibility of the mirror. He suddenly realized what Annabelle implied. “Not on your life.”

"It appears you alone can save Sarah," she said.

"Why not break the mirror?"

"I'm worried it may trap her on the other side."

"He should touch the mirror again," said Edgar. "The other time may have been a fluke."

Nigel turned and poked an index finger at the mirror. It passed through and emerged covered in slime but unhurt. Nigel wiped his finger clean on the front of Edgar's jacket.

"There's the sample you wanted." Nigel stepped back from the mirror "I don't like it. Perhaps it's one-directional. It trapped Sarah."

"Your finger and elbow passed both in and out," noted Edgar.

"We could attach a line to you, if it makes you feel any better," Annabelle added.

"But I could suffocate in that slime! I didn't sign on for this."

"Sarah, while distressed, is alive on the other side," said Annabelle. "For some reason, only you can pass through to rescue her. Perhaps she knew this from the start, which is why she insisted we recruit you."

"That's reassuring. If she's so gifted, why'd she get trapped in the first place?"

"Will you do it?" pressed Annabelle.

Nigel looked at the two of them. He turned to regard the mirror portal. Slowly, he nodded. "God help me."

As Nigel removed his jacket, vest, and tie, Edgar ran from the room in search of a rope. He returned a short while later with a long coil of hemp.

"Found this in the basement," said Edgar.

Nigel tied one end of the rope around his waist.

Edgar and Annabelle would hold the other end.

"Would a tether help a lamb being led to the slaughter?" asked Nigel.

"Thank you." Annabelle gave him a quick hug and a perfunctory kiss on the cheek. She patted his chest. "You're the only one who can rescue her."

Nigel rolled his eyes. "Lucky me." He turned, tentatively stepped up to the mirror, and took a couple of deep breaths.

"Here goes," he said. He held his breath, stepped through the glass, and disappeared.

****

Thick blood-red fog swirled around Nigel in a gale so strong, he could barely remain upright. He looked around and saw no sign of Sarah. All looked red. *Where could she be? Was it a trick to get me here? To what end?* After almost a minute, he could hold his breath no longer and exhaled. He feared choking on the slime. Instead, he discovered he could breathe. The air tasted oddly metallic but could sustain him.

"Sarah!" he shouted, but the gale swallowed his voice.

Nigel stumbled forward on the slippery terrain and yanked the rope with him. "Sarah!" he called as he moved further into this other world. He repeated her name, then stopped to listen.

Sarah's faint voice answered from the distance.

Nigel moved ahead. *How long will the rope stretch?* Perhaps distance became something altogether different in this mirror world. The fog grew thinner and a light seemed to glow up ahead. He made for it.

At long last, Nigel emerged from the mist and saw Sarah next to a young girl. Red light bathed the two from an unseen source. Like him, wind buffeted Sarah, but for some reason, the little girl looked unaffected.

Sarah's dress became a sail. It caught the hurricane-force wind and she fell. She struggled to her feet, as her hair whipped around her face. She swiped it away and watched Nigel's approach. Above her, bolts of lightning seared through the dark red sky, followed by booming claps of thunder.

In a flash of lightning, Nigel spotted hundreds of people standing upwind, hands outstretched toward Sarah and him, all with their mouths wide, as though screaming. As the fog cleared further, he could see their faces and the hideous wounds to their necks. They were of all ages—men, women, boys, and girls. Black and white. Some were naked. Others wore clothing of various economic classes. Many appeared to be sailors or fishermen in oiled trousers and jackets.

The wind did not seem to affect these people. In fact, it seemed to originate from their screams. They stood there, sentinels to Sarah's and his distress. As Nigel approached, the young girl moved away.

Nigel fought against the wind and at last reached the exhausted Sarah. "Nigel Pickford," he shouted, as he smiled and grabbed her hand. "At your service."

Sarah collapsed into his arms and croaked, "She didn't realize I'd be trapped." Sarah glanced up at the figures nearby. "They told me what's been happening. Oh, God, I know—" Sarah's eyes rolled up into her head. She fainted and became dead weight in his arms.

Nigel looked around. The hundreds who stood nearby closed their mouths and lowered their arms. The gale abruptly stopped.

Nigel slipped and fell into the muck beneath them.

He fought to keep Sarah's head up, worried still about her suffocating in the thicker stuff at their feet. When at last he managed to stand with her in his arms, he began to retrace his route by following the slime-covered rope.

****

"I see them!" yelled Annabelle. She and Edgar peered into the mirror, while still clutching their end of the rope.

"But the mirror has become solid."

Indeed, the rope merged into the mirror and would not budge. On the other side, they could see a blurry image of Nigel with Sarah in his arms. He looked panicked.

"How can that be?" asked Annabelle.

"Should I break it?" Edgar asked.

"*No!* They could be trapped forever."

****

Inside the mirror world, Nigel noticed Annabelle and Edgar did not take up the slack in the rope as he approached the portal. At the interior side of the mirror, he could see why. The rope hung suspended through the now-solid surface. He could see Annabelle and Edgar arguing on the other side but could not hear their words.

He shifted Sarah onto one shoulder and battered a hand against the glass. Each strike caused a thunderous boom and earthquake-like tremors throughout the mirror world. Nigel tried to kick the mirror, which caused a still louder sound and more intense shaking.

Nigel looked through the glass at Annabelle and Edgar. He moved Sarah, still unconscious, around in his arms, and pressed her head to his chest. He took a couple of steps back. "Hang on, kid."

****

They saw Nigel back away from the mirror.

"Is he giving up?" asked Edgar.

"No! Don't!" Annabelle shouted, hoping Nigel could hear.

Instead, Nigel, with Sarah in his arms, charged full tilt at the portal. Edgar and Annabelle dove to the side and jumped clear before Nigel and Sarah crashed through the glass and fell to the floor. The two escapees were covered in red slime and broken glass, but, though hard to tell, seemed miraculously unhurt.

Nigel looked up at Annabelle and Edgar. "I believe she's okay, only fainted."

Annabelle checked Sarah's pulse and peered under both of her eyelids. "I agree. Let's get her onto the bed, and I'll clean her up."

This time, Nigel didn't interfere when Edgar picked her up. Edgar set Sarah on her bed, and the two men left the room as Annabelle began to remove Sarah's soiled clothes.

In the hall, Nigel noticed the front of Edgar's shirt and jacket, now covered in blood-red gelatinous goo. "I guess you got more of that stuff than you bargained for. As for myself, I hoped to come out of this adventure with a clean set of clothes." He glanced down at his own attire, also covered with slime and pieces of broken glass. "Looks like I got gypped."

Back in his room, Nigel went to the washbasin and discovered soap and water dissolved the muck with ease. Still, he needed to be careful of the broken glass, which made cleaning himself a time-consuming process.

Chapter Twenty-Eight

Sarah woke with a start, as soon as Annabelle began to wash her face. She grabbed Annabelle's arm and began to cry. "We need to get a telegram to the professor and implore him to come as soon as possible. On an earlier sailing if he can make it."

Annabelle began washing Sarah's outstretched arm. "Hush now. The professor will be here soon. You've had quite a fright. We all did, but now—"

"You're not listening to me!" Sarah pushed Annabelle away and climbed off the other side of the bed. She moved toward the door. "I must warn the others—"

Annabelle rushed over and grabbed Sarah. "You're not leaving this room dressed like that!"

Sarah regarded herself for the first time and saw her attire consisted of a corset and bloomers.

"You've also got glass and slime in your hair, the latter of which seems to wash out easily."

Sarah shook herself free and picked up her dress from the floor. It looked a mess and she let it fall.

"Come," said Annabelle, "we can make quick work of this."

Sarah yielded and let Annabelle lead her to the basin.

Once Sarah got the glass removed from her hair and washed the goo from her body, she ran to the wardrobe. She saw the rope, slime and broken mirror pieces still on the floor. She began to pull on a clean dress, and Annabelle offered her assistance.

"Here," Annabelle said, "Let me help you."

"We haven't a moment to lose," said Sarah.

"As soon as you're decent."

When presentable, Sarah ran downstairs and into the kitchen. The room swam with the smell of roasted chicken and potatoes, which Maude just pulled from the oven for the group's dinner.

Sarah ran up and grabbed her. "Maude, you must take us into town immediately! We need your help! Please, it's critical!" Sarah shook Maude for emphasis.

Maude looked at her with confusion, surprise, and fear. She picked up a butcher knife and brandished it at Sarah with both hands to force Sarah back.

Annabelle entered and pulled Sarah away. "Stop, Sarah! She doesn't understand. You've frightened her!" She made a series of placating gestures.

Eventually, Maude lowered the knife and grinned somewhat sheepishly at Annabelle and Sarah.

Annabelle wrote the request for the ride onto a scrap of paper. Maude looked at the note, shrugged, and nodded. Annabelle wrote her thanks, and seeing this, Sarah scribbled *sorry*.

Maude placed the pan of chicken and roasted potatoes into the icebox and hung her apron on a peg by the back door.

Sarah and Annabelle followed Maude outside into the warmth and sunshine of the day. While Maude went to untether the horse where it grazed, Sarah ran back into the house, looking for the others. She went out onto the porch and found Edgar back at work on his contraption.

When he saw her approach, Edgar barred her access to the machine. “Don’t even consider it,” he warned.

Sarah shook her head, fought to catch her breath, and said, “I need to caution you and Nigel about the danger we’re in. I’m not sure what to do next. Annabelle and I are headed to town to wire the professor. He must catch the earliest possible ferry, he may know how to proceed.”

“Did shattering the mirror end the haunting?”

Again, Sarah shook her head. “No. We’ve got it all wrong. They’ve been trying to warn us.”

Edgar looked confused.

“Please don’t use your machine.”

Edgar shook his head in dismay, and Sarah looked to be on the verge of tears. She turned to go then stopped and turned back. “It would be best if you and Nigel came with us.”

Edgar again shook his head. “I’ve got a job to do and you’ve been acting crazy. I understand some of what you’ve been through, but I’m not going anywhere. I’m surprised you’ve convinced Annabelle. I’ll see you when you get back.”

Sarah’s tears now flowed freely down her cheeks. She stomped her foot in frustration and said, “Tell Nigel to stay away from Lenore! You as well.” Sarah turned and ran around to the rear of the house.

Maude already hitched the horse to the wagon and waited to go. Sarah and Annabelle climbed aboard, and they drove off toward town.

****

As they departed, Annabelle looked back at the

house. It dawned on her she'd not seen the house in the daylight and didn't realize it looked so rundown.

They bounced along the rutted and hole-infested road. Sarah stared straight ahead, apparently lost in thought, but Annabelle noticed Sarah scratching at one spot on her forearm where it extended from her dress. The spot became bloody, and Annabelle covered the offending hand with hers. Startled, Sarah jumped an inch or two off the wooden seat and whirled her head around to confront Annabelle.

"I know you're anxious to speak to the professor, but hurting yourself is not going to help," said Annabelle.

Sarah yanked her sleeve over the raw spot on her arm and resumed staring at the road ahead. Annabelle now saw Sarah's right leg bouncing up and down beneath her dress. She chose not to comment.

They traveled in silence for a while, save for the creaks from the wagon, the hoof-beats, and the occasional snort from the horse. They passed several swampy areas, a large pond, and the tidy scattered farmhouses they missed seeing in the dark and fog on their first night. At one point, Annabelle spotted a fox, with a chicken in its jaws, darting into the weeds alongside the road. She thought it curious, as she considered foxes to be nocturnal hunters.

At another point, a flock of sheep blocked their way. They waited for some time before the young tow-haired boy in gray knickers and an indigo shirt shooed the animals off with the help of his collie. Sarah looked beside herself at the delay and moved to get off and help, but Annabelle held her back and shook her head. "You'll frighten the sheep like you did Maude. Let them be."

Resigned but still agitated, Sarah sat back on the seat. She began to scratch at her arm again until Annabelle stopped her.

The heat of the day wore on them, and all three women perspired as they rode through the pastureland at the center of the island. Eventually, the homes became more frequent and the road better maintained. In the far distance, they could see the bay and the city of Nantucket. On the outskirts, Maude turned the wagon onto a dirt lane with rough-hewn fencing on either side.

"No!" said Sarah. She grabbed the reins and shook her head.

Maude grabbed the reins back, shook her own head, and pointed at a farmhouse and barn ahead.

Annabelle convinced Sarah to sit back on seat. "There may be someone there we can talk to."

Sarah groaned as she looked up at the afternoon sun, clearly troubled by its progress across the sky.

As they neared the farm buildings, a middle-aged Negro in coveralls and a floppy hat came out of the barn. He approached them and grabbed the horse's bridle as Maude pulled up on the reins to stop.

"Well, Maude, who you got here?" the man asked, as though he expected an answer. His daughter jerked her thumb at Sarah and Annabelle. She climbed off the wagon and went into the barn. The man pulled out a rag and wiped his hands. He offered a cleaned hand to Annabelle, who shook it. "Afternoon," he said, and introduced himself. "I'm Maude's father, Clarence Mahogany."

Annabelle climbed down from the wagon and

introduced herself. Sarah remained seated on the buckboard and simply gave a little nod of acknowledgment. "It is imperative we get to the town of Nantucket as soon as possible," said Annabelle. "We are to meet someone due in on the ferry."

"The midday ferry's come and gone," said Clarence. He took his hat off and gestured at the bay. "So your friend is either waiting for you right now, will arrive this evening, or will be on the last run later tonight." He began to unfasten the straps and removed the bit from the horse's mouth. "In any case, Dottie, here, needs a breather. She's long in the tooth. I'll take you into town after she gets some food, water, and a rest out of the sun." He began to lead the horse around to the shady side of the house as Maude emerged from the barn with a pail of water and a feed bag.

Without a word, Sarah jumped off the wagon and began to stride with determination down the driveway. Annabelle ran to her.

"You won't get there any faster by walkin'," yelled Clarence to the women. "Fact is, it'll be slower, plus you'll be hot and bothered."

Annabelle caught Sarah's hand, but Sarah shook it free and continued away from the farmhouse. This time Annabelle groaned in resignation.

Clarence called to them again as they walked away. "Unless your friend took the ferry back, he's not going anywhere. This here's an island!"

It made no difference. Sarah seemed determined to get to town without further delay.

Annabelle and she trudged along the dusty road, and before long Clarence's prediction bore true. Annabelle felt hot and bothered. "No sense in heading back now," she grumbled, "but this seems foolish when we could have ridden."

"I couldn't stand to wait. I'm eaten up with worry."

"Please tell me what weighs on you, Sarah."

"Perhaps later. I can't talk now. Let's just walk."

They heard a horse and looked back to see a wagon advancing toward them. The two women blocked the road and waved their arms for it to stop. As it approached, they saw Maude. She had hitched another horse to the wagon.

****

Nigel's washbasin became full of soapy reddish water with pieces of glass at the bottom, but now at least he felt relatively clean. He ran a comb and brush through his hair and retrieved clothes that on previous days were left on the floor or tossed across the back of the Morris chair. Out of clean clothes, he dispensed with wearing a vest, tie, and jacket. A wrinkled white shirt and pair of pants would do.

Once dressed, he regarded himself in the oval mirror above the bureau. Nigel touched it tentatively with his fingers. Solid. He wondered for a moment what might lie on the other side of his reflection. Another world? Were they staring out at him now? Nigel forced an end to those thoughts. His reflection looked rather unkempt but otherwise fine.

He went in search of Sarah and Annabelle but could not find them. He checked the main floor and finally went outside the front door onto the porch.

Edgar looked up from the dynamo when Nigel emerged from the house. Likewise cleaned up, he too went outside without a vest or jacket, as he was working in the heat of the afternoon sun. He cocked his chin at Nigel as a hello.

"Where are the others?" asked Nigel.

Edgar fitted the end of a screwdriver into a recess and tested a screw to see it was tight. "Sarah awoke in a dither. She and Annabelle have gone to meet the professor at the ferry. As for your Miss Hutchinson, I haven't seen her all day. I rarely do." Edgar set the tool down and seemed distracted, as he cast his gaze around his feet and behind him. "Sarah insisted you stay away from her. She wasn't making much sense. Blast it all!" he cursed in frustration. "Where'd I put my wrench?"

Nigel grinned at Edgar's agitation. "Fortunately," Nigel said, "Sarah is not my keeper. I wonder, could breaking the mirror have ended the haunting?"

"Sarah said no." Edgar looked up at him. "Seems my "gizmo" is our best shot."

Nigel lifted his foot, where he had hidden the tool. "You looking for this?"

Edgar appeared angry for a moment, then exhaled slowly to calm himself. He stared straight at Nigel. "Listen, I'm way behind and would appreciate your help. For starters, would you hand that to me?"

Nigel kicked the wrench in Edgar's direction. It skittered across the porch and landed in the dust at Edgar's feet.

Edgar muttered an acerbic thanks and reached down to retrieve it. Instead of "helping" further, Nigel went back inside.

In the foyer, Nigel paused for a moment so his eyes could adjust to the change in light. After a few moments, he went upstairs to look for Lenore. Nigel knocked. Not hearing a response, he entered her room and shut the door. Darkness engulfed him.

Heavy burgundy-colored curtains were drawn across the windows and French doors. The kerosene lamp next to the bed did little to cut the darkness.

"Lenore?"

"I'm here," she said in a soft voice.

Lenore stepped out of a murky corner and put her hands on either side of Nigel's face. She drew him to her. They kissed, and Lenore's tongue extended into the cavern of his mouth and began to dart around and explore. When they parted, Nigel pulled her back to him with a passionate embrace and whispered in her ear, "I can't stop thinking of you."

Lenore gave a little laugh and looked up at him. She ran her fingertips through his dark hair. "As it should be."

They kissed again and fell onto the bed. Desperate fumbling began as they worked to remove each other's clothes. Lenore made it easy; she wore only a nightgown. Nigel's garments, on the other hand, proved more difficult, so Lenore yanked down his trousers and mounted him with his pants still around his knees. She began to rock, and Nigel exploded inside her almost instantaneously. He groaned with both pleasure and disappointment.

"I'm sorry—"

Lenore put her fingers over his lips to hush him and continued to undulate. Nigel forgot his apology and moaned in ecstasy. Over the next hour, he experienced new heights of passion and the staying power to both satisfy her and have a second round himself.

****

The three arrived in town hot, tired, and covered in dust. Nevertheless, they went straight to the ferry landing. Maude dropped them off. She indicated she would be back, and drove the wagon toward the livery down the street.

They saw no sign of the professor and did not encounter him on the road, so it seemed clear he didn't catch the earlier ferry. Annabelle thought it pointless to send a telegram unless he did not arrive on the evening ferry as promised. But Sarah would hear none of it. She insisted they cable the professor, which they managed to do in the terminal.

The cable sent, and with hours to kill before the next boat's arrival, Annabelle suggested they find a place to properly clean themselves and somewhere they could eat. They waited until Maude returned, and Annabelle pantomimed her proposal.

In response, Maude led them to the Nantucket Settlement House, which allowed them the use of their facilities for a small fee. Sarah needed to be led to the sink and helped to wash, becoming almost catatonic.

After their ablutions, Sarah ate no more than a few spoonfuls of soup and refused the crab cakes or whatever else Annabelle proffered. She also quit communicating. Annabelle began to worry about Sarah's sanity. Perhaps the imprisonment in the mirror so addled her, she could not make sense of things.

After supper, Annabelle and Maude followed Sarah as she made a beeline for the ferry dock. They waited for a while in the terminal, but Sarah insisted on going outside to watch for the boat. As the day wore on, the sun slid down the horizon and came directly in line with the ferry dock. At this point, searching for the ferry meant staring into the sun.

"Sarah, come inside. The sun is giving me a

headache," snapped Annabelle. Her patience had worn thin, both with Sarah's behavior and with the ferry's delay—almost thirty minutes overdue. She indulged Sarah all afternoon, and now her head throbbed.

Finally, she could take it no longer and forced Sarah to accompany her to the pharmacy across the street from the ferry terminal. The pharmacist recommended laudanum, so Annabelle purchased a small bottle. He then encouraged her to add drops to a glass of sarsaparilla, which he happily sold her as well.

The two returned to the terminal where they met up with Maude. As they resumed waiting for the ferry, Annabelle also waited for the nostrum to ease the pain boring through her skull. It didn't seem to be working, so she took a sip right from the bottle. The profoundly bitter taste sent her running for the drinking fountain.

Sarah refused to stay in the terminal and kept going out to look for the boat, forcing Annabelle to accompany her. In Sarah's state, Annabelle did not trust her enough to leave her alone, and Maude might not understand the need to watch Sarah. Annabelle wondered if Sarah might be truly capable of harming herself.

Twenty minutes later, Annabelle yawned. She realized her head no longer ached. She smiled dreamily, though now her stomach felt a bit unsettled.

Finally, a deep horn blast announced the ferry's arrival.

Almost everyone in the terminal got up and joined them on the dock, but Maude instead began to run around the building. She turned and pantomimed that she would return with the wagon.

The disembarking of passengers and wagons did

not go smoothly. One horse, attached to an overloaded wagon, reared as it exited the boat. The wagon tipped over and spilled a load of lumber and nails. A two-by-four bounced up and struck an obese woman on the forehead. The woman tumbled backward onto a group of passengers who screamed with fright. The same two ferry workers who belittled Edgar the other night came to the woman's aid and carted her off to the terminal. Blood dripped from the woman's ears. Other deck hands righted the wagon and cleared the debris from the dock. They put some things back on the wagon and pitched other items off the dock into the water, much to the ire of the owner.

The evening sun became too bright for Sarah and Annabelle to stare in the direction of the ferry for any length of time, even when they raised their hands to shade their eyes. Sarah began edging forward toward the boat. Annabelle smiled and followed. She felt remarkably good, almost euphoric.

At last, about halfway down the pier, Professor James seemed to step out of the sun and stood before them.

Sarah ran up and threw her arms around him. "It's much worse than we realized," she sobbed.

****

Edgar stepped back from the machine and wiped grease from his hands with a rag. Behind him, the sun became a fiery red ball as it sank toward the horizon. Much of the sky turned a deep shade of crimson. Edgar looked up at the sunset and let out a tired sigh.

He surveyed his handiwork. From one end of the cast-iron dynamo extended a long bicycle chain. The chain attached to a sprocket on a bicycle whose rear axle sat on a stand, elevating the wheel off the ground. From the other end of the dynamo ran copper wire which wrapped around the house several times.

****

Nigel and Lenore lay naked together in her bed. Nigel snored softly, and Lenore watched him sleep.

He stirred, opened his eyes, and smiled.

"I don't know when Edgar will have his contraption finished," he murmured, "but we should leave the house. It may be dangerous."

"You're right," she replied and stroked his face. "You should leave."

Nigel gathered her to him and kissed her. "*We* should go."

"Of course." She smiled and kissed him back.

The two rose from the bed and dressed. They helped each other in post-coital intimacy. Lenore buttoned his shirt from the bottom up and kissed him with increased intensity with each button. When she asked for help with her corset, she placed his hands over each of her breasts. Again, he became aroused but fought the urge to throw her back onto the bed—a sense of prudence really did dictate they leave. Once clad, they emerged from Lenore's room and went downstairs.

Nigel opened the front door. Crimson light from the setting sun bathed his features. Lenore pushed the door shut and put a hand to his cheek.

"I'll join you outside in a moment, dear-heart. In case the house gets damaged, I want to gather a few mementos."

"Don't be long."

Lenore kissed him, and he went out onto the porch.

"I was about to come looking for you," said Edgar.

He donned a pair of elbow-length rubber gloves, placed a pair of goggles over his eyes, and waved his rubberized hands before his completed machine to show it off.

But before Nigel could appraise it fully, he spotted a wagon racing toward the house through the twilight. He recognized the professor on the buckboard next to the cook. The man held his hat on his head with one hand and grasped the seat with the other. Annabelle and Sarah bounced around in the back. The cook pulled the wagon before the house and brought it to a stop.

Nigel crossed the porch and ducked beneath the strands of copper wire. He walked past Edgar and out into the drive to meet the others. The professor, Annabelle, and Sarah climbed off the wagon and approached him.

"You're just in time!" shouted Edgar.

The professor crossed the drive to Nigel and stuck out his hand. Nigel took it, and they shook with vigor.

"I understand you saved our Sarah's life. I can't tell you how grateful we are you joined our troop."

Nigel looked embarrassed and released the professor's hand. "About that—I've decided to part company and will remain here." He lowered his eyes. "Miss Hutchinson and I have developed a very deep regard for each other. But I want to thank you all for rescuing me from the streets and giving me back my life—one I all but lost."

Behind Nigel, Edgar shouted, "It's…it's working!"

Nigel turned to see Edgar maniacally pedaling his contraption and the house enveloped in a blue electrical hue. Electric crackling noises began and increased in volume. The air stank of ozone.

"It's working!" Edgar shouted though he was out of breath. "By God, I knew it!"

Panic flashed across Nigel's face as he glanced around. "Where's Lenore?"

Nigel began charging for the house, but Annabelle grabbed his arm.

"Stop!" she shouted. "It isn't safe!"

"To hell with that!" Nigel broke free and ran to the porch. Nearly there, the electrical charge threw him back fifteen feet through the air. He crashed down onto the dirt and gravel drive. Nigel struggled to his feet and shook his head clear. He began to stumble back toward the house.

Annabelle ran to Edgar and shouted, "Stop!"

Edgar tore off his goggles. "I have! It's continuing on its own."

The house continued to crackle and glow with the blue current.

Nigel grabbed one of the boards from the packing crate. He approached the copper wires baring his way and began to strike at them like a madman. Finally, the wires broke and the blue current disappeared.

Sarah stepped forward and closed her eyes. She raised her right palm toward the house. "They're gone," she announced. "The house is clear."

Nigel staggered inside. He lurched into the foyer and screamed, "Lenore!" The silence was ominous. He stumbled into the library. Unoccupied. Tears ran from his eyes. "Lenore!" he screamed again.

He considered checking the other rooms on the main floor, but something drew him upstairs. He reached the second floor and clumsily ran down the hall, tripping in his haste. He fell face-first onto the carpet, next to the still-wet wine stain from the night before. Crying freely now, he drew in a ragged breath and his lungs filled with the scent of stale wine. It made him want to vomit.

Nigel stood and ran down the hall. He threw open Lenore's door. His voice caught in his throat, but as he entered, he managed to croak, "Lenore!" The door swung shut behind him.

Lenore stood naked with her back to him in the open doorway to her veranda. She'd drawn back the curtains and now stared out at the darkening horizon.

Her unbound white hair writhed, Medusa-like, around her head in the breeze.

"Thank God, you're all right!" he said as he drew his dirty sleeve across his face to wipe away the tears.

"I don't think God had much to do with it," she said, still staring out the window.

Nigel approached her from behind, reached around on either side and cupped her breasts in his hands. He pressed his cheek against the left side of her head and let her hair and lavender scent wash over him.

Lenore turned and smiled at Nigel. They kissed. Her tongue once again snaked into his mouth and met his own. He pressed against her and again breathed in her scent. They kissed with a heady intensity, exorcizing any trace of nausea. She intoxicated him. He wanted her more than anything.

They drew back for a moment, though still in each other's arms.

"Look at you," she laughed. "You're filthy." Lenore tore open the front of his shirt, and buttons ricocheted around the room. She yanked his shirt free, and they embraced again. Lenore nuzzled his neck, and they edged toward the bed.

"The ghosts," said Nigel, "they're all gone! You're free."

"I know. I have you and the rest of the group to thank."

"I hope to claim a special reward."

"Oh, you shall."

Lenore pushed him backward onto the bed and climbed on top. She straddled him and pinned his arms to the mattress. Her breasts hung down almost to Nigel's mouth, and he raised his head to playfully kiss them. He looked up at her face and froze.

Her smile was hungry. Feral. Her red eyes began to glow. "You can't imagine how inconvenient it is when my victims come back to haunt me!"

Lenore's eyes looked like two fiery red coals. Fangs revealed themselves as her smile became a snarl.

A stringy drop of cold saliva fell from her mouth and landed on Nigel's right cheek.

Lenore slurped back her spittle and drew a long icy tongue along the length of his throat.

"*No!*" he cried in disbelief and fear. Too late. Nigel ineffectually jerked his head back and forth as he struggled to break free.

Lenore bent down toward Nigel, fangs bared. Her now frigid breath burned across the skin of his neck. Behind her came muffled yelling from out in the hall then a crash as the door burst open. Lenore stopped a fraction of an inch from his throat.

He could hear the voice of the professor, panting, fighting for breath. "Remember," he huffed, "through the heart!"

He heard Edgar yell and the sound of him charging

across the room. Then came screams from Annabelle and Sarah. With perfect timing, Lenore whipped around as Edgar approached and batted him aside. Edgar flew through the air and landed on his back. He slid along the wooden floor and forced a red Persian rug to buckle and curl before him. Somehow, he'd managed to keep a grip on a spear-like board from the packing crate. But as he struggled to get up, Lenore sprang from the bed and landed on him, driving him back to the floor. The spear went flying.

Still on top of Edgar, Lenore looked up at the others in the doorway and roared. She leaned down, fangs bared again, this time to tear at Edgar's throat. Then she lurched back with an almost orgasmic gasp.

"Harder!" screamed the professor. "Push harder, man!"

Nigel gave a huge grunt, and the sharp piece of wood jutted out from below Lenore's left breast with a wet sickening pop. Black blood oozed around the wound.

Lenore shrieked and arched her back in pain. Her hands flailed behind her but were unable to remove the spear. After several moments they slowed to a stop and dropped to her side. Her lower jaw became slack and a foot-long flaccid tongue lolled out and dripped a milky white drool. Her eyes faded from two fiery coals to become the color of dried blood. The lids closed, and she collapsed forward.

As Lenore's body fell, Edgar was about to be impaled with the portion of the spear protruding from her chest. Nigel grabbed Lenore in a final macabre embrace and twisted her away. He looked down at Lenore in his arms. Her features reverted back to the woman with whom he fell in love. No longer a vampire but truly dead.

Edgar pushed himself up from the floor and onto his knees. He ran his hands over his throat to check it remained whole. Edgar raised his head and met Nigel's gaze. He gave a nod of thanks.

Lenore slipped from Nigel's grip and fell to the floor with a thud. He regarded the black blood on his hands, lifted his head, and howled, "Nooo!"

Chapter Twenty-Nine

All the shades were raised in the dining room, the first time since they arrived, and it became a bright naturally-lit room. Dust motes danced in the morning light streaming in through the windows. Nigel regarded the moats with mindless fascination. They seemed to move by their own accord, as though animated and purposeful, despite their being lifeless specks.

"Mr. Pickford?"

Nigel snapped to, leaving his reverie for the cold comfort of reality. "Yes?"

"Is there anything more you wish to add?" Sergeant Sean O'Connell held his pencil poised above his small notebook.

"No," Nigel said as he shook his head. The movement hurt, and he winced. In fact, he hurt all over. He also felt drained, an automaton going through the motions.

The officer flipped the cover closed on his notebook and put it and his pencil into his uniform's breast pocket. He stood and retrieved his round-topped helmet from the table beside him. On the other side of the table, Nigel stood up as well.

"That should do it, sir. An incredible story, if I do say so. But you're all tellin' the same tale, and all the bodies we're diggin' up speak for themselves, in a manner of speakin'."

"What bodies?" asked Nigel. His face blanched further than the wan color he wore since last night. He started to feel dizzy. "Her parents? The dog?"

"Your Miss Bradbury showed us where to dig. Some were found in the basement, others outside. Bodies lay stacked like cordwood, in a manner of speakin', beneath where Miss Hutchinson told you she buried her dog. All of 'em with terrible neck wounds, the same wounds as on the bodies of fishermen who have been washin' ashore for years. We found the minister I've been lookin' for buried in the basement. The way I see it, you're lucky to be alive."

Nigel felt queasy and about to pass out. "I need air!" he managed before he dashed out the door. He ran by two policemen smoking and laughing in the foyer. They looked startled when an ill-looking Nigel burst from the dining room. One of the policemen chuckled. "Sean, did you recite your limerick about the whore from Azores?"

Nigel finally got the front door open and ran outside. The bright morning light blinded him, but the cool air helped to relieve the nausea. Dazed, he moved across the porch and sat on the steps. He put his head into his hands and began to cry.

"You all right, considering?" asked Edgar

Embarrassed, Nigel swiped away his tears. He raised his head and saw Edgar sitting next to him. Edgar held a shovel before him, blade up, like a scepter.

In the distance, policemen still dug in the family plot. A pair of officers laid a draped body next to a dozen more already in the drive.

"You all right?" Edgar repeated.

Nigel made a wan smile and imitated the sergeant.

"In a manner of speakin'."

Edgar stood and looked in the direction of the bodies. He glanced back at Nigel. "What now?"

"I either get drunk or start making amends." Nigel heaved his shoulders in a heavy sigh and stared at Edgar. "For a start, I owe you an apology. You tried to save my life."

"Twice, but who's counting."

"I've been wrong about a lot of things."

"Can I quote you?" Annabelle said from behind.

Nigel craned his neck around and saw Annabelle, Sarah, and Professor James now stood on the porch. Nigel rose to his feet and took a step back so he faced them all.

"I'm hoping you were wrong about leaving our group." Annabelle smiled.

"I don't seem to be much good at anything."

"You saved me." Sarah ran to Nigel and hugged him.

"I don't know—"

"None of us do," said the professor, as he and Annabelle approached him. "That's what we are about. To shine the light of science on what has been hidden, feared, or misunderstood. We want you to be a part of this."

"I don't know what to say."

"Then we'll speak no more of resigning. I'll chalk it up to a momentary lapse of judgment. Welcome back." The professor smiled and stuck out his hand.

Grinning ruefully, Nigel reached around Sarah, who still hugged him, to shake the professor's hand.

The professor stepped back, glanced up at the bright blue sky, and gave a little sigh himself. He looked back at Nigel. "After a well-deserved respite, our next case will be in Petersburg, Virginia. It's near the Fort Stedman Battlefield—a place where I believe you have some familiarity."

Nigel's smile evaporated.

A word from the author…

The supernatural always had the allure of forbidden fruit, ever since my mother refused to allow me, as a boy, to watch creature features on late night TV. She caved in. (Well, not literally.)

As a child, fresh snow provided me the opportunity to walk out onto neighbors' lawns halfway and then make paw prints with my fingers as far as I could stretch. I would retrace the paw and boot prints, then fetch the neighbor kids and point out that someone turned into a werewolf on their front lawn. (They were skeptical.)

I have pursued many interests over the years, but the supernatural always called to me. You could say I was haunted. Finally, following the siren's call, I wrote *The Eidola Project*, based on a germ of an idea I had as a teenager.

Ultimately, I hope my book gives you the creeps, and I mean that in the best way possible.

roberthe roldauthor.com

facebook.com/RobertHeroldauthor/

~

P.S., If you would be so kind, please write a review and post it wherever readers may go. Reviews are golden to writers. Thank you so much!

P.P.S., For those of you belonging to a literary coven, *er, book group*, discussion questions are available on my website.

P.P.P.S., A free short story is also available to those going to my website!